A Cockney Queen

For an hour or two after Adelaide was crowned, there was a wild confusion of excitement and grief throughout the city. Thousands of people had seen it happen, but it was still scarcely believable; it wasn't until Adelaide had recovered enough to ride down the Rock in the funicular railway that it began to sink in. The open barouche that had been going to take Rudolf back to the palace as king now had to take her alone as queen, and she sat in it, pale and shivering now that the shock of it was reaching her, with the iron crown on her dark hair and an expression that was indomitable. She was ravaged; she could never hide the play of thoughts over her face; and that, as Jim was coming to see, was her strongest hold over the people–over her subjects. She could hide nothing, so they believed her.

Also by Philip Pullman:

The Sally Lockhart Trilogy:

The Ruby in the Smoke

The Shadow in the North

The Tiger in the Well

The Broken Bridge

The White Mercedes

The Golden Compass

The Subtle Knife

Count Karlstein

THE TIN PRINCESS

PHILIP PULLMAN

A Knopf Paperback
Alfred A. Knopf
New York

A KNOPF PAPERBACK PUBLISHED BY ALFRED A. KNOPF, INC.

www.randomhouse.com/kids

Library of Congress Cataloging-in-Publication Data
Pullman, Philip.
The tin princess / by Philip Pullman.
p. cm.
Summary: In 1882 sixteen-year-old Becky applies for a tutoring job in London and becomes embroiled in assassination, intrigue, and dangerous politics in the small European kingdom of Razkavia.
[1. Adventure and adventurers–Fiction.] I. Title.
PZ7.P968Tm 1994 92-38305 [Fic]–dc20

ISBN 0-679-87615-4 (pbk.)

First Knopf Paperback edition: April 1997
Printed in the United States of America
10 9 8 7 6 5 4

For Gordon Dennis,
with gratitude and affection

•

Thanks to Tom
for help with the family tree

Characters in ***The Tin Princess,***
in the order in which they appear

Rebecca Winter (Becky), age 16
James Taylor (Jim), a consulting detective
Adelaide Bevan, a young woman living in St. John's Wood
Herr Strauss, otherwise Prince Rudolf of Razkavia
Sally Lockhart Goldberg, a financial consultant
Daniel Goldberg, Sally's husband, a political journalist
Charlie, Dermot, Liam, and other members of a street gang known as the Irish Guards
Count Thalgau, Razkavian ambassador to the Court of St. James (i.e., Great Britain)
Countess Thalgau
Frau Winter, Becky's mother, an artist
Carmen Isabella Ruiz y Soler, an actress
Prince Otto von Bismarck, Chancellor of Germany
Gerson von Bleichröder, a Berlin banker
Julius, his secretary
King Wilhelm of Razkavia, Prince Rudolf's father
Baron Gödel, Chamberlain, head of the royal household
Karl von Gaisberg, a student, member of the Richterbund
Glatz, a student over-excited by politics
Count Otto von Schwartzberg, Prince Rudolf's cousin, a huntsman
Anton, Friedrich, Fritz, Hans, Heinrich, Jan, Michael, Willi, students, members of the Richterbund
Alois Egger, a cigar merchant
The Archbishop of Razkavia
Frau Busch, a huntsman's widow
Herr Bangemann, a clerk in the Razkavian Ministry of Foreign Affairs

Prince Leopold of Razkavia
Matyas, landlord of the Café Florestan
Private Schweigner, a sentry of the Eagle Guard
Corporal Kogler, a sentry of the Eagle Guard
Miroslav and Josef, two elderly brothers who are river thieves

...and various servants, soldiers, citizens, diplomats, doctors, ticket collectors, mining engineers, palace officials, butchers' boys, funicular railway stationmasters, clerks, musicians, telegraph operators, landladies, and assassins

Family Tree of the Ruling House of Razkavia

(monarchs in capitals)

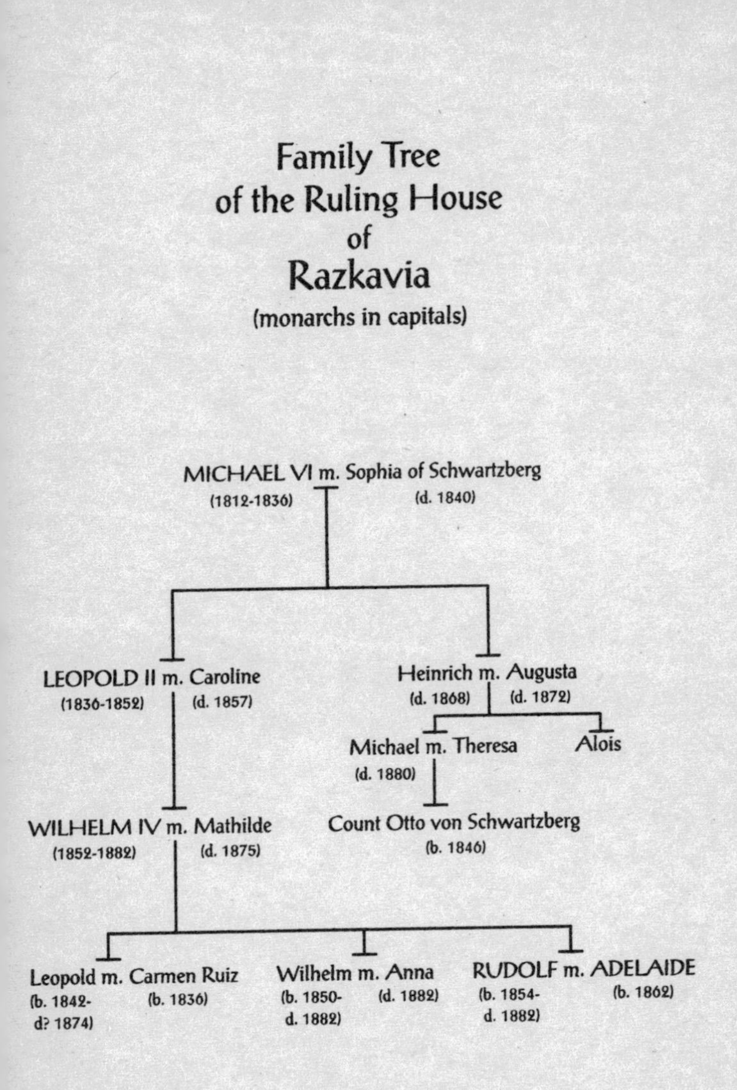

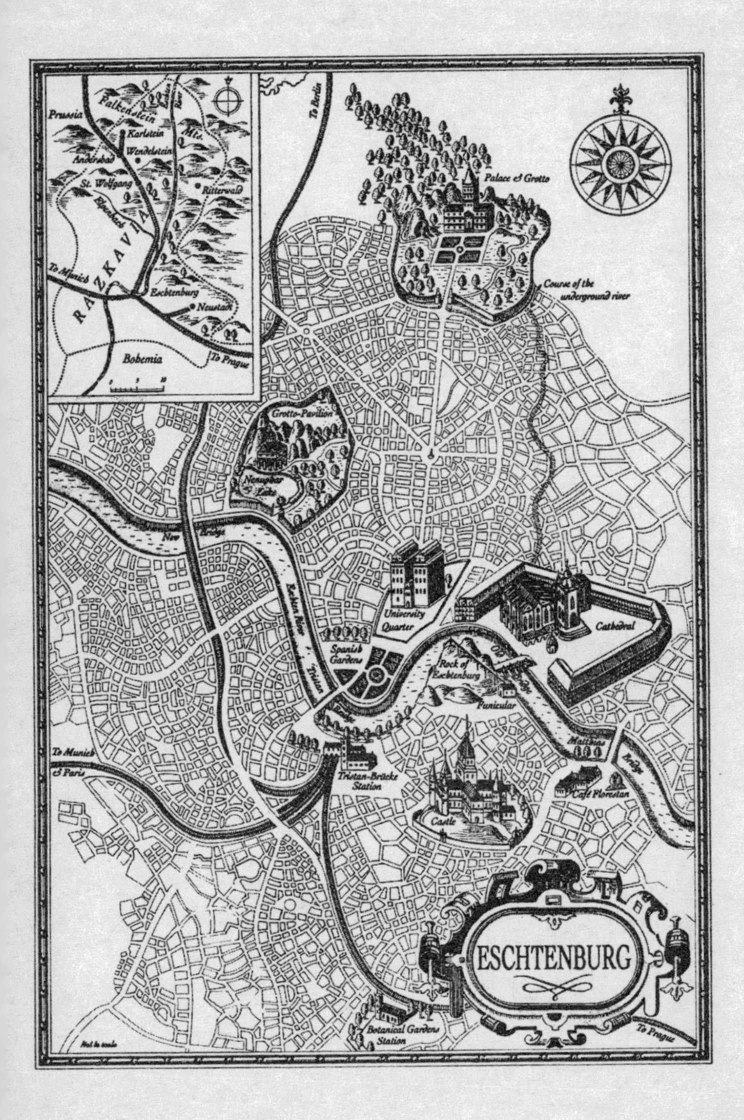
Prussia
Falkenstein
Mts.
Karlstein
Wendelstein
Anderebad
St. Wolfgang
Ritterwald
Elpenbach
RAZKAVIA
To Munich
Eschtenburg
Neustadt
Bohemia
To Prague
0 5 10
To Berlin
Palace & Grotto
Course of the underground river
Grotto-Pavilion
Nenuphar Lake
New Bridge
Eschten River
Tristan
University Quarter
Cathedral
Spanish Gardens
Rock of Eschtenburg
Funicular
Old Bridge
Matthias Bridge
To Munich & Paris
Tristan-Brücke Station
Café Florestan
Castle
ESCHTENBURG
Botanical Gardens Station
To Prague

1
The Infernal Machine

Rebecca Winter, gifted, cheerful, and poor, had lived sixteen years without once seeing a bomb go off. She might have seen one; London, in 1882, was no less explosive than it is now, for dynamiting was already a vigorous branch of politics. But Becky's path had never crossed a bomb, which is why, on that sunny May morning, she was thinking of something else entirely; namely, German verbs.

The sun was bright and the sky was dotted with fat little clouds like dabs of flake white on a wash of ultramarine, and Becky was walking down a tree-lined road in St. John's Wood in north London. She was on her way to meet her new pupil—her first pupil, in fact—and she was anxious to make a good impression and acquit herself well.

Her cloak was a little shabby and her bonnet was unfashionable, and there was a hole in the sole of her right boot. But that didn't matter. The road was dry and the air was fresh, and that young man in the straw boater had given her what might have been an interested look, and Becky felt splendid, for she was an independent woman—or nearly, anyway. Her head high, she ignored the speculative young man in the boater, checked the road sign, and turned up into an avenue lined with comfortable villas.

German was Becky's first language. Her second was English, her third Italian, her fourth French, her fifth Spanish; she was in the process of mastering Russian, and she could swear in Polish and Lithuanian. She lived with her mother and grandmother in a plain boardinghouse in the most modest corner of Maida Vale, where her mother worked as an illustrator of cheap novels and sensational periodicals. They had lived there ever since they'd been forced into exile from central Europe, when Becky was three, sustained by each other's diligence and by the local network of exiles: a poor, noisy, quarrelsome, generous, vigorously gifted bunch of people from almost every country in Europe. It was as natural to Becky to think in several languages as it was to assume that she would have to earn a living; it seemed only sensible to put the two things together.

At the same time, she chafed at the limitations hemming her in. Like all people with an unromantic appearance (just on the sturdy side of plump, with bright black inquisitive eyes, cheeks that flushed too easily, unruly dark hair) she had, she was sure, the soul of a brigand. She hungered for romance. The only romance she'd known so far had been a liaison with a butcher's boy when she was twelve. He had sold her a cigarette in exchange for a kiss, but she hadn't even smoked it all, because he said it was dangerous for women to smoke cigarettes in case they went mad. So they sat in the bushes and shared it, and she was sick over his boots, which served him right. Somehow, though, it hadn't satisfied her soul. She longed for cutlasses, pistols, and brandy; she had to make do with coffee, and pencils, and verbs.

But there was a consolation in the verbs. She was genuinely fascinated by how languages worked, and if she couldn't live with a band of robbers in a Sicilian cave, she was prepared to study linguistics and philology at university. But that cost money. So she had done what many of her fellow exiles did, and placed an advertisement offering her services as a language tutor, specializing in German and Italian.

It had drawn a reply almost at once.

It was a curious reply, too. A young gentleman, who had insisted on speaking English though it was clear to both Becky and her mother that he'd have been happier in German, had engaged her to come each morning to his villa at number 43, Church Road, St. John's Wood, and tutor a Miss Bevan. The money he offered was ample, his embarrassment (he was a very young man) was plain. Becky and her mother had spent hours afterward in speculating about him. Becky was sure he was an anarchist; her mother equally sure that he was a nobleman, or even a prince.

"I have seen princes, and you have not," she said. "Believe me, he's a prince. And as for her..."

They couldn't begin to guess about Miss Bevan. Was she young? Old? A child? A beautiful sinister spy?

Well, Becky thought, she'd soon find out. She turned into Church Road, and was about to open the gate of number 43, which was a white-painted villa with a front path shadowed by heavy laurels, when someone said, "Excuse me, miss."

She stopped in surprise. It was the young man in the straw boater. How had he arrived in front of her?

He was in his early twenties, with a vivid, intelligent expression, green eyes, and hair the same color as his hat. There was an air about him she couldn't quite place: he was a gentleman, to judge by his appearance, but something about his confident manner spoke of acquaintance with stables, and stage doors, and low public houses.

"Yes?" she said.

"Do you happen to know the young lady who lives in this house?"

"Miss Bevan? As a matter of fact, no, not yet. I've been engaged to teach her German. But who are you? And what business is it of yours?"

He produced a card from his waistcoat pocket. It said J. TAYLOR, CONSULTING DETECTIVE, and gave the address of a photographic firm in Twickenham. Becky felt slightly unreal.

"You're a *detective?* What on earth are you detecting?"

"I think your Miss Bevan might be someone I've been looking for," he said. "I'm sorry to take up your time. May I ask your name?"

"Miss Rebecca Winter," Becky said frostily. "Excuse me, please."

He stood aside with a slight satirical bow, replaced his straw hat at a jaunty angle, and walked away. Becky blinked. She took a deep breath, walked up the path, and rang the bell.

A pert maid let Becky in, and let her know by a glance what she thought of her figure. Becky could raise a disdainful eyebrow when she wanted to, and she did so now, spoiling the effect slightly by tripping on the rug at the foot of the stairs.

"Wait in here," said the maid, showing her into a sitting room off the landing, and shutting the door behind her.

Becky found herself in a pretty little room facing the front of the house. The window was open, and Becky could see blue sky and green leaves, and smell the fresh air. The furniture was expensive, but too big, and crowded the room oppressively. There were no books, and the pictures were dull; the only interesting thing in the room was a stereoscope. Becky picked it up and looked at the slide in the frame. It was a picture of a little girl in ragged clothes sitting on the knee of a thin man with a huge mustache, and printed on the back were the words of a sentimental song.

"What the bloody hell are you doing?"

Becky nearly dropped the stereoscope, and spun around to see a young woman in the doorway, angry and dark and suspicious.

"I'm sorry," Becky said. "Miss Bevan, I presume?"

"Who are you?"

"Miss Winter. Becky Winter. Your tutor."

"What were you doing with that?" she said, frowning at the stereoscope.

"I just love stereographs. I know I shouldn't have touched it."

"H'mm," said Miss Bevan, and came into the room. She looked Becky up and down, and then sat in an armchair by the open window, leaning back languidly and watching Becky with lazy amusement.

She wasn't altogether pretty; she was too thin for that, and there was a sharpness about her face, and something challenging in her manner. She was gaudily overdressed, and her voice was harsh and cockney—but there was some quality about her that Becky couldn't help being caught by, a hint of vulnerability, a softness under the scorn. Her eyes were lovely, dark and enormous, and she moved with the grace of a cat.

"What's this tutoring lark then?" she said.

"I was engaged by a Herr Strauss to come and teach you German."

"Prove it."

Becky blinked. "But didn't you know?"

"Anyone could come in here and spin a yarn like that. You might be an assassin or summing. You might have a gun in that bag of yours. How do I know who you are?"

"Oh, really—I've got books in here, look. Didn't he tell you I was coming?"

"Might've."

Miss Bevan stretched lithely and relaxed again. She wasn't

really suspicious, Becky thought, just bored. She looked about nineteen or twenty, and now that Becky had seen her, she could guess at the relationship between her and the mysterious Herr Strauss. St. John's Wood was notorious as a place where rich gentlemen set up their mistresses in households of their own.

"What you blushing for?" inquired Miss Bevan.

"I'm not. Look, we'd better begin. Have you done any German—"

"Oh, pooh. Who was that bloke at the gate?"

"The young man in the straw hat? A detective. He gave me his card."

She handed it to Miss Bevan, who frowned at it and dropped it on the bamboo table beside her.

"Detective," she said wearily. "Tosh. Probably a reporter. Here, can you play Halma?"

"Yes, but—"

"Or better still this 'un here. I got it Monday, and I ain't played it yet. I forget what it's called..."

She jumped up and reached to a shelf that was full of colored cardboard boxes of children's board games.

"I plays 'em with Herr Strauss of an evening," she said. "What's this one called?"

She was squinting at it as if she were too vain to wear spectacles.

"It's called Ludo, or Parcheesi," Becky said. "But hadn't we—"

"D'you know how to play it?"

"Well, we could read the instructions, but hadn't I better start teaching you German? After all, Herr Strauss is paying me to."

"How much?"

"Half a crown for an hour."

"Well, I'll pay you twice that to play Halma with me. Go on."

"No. I'll play with you for nothing, but I must teach you as well. I made an agreement with Herr Strauss."

Miss Bevan scowled and slumped back on the sofa. She eyed Becky appraisingly.

"You're honest, ain't yer?" she said.

"I don't know. I've never been tempted to be dishonest. Why?"

"Shall I tell you a secret?"

"If you like. But you hardly know me."

"I don't know anyone else," said Miss Bevan bitterly. "Only the cook and the bootboy and the parlormaid, sly scheming bitch that she is, and I wouldn't tell her the time of day, even s'posing I knew it. No, it's driving me wild, cooped up here like a hen. I can't read and I can't write..."

"Is that the secret?"

"That's part of it. The prince ought to've got you to teach me that, instead of German."

"The prince?" said Becky. "D'you mean Herr Strauss? Is that the rest of the secret?"

"Part of the rest. You guessed anyway, didn't yer?"

"My mother did. Prince what, of where?"

"Prince Rudolf of Razkavia. Bet you never heard of it."

Becky blinked, and felt a little breathless.

"Yes. I have heard of it. But why...I mean...I thought..."

"And he's in danger. I don't know as he ought to've trusted *you*. I don't know as *I* ought. You might be a socialist, or worse."

"What's wrong with socialists?" Becky said, dazed.

"I hate 'em. I'm a Conservative—always have been."

"But you're a woman! You haven't even got a vote!"

"Huh! You don't need a vote to prove you're loyal. If people vote for socialism, then they obviously don't know what's good for 'em. It's kings and queens and princes we ought to have.

And Conservatives. And princesses. Even if they can't bloody read..."

Becky was sure that she'd misheard.

"Wait a minute. Did you say *princess?*"

"Yeah. We're married, him and me. I'm a princess."

Becky stared.

Miss Bevan gave a short laugh. "Look, I'll prove it," she said, and got up from the sofa to open a drawer in a walnut bureau.

She brought out a piece of paper which, Becky saw when she unfolded it, was a certificate of marriage. The wedding had taken place in St. Patrick's Catholic Church in Hickson Street, Manchester, between Miss Adelaide Bevan and His Royal Highness Prince Rudolf Eugen Wilhelm August Josef von und zu Eschten und Rittersthal. The witnesses were a Mr. Albert Suggs and a Miss Emily Thwaite. The prince had signed himself Rudolf; she had signed herself even more simply *X.*

"Is that the right one? I ain't given you the laundry list by mistake?"

She sounded bitter. Becky handed the certificate back, wondering if she ought to curtsy.

"I'm flabbergasted," she said.

"Are you? Well, I'm buggered. I just dunno what I'm going to do."

"But how...why...?"

"He insisted. And he's such a nice man. When you seen and done all the things I have, you don't say no when you get a chance of something better. I should of, though. I know I should of."

"But...why Manchester?"

"Out of the way, see? It had to be a Catholic church, naturally, and he didn't want anyone to find out and prevent it, so that meant we couldn't do it in London, just in case. We went to this poky little dusty church behind a factory. Them witnesses, we just fetched 'em in off the street, they didn't know nothing about it. And the priest was a doddery old man smelling of whiskey. He kept wiping his nose on his sleeve and hoping we wouldn't notice. But it's legal. Everything's watertight. I'm a bloody princess, Becky. Can I call you Becky? You don't have to call me Your Highness. Adelaide'll do."

"But...does anyone else know about it? What about the royal family? Or the court? Or the people? What are they going to say when they find out?"

Miss Bevan threw up her hands and flounced back to the sofa.

"Dunno," she said.

Becky was goggling. The marriage of a prince was a matter for international politics. Kings and queens and statesmen were involved; they had to consult ambassadors, draw up treaties, consider every dynastic and diplomatic implication. What had he been thinking of, this prince, to take his illiterate cockney mistress up to Manchester and marry her in secret? Perhaps he was as naive as she'd been, puffing at her one cigarette in the shrubbery with her beefy lover.

And besides...

"You thought I wouldn't have heard of Razkavia," she said diffidently. "Well, I had, because I was born there. I'm a Razkavian citizen."

Miss Bevan stared. Then she flew into a passion.

"You're a spy!" she cried, and leapt up to stamp furiously on the polished floor. "You come here to prod your blooming nose in, didn't yer? Who's paying yer? Eh? Whose side you on? The Germans? The Russians? If I had a gun I'd shoot you where you sit, you baggage, you crawly slimy hypocrite. Bloody sauce! How dare you come in here pretending butter wouldn't melt, and all the time—"

"Shut your pan," said Becky hotly. It was an expression she'd heard, but never used, and it worked. Miss Bevan blinked and shut up mutinously. Becky went on: "Don't you dare get angry with me. I *am* Razkavian, and I had no idea who the prince was, and I'm certainly not a spy. Do you think I'm likely to betray my own prince now that I know who he is?"

"What you doing in this country then?"

"We're in exile."

"Why?"

"Nothing to do with you."

"Yes, it is, 'cause I'm a bloody princess, ain't I? I got a right to know who's teaching me. Sit down, go on. Stop scowling at me. I don't think you're a spy, really, you blush too easy."

Becky sniffed and sat down frostily; she hadn't been aware she'd stood up.

"All right," she said, "I'll tell you why we're in exile. My father was a lawyer and he tried to start a movement for democracy, and they arrested him and put him in jail. He caught typhus and died. So my mother took me and my grandmother and we came to live here. That's all."

"You're not likely to be on the side of the prince then, are yer?"

"It wasn't the royal family who locked him up, it was the court. I've got no grudge against Prince Rudolf."

Miss Bevan, or Princess Adelaide, raised an elegant eyebrow, but finally nodded and sat down, sullenly plucking at a thread on her dress. Then she looked at Becky helplessly.

"What can I *do*?" she said.

Becky blew out her cheeks in bewilderment.

"Well...to start with, you'd better learn to read. And write.

You can't go on signing things with an *X*."

"S'pose not." She sat up. "Go on then. When we gonna start?"

Becky looked around. There were no books in the room, but the Ludo board lay open in front of them.

"You can start by learning to read the rules of games. You know what they're about, so that's a way in. And colors—here we are—that's nice and easy. This says *Red*..."

They spent half an hour on that, by which time Adelaide could read *Start, Home, Finish,* and the four colors.

"We'll have to do writing too," Becky told her. "I'll look for a copybook this afternoon. You can learn the most elegant hand I can find. In fact, you'll have to learn all kinds of things, won't you? You need more than a reading and writing teacher. You need—"

But she never finished the sentence, for that was the moment when Becky's first bomb went off.

There was a powerful *Bang!* and a blast of air that blew the curtains up and slammed the window shut, breaking all the glass. Both girls ducked instinctively, Becky grabbing for the papers on the table and Adelaide turning to crouch by the sofa, wide-eyed.

After the first shock, Becky leapt up to see what had happened. Adelaide joined her at the window. Only a second before the explosion, Becky had been aware of the sounds of a carriage drawing up outside the house, a horse blowing hard and shaking its head. Now, as the dust that had risen in a great cloud drifted over the dry road and the laurels, she saw them both—shattered. The horse lay twitching in the shafts, messily, and the coachman lay still. Halfway up the garden path, unharmed, mesmerized, stood the figure of Herr Strauss, Prince Rudolf of Razkavia.

For a moment no one moved. Then the prince turned to look up at the window, his eyes seeking Adelaide's, and the entire road seemed to come to life: doors opened, servants appeared at gateways, a nursemaid with her two small charges craned to see, a stout gentleman with a walking stick ran clumsily up, a butcher's boy with a basket of meat cast a professional eye at the horse. From nowhere the straw-hatted detective, J. Taylor, appeared at the side of the prince and spoke quietly.

"That's the detective," said Becky. Her voice was shaking.

Adelaide said nothing. She was watching with fierce concentration. J. Taylor glanced out at the road and snapped his fingers at the butcher's boy, who dropped his basket inside the gate and took off his cap.

"Go and find a copper," they heard J. Taylor tell him. "Quick as you like. We'll need a doctor, too, to certify the death. Do that in under ten minutes, and there's five bob for you. Hop it."

"I've seen him before," Adelaide said quietly. "I *know* I have."

J. Taylor seemed to know how to take charge of things; he appointed the stout gentleman to keep guard over the shattered carriage, he tore a curtain loose from the broken door and laid it gently over the dead man, he took a clasp knife from his pocket and did something to the horse, which fell still. He wiped the knife clean and stood up, his eyes meeting Becky's and moving to look expressionlessly at Adelaide; and then he joined the prince and entered the house.

"You gone pale," said Adelaide critically.

"Hardly surprising," said Becky.

"Doesn't suit yer. Listen, when Rudi—the prince—comes in, you pretend you don't know who he is."

Becky was about to argue, but there came a knock on the door, and the prince himself came in.

"My dear..." he said.

Adelaide ran to him almost protectively, but stopped. Behind the prince was the jaunty figure of the straw-hatted detective, serious now, and as he stepped into the doorway Becky had the most curious sensation, because J. Taylor and Adelaide were looking at each other with an almost electric intensity.

The moment passed.

The prince, who seemed dazed—at all events, he hadn't seen what Becky had, that fierce reciprocal glance—gathered himself and said, "My dear. I am sorry to interrupt your lesson, but I must ask Miss Winter to leave us now. As you have seen, Miss Winter, I am in some danger. I think it has passed for the moment, but I would not want to expose you to any more of it. This gentleman will escort you home."

Adelaide said to Becky, "Stay a moment. She'll come down in a minute, Rudi," she added, and pushed the door to, shutting the men out. Then in a fierce whisper she said "What's his name? That feller in the straw hat? What's he called?"

"I gave you his card—oh, of course, you can't read it," said Becky, and went to pick it up from the little bamboo table. "J. Taylor, Consulting Detective, care of Garland and Lockhart, Photographers, Orchard House, Twickenham...What's the matter?"

Because her pupil had clutched a hand to her heart, and gone pale. Her great dark eyes were wide. Then she snatched the card from Becky and sank into a chair as the color rose in her cheeks again.

"You'd best go," she said hoarsely. "Go on. He'll be waiting. But you come back, you hear?"

"I promise," Becky said.

Bemused, she left the room and went downstairs, to find the prince standing anxiously in the hall. She tried to remember not to curtsy as he nodded to her, and then went out to join J. Taylor, Consulting Detective, in the garden.

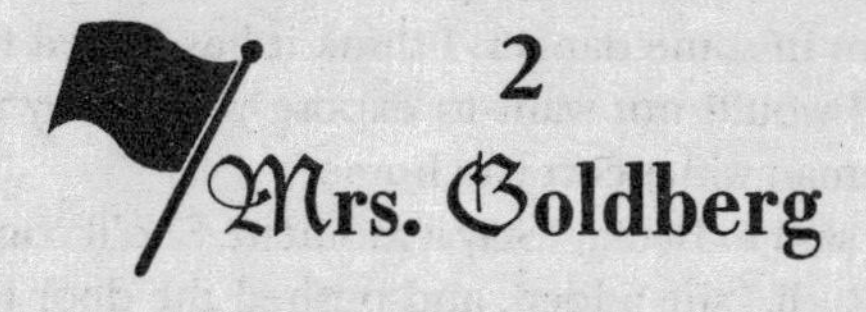

2
Mrs. Goldberg

Becky was first to the garden gate; J. Taylor was discussing something with the prince. As she stood there waiting, the butcher's boy came panting up red-faced, and stopped in surprise when he saw her.

"Oh! It's you!" he said. "D'you see the explosion, then? See the dead bloke? All his tripes and giblets hanging out?"

"Don't be disgusting."

"Here, you all right for cigarettes? Fancy a smoke in the bushes again? Eh?"

She turned away. J. Taylor came up, and the butcher's boy turned his attention to him instead.

"I found a copper," he said. "A big fat one. He'll be here in a minute. Five bob you said, didn't yer?"

J. Taylor gave him a couple of coins, and walked away with Becky.

"Shouldn't you wait for the police?" said Becky.

"Herr Strauss will deal with them. He's got my card; they can find me if they want me. And it's not as if I actually saw the bombers; no one did. They'll have used an infernal machine."

"A what?"

"A clockwork timer to explode the dynamite. They don't have to throw bombs any more, that's old-fashioned. Where are you going, Miss Winter? Can I escort you anywhere?"

They were halfway down Church Road by this time, and Becky found that she was shaking helplessly. She didn't know whether to trust him or not; but the prince obviously did, and...

Her head began to swim, and he took her arm.

"Here, sit on this bench. Put your head down, that's it. It's shock; only natural. You'll feel better in a minute or two."

"Thank you," Becky muttered. "I feel very foolish."

"Well, you don't look it. Stop worrying."

"That poor coachman..."

More and more people were gathering back along the road, outside the house. Someone was cutting the reins to free the dead horse from the shafts of the carriage; a policeman was lumbering up from the other end of the road.

"Are you really a detective?" Becky said.

"Yes. Among other things. I've been looking for that young lady for...oh, ten years, since we were kids. I thought she was lost for good. But a month or two ago I caught sight of a face that reminded me of her, and I traced her to that house. I was going to call and surprise her, but then I realized what the lay was, and I thought I'd be discreet. She was called Adelaide..."

"She still is."

"What's she doing chumming with a prince?"

Becky looked up sharply. "How do you know he's a prince?"

"It's not hard to find out. Servants talk; you can look up coats of arms. I made his acquaintance a week or two ago, which is why he knew who I was this morning. I wanted to be sure he was treating Adelaide right, you see. He's in love with her, poor guppy; innocent as a baby. I'm concerned, because if he's in political trouble, I don't want him dragging her into it."

"She's in already," Becky said. "She's married to him."

"*What?*"

"She showed me the marriage certificate...I suppose it doesn't matter my telling you, if you know her," Becky added doubtfully.

His eyes flared with anger. "Irresponsible half-wit! He *does* need looking after! Pitching her into a situation like this...It'd be hard even for a girl born to the princess trade. What does he expect of her, for God's sake?"

"He didn't force her into it. It was her choice too, I suppose. She knows who you are, by the way."

He looked at her intently. She told him of Adelaide's reaction when she'd learned his name from the card, and he nodded.

"She'd know Garland and Lockhart too," he said. "No doubt it's her. After all this time...I'm blowed."

"Who are Garland and Lockhart?"

He looked up the road, consulted a watch, snapped it shut and stood up.

"Listen, Miss Winter. I think we'd better work together for a while. If you're not busy for the next hour or two, can I take you to Twickenham and introduce you to an old friend of mine? She'll vouch for me, and for Adelaide, and it'll give us a chance to tell you the whole story."

Becky was far from sure about the propriety of this. But he seemed honest, and she was vastly intrigued, and after all the more she knew the more she could help Adelaide.

"Very well," she said.

In the train he told her how, years before, he had been an office boy in the financial heart of London, and had helped a young lady called Sally Lockhart solve the mystery of her father's murder. It was a murky story, with Chinese secret societies and opium and an enormous ruby mixed up in it. The nine-year-old Adelaide had been the maidservant (more of a slave, really) of a vile old woman called Mrs. Holland, who had played a part in Sally Lockhart's story, and after the mystery was cleared up and the villains disposed of, Adelaide vanished. They'd been afraid she was dead, until J. Taylor had caught a glimpse of Adelaide a month before, and traced her to number 43, Church Road, and met the prince.

Becky said, "Is Miss Lockhart the friend I'm going to meet?"

"Yes. She's Mrs. Goldberg now."

Sally (Mr. Taylor called her that) was a crack shot with a pistol, apparently. She worked as a financial consultant, and she was married to the political journalist Daniel Goldberg, who had helped to rescue Sally's little daughter when she was kidnapped the year before.

He told all this in the simplest, most matter-of-fact way, as if kidnappings and opium dens were everyday features of life. Becky was more impressed by this than if he'd tried to play it up. Then she realized what Mr. Taylor had said about a child.

"Did you say that Mrs. Goldberg had a child? Before...before she was married?"

"Yes. It happens, you know. Little Harriet was Fred Garland's daughter; he died in a fire. He was with me the night Adelaide disappeared. She'll remember him, I'm sure."

That set the seal on it: Becky was fascinated. If you were a single woman, you needed great strength of character to have a child and remain respectable. She found herself looking forward to meeting this gun-toting female desperado Mrs. Goldberg, and finding out how she did it.

Orchard House, in Twickenham, stood at the end of a quiet

tree-lined road near the river: a big Regency villa covered in white stucco, with a gravel drive and a stable block off to the left. There was a light ironwork balcony, and a glass-covered veranda to the side, overlooking a wide garden. It seemed an odd place to run a detective agency from.

"Well, we're an odd crew," said J. Taylor. "I've got an office in the Edgware Road, but I haven't had the cards printed for that yet. This is home rather than workplace."

He showed her into a comfortable, jumbled kind of room—a mixture of studio, workshop, and sitting room, with French windows open wide to let the sun in. There was a cabinet containing blue china, there was a wall of bookshelves, there was a grand piano, and hanging by the door, something that drew Becky like a magnet—an oil sketch of a French river on a sunny morning, with the fresh light almost laughing as it touched the blossoms on the trees and sparkled on the water.

"Pissarro!" she said, before she could help herself. "Oh! I do beg your pardon..."

Seated on the sofa by the French windows was a young woman with blond hair and dark brown eyes. She was biting through a strand of thin navy-blue wool from the bulky piece of knitting on her lap.

"Hello, Jim," she said. "Who's this?"

"This is Miss Winter. She's brought me luck. Miss Winter, this is Mrs. Goldberg."

Mrs. Goldberg stood up to shake hands. She was slim and pretty, and younger than Becky had expected. She had the same direct, vivid, friendly curiosity in her expression as J. Taylor did, almost as if they were brother and sister.

"And yes, it is by Pissarro," Mrs. Goldberg said. "I bought it last week. Have I made a good choice?"

"It's lovely. Monsieur Pissarro stays with some friends of my mother's when he comes to London, and we know him slightly, that's how I recognized his style..."

Mrs. Goldberg was still holding her knitting, and Becky was staring at it, rudely, because the woman she'd heard about on the train, this daring adventuress who fired pistols and married socialists and had a child out of wedlock, was hardly the sort of person to *knit,* surely?

Mrs. Goldberg saw where she was looking, smiled, and tossed the bundle to J. Taylor.

"I don't believe it," he said, holding it up against himself: a fisherman's jersey. "It blooming fits, as well."

Mrs. Goldberg laughed. "Jim bet me five pounds I couldn't do it," she said. "It's taken me nearly a year, but I wasn't going to let it beat me. Come on, dub up," she said to him, holding out a hand.

He counted out five sovereigns. "Don't bet with women," he said to Becky. "Here, Sal, we've walked into a prime lark here. It *is* Adelaide, and she's married to the prince. Miss Winter's her language tutor. Oh, and someone tried to blow him up this morning."

"They didn't succeed, I hope?"

"There was a bomb in his carriage," Becky said. "An infernal machine, Mr. Taylor thinks."

"A bomb?" said Mrs. Goldberg. "I've never heard a bomb explode. What sort of noise does it make?"

"D'you know, I can't remember. A bang, obviously, but whether it was a sharp one or a deep one or a whooshy one, I couldn't say. I was upstairs in the sitting room with Miss Bevan, and it blew the glass out of the window. It made a lot of dust..."

"Miss Bevan? Is that what Adelaide calls herself?"

"Yes. But..." Becky felt a moment's doubt again; should she be exposing Adelaide's secrets to these strangers? But she'd seldom felt so welcome, seldom met people she trusted so instinctively.

Mrs. Goldberg saw her hesitation, and took a stereoscope from the sideboard, fitting a slide into the frame before handing it to Becky. The first picture showed a little girl with enormous dark eyes dressed as a kitchenmaid, and the next showed her as a flower girl, and then as a Biblical maiden, and then as a fairy, and then as Little Nell. Was she Miss Bevan? It was hard to say. Then Mrs. Goldberg handed her another.

"Yes! It's her!"

It was the very one she'd seen earlier that morning in Miss Bevan's own room: the little girl on the man's knee, and the sentimental song. She told Mrs. Goldberg about it, and the other woman clapped her hands with delight.

"I don't believe it!" she said. "Adelaide…We thought she was dead, we thought she'd vanished forever…"

"Why did you take so many pictures?"

"It was when we were starting out. We sold them individually, at first, and then we made sets—Scenes from Dickens, Scenes from Shakespeare, Castles of Britain, Corners of Old London, and so on. But Adelaide had vanished by that time, so she was only in the early ones. And she's kept it…"

Becky told her about how Adelaide had reacted on hearing the names Taylor and Garland and Lockhart.

"No doubt about it," said Mrs. Goldberg. "And she's married to the Prince of Razkavia…Where *is* Razkavia? Dan would know. He's probably been arrested there more than once. My husband," she added to Becky. "Not a criminal, a politician."

"I know where Razkavia is," Becky said. "As a matter of fact, I was born there. I suppose I'm still a citizen."

She was pleased with the modest sensation she caused. Mrs. Goldberg and Mr. Taylor looked at each other, speechless, and then a broad grin broke out on his face and a warm smile on hers.

"That settles it," Mrs. Goldberg said. "You'll have to stay to lunch now, and tell us all about it. This is too good to miss, isn't it, Jim?"

Lunch was a casual affair, to Becky's relief. Within half an hour she found herself feeling that she'd known these odd, sharp, teasing, friendly people all her life, and she told them everything she knew about the little kingdom that was her birthplace.

"It's hardly bigger than Berkshire. Between Prussia and Bohemia, so it's sort of squashed between Germany and Austria-Hungary. There were dozens of those little kingdoms once, but most of them have been gobbled up now. Except Razkavia. It goes all the way back to 1253..."

She told them what she remembered of the story of the Red Eagle. Razkavia had been invaded by Ottokar the Second, the king of Bohemia, but a nobleman called Walter von Eschten and one hundred knights took a stand on a great rock in a bend of the Eschten River, fighting under a banner bearing a red eagle, and all Ottokar's forces couldn't dislodge them. At night, knowing the mountains so well, Walter and his men slipped out silently, without their armor so as not to make a noise, and destroyed all the Bohemians' supplies. Ottokar's knights clanked about helplessly, hot and hungry and totally baffled, until Walter drew them into battle at his castle of Wendelstein, where most of the invaders were killed.

Ottokar kept his distance after that, and so did everyone else; and the red eagle banner, the *Adlerfahne*, had flown over the Rock of Eschtenburg ever since. While the eagle flies, Razkavia will be free, said Walter von Eschten, and so it was. The banner was taken down for two reasons only: one was to keep it repaired (there wasn't an original thread left, but it was still the same banner) and the other was for a coronation, when it was taken to the cathedral to be blessed, and then carried by the new king back across the ancient bridge to the Rock of Eschtenburg, to fly again. That was why the king of Razkavia was sometimes called the *Adlerträger*, the Eagle-bearer. For Razkavians the Red Eagle wasn't just a flag; it was their very identity. If it were ever to fall, ever to touch the ground...No one even dared to think of it.

The country wasn't especially prosperous. There had once been rich mines in the Karlstein Mountains, producing copper and a little silver, but as long as two centuries before, they had begun to run out, at least of copper. There was plenty of some ore that looked like copper but wasn't, and which poisoned the miners who worked it. It was so useless and unpleasant that they called it *Kupfer-Nickel*, or devil's copper, and left it well alone. Much later someone discovered that *Kupfer-Nickel* was a compound of arsenic and a new metal, which they called nickel, and by the beginning of the nineteenth century they'd found some uses for it, so the mines of Karlstein began to work again.

But for centuries there was nothing to be gained from Razkavia, so the surrounding nations left it alone. The people milked the cows that grazed on the upland pastures, made wine from the grapes that grew on the slopes of the Elpenbach Valley, and hunted the game in the forests. In the capital, Eschtenburg, there was an opera house, where the composer Weber had once conducted; there was a theater and a cathedral and a pretty baroque palace, all fantastic columns and fountains and icing-sugar plasterwork; and there was a park with a grotto-pavilion built by Razkavia's one mad king, who had been fairly harmless, as mad kings went. In the 1840s, the younger set of the aristocracy, tired of the stuffy life around the king and his conservative court, tried to establish a little spa called Andersbad, down the Elpenbach Valley, as a center of fashion. There was a casino; Johann Strauss had played there with his orchestra, and they'd even paid him to write an Andersbad Waltz, although it wasn't one of his best. There were a few tourists, even occasionally a visiting king or grand duke, but not enough to spoil it.

In fact, Razkavia was one of the most pleasant places in Europe. The forests were deep and romantic, the Elpenbach Valley was picturesque. Eschtenburg with the rock and the banner was medieval and baroque and artistic; Andersbad was raffish and amusing; the beer was good, the game was abundant, and the people were hospitable.

"Sounds delightful," said Mrs. Goldberg. "But you're not living there now..."

"We're in exile, Mama and I and my grandmother. You see, when I was young, my father and some of his friends—he was a lawyer—tried to set up a political party. A liberal party. They wanted to bring about a more democratic system, because there was no parliament or senate or anything. But they put him in prison, and he caught typhus and died. So Mama took me and Granny away and we've lived here ever since. She won't go back. It's more democratic now, apparently, but there's the danger from the two Great Powers."

"What do they want?" said Mr. Taylor.

"The nickel from the mines. I think you make an alloy with it, for gun barrels or armor plating or something. Both powers are sort of hovering, ready to pounce. Germany could conquer the place in about an hour and a half, and so could Austria-Hungary, but if either of them did they'd have trouble with the other one, so they're holding off, so far. Mama thinks we're safer here."

"She's probably right," said Mrs. Goldberg. "And Adelaide—little Adelaide! Married to the prince..."

She shook her head in wonderment.

"It'll have to be a morganatic marriage," said Becky.

"What's that?" said J. Taylor.

"Legal," said Mrs. Goldberg, "but limited. If she has any children, they don't inherit. That's right, isn't it?"

Becky nodded. "There was a king of Razkavia called Michael the Second who was mad. He wanted to marry a swan. So they let him, but it had to be morganatic."

"Quite right," said Mr. Taylor. "Wouldn't do to have an egg on the throne. But it's a bit of a coincidence, isn't it? Prince Rudolf picking one of his own subjects as a language tutor for his wife, I mean."

"Not so much really. There's quite a lot of us in Maida Vale, people who've left Razkavia for one reason or another. I know at least a dozen. Writers, painters, people like that. One of the ways we can earn money is teaching German, and Maida Vale's only a short walk away from Church Road. The prince could have picked any of us without knowing where we came from."

"And you," said Mrs. Goldberg. "What do you want to do with your life?"

That was a question not often asked of girls, in Becky's experience, and she wasn't sure what sort of answer to give. She liked the idea of sweeping into a lecture, austere, gowned, majestic, and being addressed as Dr. Winter. But then she also liked the idea of presiding over a bar in a shantytown, with a cigar in her mouth, a diamond in her ear, and a gun in her belt. It was difficult to decide.

"I've got to earn some money," she said. "I want to go to university, but I've got to help Mama too. She illustrates stories for magazines. But now I'm involved with this...I promised I'd go back to Miss Bevan. Adelaide. The princess. She needs to learn, and I want to help her. And besides, I'm curious. Prince Rudolf is a descendant of Walter von Eschten, you see. And that means a lot to me. Because I *am* Razkavian, after all, in spite of what they did to my father; and if people are trying to blow up my royal family..."

"Yes?" said Mr. Taylor.

"Well, I want to try and stop them."

"Good for you," he said. "But you want to keep away from dynamite."

"You know, I'd love to see how this turns out," said Mrs. Goldberg, with real longing in her voice. "But I'm off to America with my husband the day after tomorrow. He's going to study labor relations in Chicago, and I want to look at the stock market in New York; we're going to be away some time...Listen, Rebecca—may I call you Rebecca?"

"Becky."

"Becky, then: give my love to Adelaide. And trust Jim—Mr. Taylor—and take his advice. He's saved my life three times already. I hope he never has to save yours, but if he has to, you can be sure he'll do it. And the best of luck!"

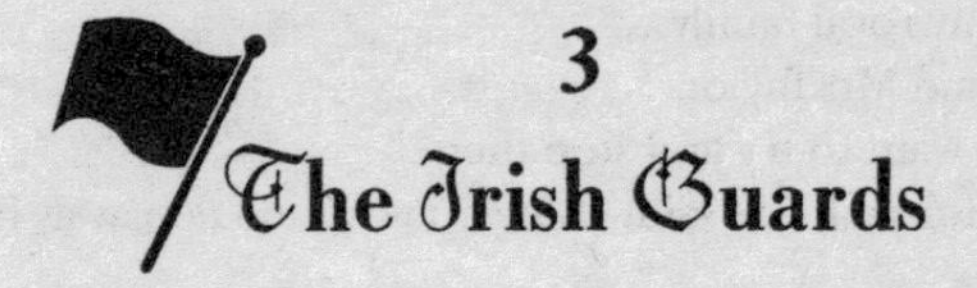

3
The Irish Guards

Jim Taylor was twenty-three. As he'd told Becky, he and Sally Goldberg had shared a number of adventures and a considerable amount of danger; and he did work as a detective, though that was only one among many ways he had of earning money. He also wrote stories for the shockers and the bloods—cheap magazines of the sort Becky's mother illustrated—though he had higher literary ambitions than that. He gambled; he'd been a European courier; he'd been a bodyguard; in short, he had a variety of livings, and he knew a great deal about the more colorful, which is to say the less law-abiding, side of London.

But he knew little about European politics. After he'd escorted Becky back to Maida Vale, he took the omnibus to Soho and climbed to the third floor of a dingy boardinghouse-cum-socialist club in Dean Street, where he found Sally's husband, Daniel Goldberg, with a pungent cigar clamped between his teeth, packing books for his trip to America.

"Ever been to Razkavia, Dan?"

"I passed through it once. Don't drink the water in the spa

there—it'll give you a gripe in the guts that'll lay you out for a week. Why?"

Jim told him. Goldberg stopped packing to listen.

"Well, I'm damned," he said. "How do you do it? How do you keep finding trouble like that?"

"Just luck. But what I want to know is, who'd want to blow him up? Anarchists, d'you reckon?"

"Pah! Who can say? Half of them are crazy, and the other half are ineffectual. You've spoken to the prince himself, you tell me. What does he think?"

"He thinks it might be his cousin Otto. Count Otto von Schwartzberg. He gave me a photograph..."

Jim fished in his waistcoat pocket and brought out a picture of a group of men, including the prince himself, wearing short Austrian-style jackets and hats decked with feathers and brushes of badger hair, posing outside a hunting lodge with a heap of dead stags at their feet. Some of them were carrying rifles.

"That's Otto with the crossbow," he said, pointing to a tall man, dark-eyebrowed and heavy-mustached, with a ferocious glitter in his eye and a scar down his cheek. "Apparently he killed a bear once with his...bare hands. He'd shot the cub, and the mother attacked him before he could reload. He tore her lower jaw from her head and then beat out her brains with a rock. He was covered in terrible wounds, and he stood and laughed. He's next in line to the throne, after Rudolf. The prince is frightened of him, that's plain enough; but I don't know, there's something that doesn't make sense about it."

"I agree," said Goldberg. "Always look for the politics first. The country will fall to one of the Great Powers eventually, and take it from me, that's what this is all about. As for the wild man who tears the heads off bears—no, he doesn't sound like a bomber. Pass me that book—the one you've got your feet on. That expensive one with the beautiful binding."

Jim took his feet off the table and handed Goldberg the scruffy directory he was referring to. Goldberg flicked through the pages and ran a finger down a column.

"Here we are," he said. "This is a couple of years out of date, but the place isn't a democracy; the same men will still be in charge."

He handed back the book. Straining his German, Jim read a brief description of the kingdom of Razkavia, with the names and residences of the king, the crown prince, and Prince Rudolf, and the names of various officials such as the chancellor, the mayor of Eschtenburg, the inspector of mines, the chief of police, and so on.

"And your prince is not the first in line to the throne?" Goldberg said.

"No. That's his elder brother, Wilhelm. Who's married, but without children; so Prince Rudolf would be next. But just to get it straight, Dan: who would *you* suspect of leaving a bomb in his carriage? Who should I watch out for?"

"Well, you can forget the werewolf of Schwartzberg. He's interesting, but anthropologically, not politically. It won't be him. There'll be someone obscure working quietly to provoke a crisis, so as to give Prince von Bismarck in Berlin or Emperor Franz-Josef in Vienna the excuse to send in a regiment and annex the place. And once they do, nothing much will change. The king will become a duke of some kind, keep his palace and his hunting lodge; Otto von Schwartzberg will go on biting animals in half; but all the nickel from the mines will be trundling busily along a railway line to one place or the other. My bet is Germany. It'll end up in Krupp's artillery works, in Essen."

"You're an optimistic bleeder, aren't you?"

"Realistic, dear boy. It's being right all the time that keeps me cheerful. You want that book? I won't need it in Chicago. Incidentally, I know a little story about Eschtenburg, the capital of Razkavia. The streets there are so crooked and ancient and narrow that they have no names, and the houses are numbered not according to where they are but according to when they were built, so you have number three next to number forty-six, and so on. Anyway, it seems that the Devil went there once, and couldn't find his way out. Which means, of course, that he's still there. I think I'd rather be in Chicago."

A year or two before, Jim had made the acquaintance of a gang of Irish street urchins from Lambeth. They were a brawling, foulmouthed, filthy crew, but he'd never seen better in a fight for cunning and tenacity; if rats bred with terriers, they'd produce offspring like this. Jim had used them on a number of different jobs, and he always paid them well, so they naturally respected him as a sound judge of value, as well as a masher and a swell.

As soon as he'd realized that the prince was in danger, he'd set them to guarding the villa in St. John's Wood—without anyone's knowing they were there, of course. They were to hide in the shrubbery of an empty villa overlooking Adelaide's house and in case of trouble, raise a hullabaloo. That very morning, Jim had checked with them first after the explosion; they hadn't seen anyone throwing a bomb, which was how he knew it had been an infernal machine.

Later that evening, when the prince was attending a soirée at the Brazilian Embassy, Jim paid the Irish Guards a visit of inspection. They were in fine fettle. Too fine, in fact; they'd found the local ruffians no match for them, and when Jim arrived at their hideout, they were crowing about a victory over a butcher's boy, and roasting some juicy-looking sausages over a smoky fire.

"But we're living off the land!" protested Liam, when Jim told them off. "Sure and isn't that what your guerrilla fighters are supposed to do?"

"You're supposed to keep out of sight. Save your fighting till this job's over. Is the lady at home?"

"She's been out for a drive," said a little boy called Charlie. "She came back about an hour ago. Say, Mr. Taylor, d'ye know about the skivvy?"

"What about her?"

"She's got a mash."

"He's an Alphonse!"

"He's a mackerel, if ever I saw one."

"All right, keep your voices down," said Jim. "What's he do, this fellow?"

"He calls each night after dark," said Liam. "She slips out and they have a yarn in the bushes. I thought maybe we could tap him on the coconut, what d'ye say? Go through his pockets."

"What I say is, don't. Why don't you follow him, see where he comes from?"

"Psst!" came from the lookout, and Jim clambered over the tangle of legs to see where he was pointing. "There he is now..."

The road was lit by gas, but the laurels overhanging Adelaide's garden shadowed it heavily. Jim could just make out a dark figure slipping along the side of the house and vanishing into the darkness. A second or two later came a gleam of light as the kitchen door opened and shut again.

"All right," said Jim. "Let's go and listen. Me, Liam, Charlie, and Sean. If I shout, then we grab him. If not, keep out of sight and don't let him hear you."

The Irish Guards were good. They slipped across the road like cats, and within a few seconds they and Jim were under the trees in Adelaide's garden. Jim felt a hand on his arm, and Liam whispered, "Listen."

Two voices were murmuring close by. The girl was saying, "...And she told that perky dell she was *married* to him!"

"Married?" said the other voice. Jim felt a strange prickle along his hairline, because something was *wrong* with that voice; was it foreign? Or was it something else?

"And I got this."

There was a rustle of paper, and a little flash of light as the man struck a match. Jim could see Liam's eyes glitter.

"A marriage certificate..." the man said. "What is this mark?"

"X. It's her signature. She's too bleedin' ignorant to read and write, so she's got to make an *X*. But that's her name, look, it's all legal."

The man said, "Ahh..."

There was the chink of coins. While they were distracted, Jim whispered, "As soon as she goes back in, we'll have him. I want that paper—it's vital. And I don't want him yelling."

He didn't have to tell them any more. Like most boys his age, Liam wore a silk muffler, which had all kinds of uses. He slipped it off, stooped and felt for a stone, and tied it into one end so that he could swing the muffler round the man's neck as a garrote. The other boys crept away to hide by the gate.

They didn't have to wait for long. The man said quietly, "Same time tomorrow?"

"All right. I'll see what else I can find. But I want more money'n this next time."

"You shall have it," he said.

The maid turned away and flitted back along the side of the house. The man stayed where he was for a minute, lighting a cigarette while Liam fretted and twitched beside Jim; and then the man moved away toward the garden gate.

Two paces, and Liam was behind him, the muffler swinging through the air with a silken hiss. It lashed around the man's throat, Liam tugged backward and Jim threw himself at the man's knees, and there was a lashing, gasping, kicking, choking confusion for a few seconds until the maid's visitor was pinioned facedown on the patch of grass under the laurels, with Liam kneeling on his back and the other two boys holding his legs and arms.

"Right, listen," Jim whispered. "My friend's going to stop strangling you as soon as you nod."

The man's head jerked frenziedly, and Liam loosened the muffler.

"What do you want?" came a hoarse gasp.

"That paper the maid's just given you. Turn him over, lads."

They rolled him over onto his back, and Jim felt in his pockets. As Jim searched, the feeling of *something not right* deepened suddenly into a strange suspicion. He hesitated, and the man's eyes—large, dark, expressive—flashed in the gloom. Then Jim found the paper, in the waistcoat pocket, and tucked it in his own pocket before sitting back on his haunches.

Liam stood up and slipped the muffler back around his neck. The other boys let go. The spy got up slowly, crouched like a cat, with a sleek feral grace. And then something glittered in his hand.

Jim had time to spring backward, but not quite time enough to avoid the slashing knife blade. It caught him across the knuckles of his right hand: a heavy dull pain that turned almost at once into a blazing sharpness. He cursed and rolled sideways as the other leapt at him, and then sprang up again, whipping his right arm out of his jacket and bundling it around the left automatically, as you always did against a knife, but Jim had no weapon.

Liam swung his muffler again. The spy dodged out of range, and then Jim heard several things at once: hooves and carriage wheels from the road, a window flying open above him. He paused, and the spy turned and darted out of the garden.

"After him, boys!" Jim shouted. "Follow him as far as he goes!"

Liam yelled across to the others in the hideout, and Jim reached the gate to see the man fleeing down the road, pursued by a line of small boys whooping their Lambeth war cries.

And then Jim realized that the prince was standing beside him. He'd just got out of the carriage, and he was in full fig: white tie, tails, glittering decorations around his neck, and a face that looked ravaged.

"What has happened?" he said. "Is she safe?"

"It was a spy. Yes, she's safe—so far. But we've got to talk, you and I."

"You are bleeding," said the prince, and Jim found that blood was pouring thickly from the cut over his knuckles. It was hurting damnably.

"I thought you were at the Brazilian Embassy, sir?" he said, wrapping a handkerchief around his hand.

"I was—but something has happened—and a spy as well? *Ach*, this is too much—"

"Let's go inside," Jim said, and then, to the coachman goggling from the box, "Go and find a policeman, quick as you like."

The man cracked his whip and set off. As soon as they were in the house, Jim took the prince into the parlor and sent for the maid. She was frightened, but she looked from one to the other with a narrow, calculating flick of the eyes. Jim took her measure at once.

"You're a thief," he said to her, "and a copper's coming to

take you away in a minute. But how long you spend in jail depends on whether you tell us the truth now. Who was that person you were speaking to?"

"I dunno," she said, with a lift of her chin. "They won't send me to jail."

"Maybe not. This is treason, after all, and that usually means the rope. You fancy standing in the dock when the judge puts the black cap on? Eh?"

Bluff, but it worked. Her eyes widened, and she gave a little gasp of dismay.

"I—I dunno who he is—he give me five sovereigns, but I never meant no harm—I thought it wouldn't matter..."

She wasn't honest, but she had little else to tell. Jim locked her in the scullery, and went back to find the prince pacing nervously, chewing a fingernail.

"What did she steal?" he said.

"This," said Jim, taking out the marriage certificate.

The prince put his hands to his head. He looked wild-eyed with despair—but then, thought Jim, the poor mooncalf had looked like that when he came in; something else was up.

"Why didn't you tell me, sir?" he said. "Why keep me in the dark? I'm working for you, remember?"

The prince stood there in his evening finery, with the Cross of St. This and the Order of the Golden That twinkling in the lamplight, and looked overwhelmed. It was all too much for him. And then he told Jim why he'd come home early.

"I had to leave the soirée. There was a message—terrible news. My brother the crown prince and his wife, Princess Anna—both shot. He is dead and she is not expected to live. I must return at once. I came here to...warn my wife...I have asked the ambassador and his wife to be here in twenty minutes. They do not know why."

At that moment the door opened, and Adelaide came in. Jim felt a shock in his heart, as if his soul were leaping from his body to fly to her. Those great dark eyes, that slender figure, that vivid face alert with speculation and mischief and underpinned with melancholy or apprehension...He knew that very second that wherever this game led, he'd be in it all the way. His spirit soared and then plunged downward at once, as he remembered that she was married, that she was a princess, and that he was her husband's man.

"Hello, Jim," she said softly.

"Little Adelaide," he said, and his voice was shaking. "Where you been all this time?"

She glanced at the prince, took in something of his expression, then looked down at Jim's hand.

"You're hurt," she said, concerned, and stepped forward to look more closely and untie the handkerchief Jim had bound roughly around it. "Let me do this properly—you got to wash it—Rudi, what's going on? What's the matter?"

While she rang a bell and sent the cook for a bowl of hot water, the prince told her what had happened in Razkavia.

"So I am the heir to the throne," he said. "When my father dies, I will be king. In a few minutes the ambassador will be here. I have asked him to bring his wife; they must both know. And then we must go, straightaway."

"To Razkavia?"

"Of course. I shall not go without you. You must come, Adelaide. So must you, Mr. Taylor."

Adelaide flashed a dark look at Jim, then back at her husband. "I'm not going without Becky."

Everything was happening at once. The cook brought in a bowl of water and some clean flannel, and simultaneously there was a rap at the door, and as Jim looked out of the window he saw a policeman standing on the path, and the lights of a carriage pulling up.

"Come on upstairs," said Adelaide, taking the bowl, and Jim followed, leaving the prince to tell the policeman the charge against the maidservant and to receive the ambassador and his wife in the parlor. *God knows what they must be thinking,* Jim thought; *well, they'll find out in a minute...*

Adelaide knelt on the floor, dabbing painfully at his hand and binding it up, while they talked quietly and urgently, like guilty children.

"What's going to happen, Jim? I *can't* be a bloody princess—"

"You are one. Shut up. Where've you *been?* What happened after we lost you? That night when we were running away from Mrs. Holland—"

"On the wharf there—you and Mr. Garland fighting the big man—"

"We killed him. He bloody near killed us, too. What'd you run away for?"

"Dunno. I was just so scared. Oh, Jim, I been doing terrible things—"

"How'd you get hitched like this?"

"He asked me. He's in love with me."

"I can tell. But how'd you meet him?"

"I used—I was...I'm ashamed, I can't tell you."

"This is the only chance you're going to get, Adelaide, because they'll be up here in a minute, and then we'll never be alone together again, you realize that? You been on the game, haven't you?"

She nodded. Her little face was flushed with sorrow, and he longed to kiss her; and then he swore to himself that while the prince was alive he'd never let this happen again, never let their hands touch as they were doing now, never get within six feet of her. There was love, and there was honor, and when they clashed, it broke your heart.

"I got lost, Jim. I didn't know what I was doing. I begged, I stole, I near starved...Finally I ended up in a house in Shepherd Market. You know the sort I mean. This old woman called Mrs. Catlett, she had half a dozen girls. She weren't bad, she had a doctor what called every month to keep us healthy...And one day this German nobleman come in with a party of friends. He was showing them around, like tourists. One of 'em was the prince. I could tell he was uncomfortable, he didn't want that kind of thing, but he was nice and we just talked, and...I suppose he fell in love there and then. He ain't had much affection, poor thing. So anyway, he paid Mrs. Catlett a lot of money, for taking me away, like, and he set me up here. And then we was married. He wouldn't take no for an answer. I...I used to go up Bloomsbury all the time at first, you know. I used to stand across the road and look at Garland's, at the shop..."

"Why didn't you come in, you crazy goose? You know we had detectives combing bloody London for you?"

"I was scared I'd done something wrong. Then later on, when I plucked up me courage and I went there, it was all burnt down..."

"Fred died in the fire."

"He never...Oh, God...What about Miss Lockhart? And Trembler?"

"Miss Lockhart's married now. She's Mrs. Goldberg. And old Trembler married a rich widow. He keeps a boardinghouse in Islington."

Then she said again, "Jim, what's going to happen? I *can't* go and be a princess, I can't do it..."

"You married him. You got to face it. You can't back out of a thing like that. But I'll be there, and Becky—"

"Will she come? I won't go without her, I swear it."

"Yeah, 'course she'll come," said Jim, privately uncertain. "Here—listen—they're coming up the stairs. Chin up, gal. We been in worse places than this. Remember the Animal Charcoal Works?"

She gave a tight nervous smile, and Jim's heart wept.

There was a brief knock, and the door opened. Jim stood up as the prince came in. The elderly man who followed him blinked once or twice in surprise at the young man with the disordered hair and the torn jacket, at the dark-eyed girl smoothing her skirts, at the bowl of bloody water on the floor; then he clicked his heels and bowed. He was a stout, red-faced, bristle-haired military man with a dueling scar on his cheek, a mighty mustache, and a chest full of medals. His wife, massive and icy, glittered like an opera house.

The prince closed the door.

"We shall speak in English," he began. He was pale, and he sounded nervous, but he went on steadily, "This is not the way in which I would have wished to break such news. However, it cannot be helped. Adelaide, this is the ambassador, Count Thalgau, and Her Grace the countess."

Jim noticed that both of them were immediately aware of the way he made the introduction: they were introduced to her, not she to them, so she must be their social superior. There was a bristle of surprise, and then it was his turn.

"Count Thalgau, this is my trusted secretary and adviser, Mr. James Taylor. As you can see, he has been wounded in my service this evening already."

An approving kind of bristle this time, followed by a click of heels and a nod. Jim couldn't shake hands, but he managed a respectful Prussian-style jerk of the head. Behind all the politeness he could sense a colossal curiosity building up like steam in a boiler.

The prince reached for Adelaide's hand, and drew it through his arm.

"And this is my wife, Adelaide, and your princess," he said.

The count took a step backward; the countess's mouth fell open. Then the old man exploded.

"God in Heaven! Married! *Married!* Are you mad, sir? Have you lost your wits? The marriage of a prince—now a crown prince, by God! The heir to a throne!—is not a matter for lovesick adolescents and moonstruck poets, by God! It is a matter for diplomatists and statesmen! Good God! The very future of Razkavia depends on the alliance you contract with your marriage—*ach! Mein Gott!*"

"And that is a very good reason," said the prince, pale but steady under fire, "if I needed any other than my love for her, for justifying my marriage to this lady. Any diplomatic marriage I contracted would be taken as a signal of my political position, and that would be fatal. Now I have the freedom to act in the best way for Razkavia, without being tied up by an alliance which might split the country."

"Ach! Sancta simplicitas!" moaned the count. "But—the lady's family—who is she?"

The prince looked down at Adelaide, and said, "My wife is of English blood. As far as I can recall, there has been nothing but friendship between the peoples of England and Razkavia. There is nothing now to prevent our marriage."

"Prevent it, no. Dissolve it, yes. We shall apply to the Vatican at once. The cardinal-archbishop will do as—"

"Never!" said the prince, and then switched to German. In a high, angry tone, he said, "It is not your place, Count Thalgau, to seek to undo the decisions of princes. If I had asked you for advice, I would listen to you with respect—but I have not. I do not seek your advice. I require your loyalty. You have been a faithful friend of my family; do not betray me now. I love this lady as my soul. Nothing will part us but death—certainly not some squalid arrangement patched up by the Vatican. Do you understand?"

Jim understood enough German to follow that, and for the first time he saw something royal in the prince. The count closed his eyes. Then he rubbed his temples and said, "Well, if it is done, it is done. But of course it will be morganatic. The royal line of the Eschtenburgs will come to an end in you. King August the Second—"

"It cannot be morganatic."

"Why not?"

"Because we were married in this country. English law makes no provision for morganatic marriage. My wife has the rank of princess."

Only the fact that the prince was still standing prevented the ambassador from sinking into a chair. As it was, he tottered, and then Adelaide spoke.

"Your Excellency," she said in her little cockney voice, "I understand your surprise. I am very glad to meet you; my husband has often told me of his admiration for you and your exploits in battle. I look forward to hearing more about them. Would you and the countess care to sit down? And perhaps Mr. Taylor would be good enough to send for some refreshments?"

Nicely done, gal, Jim thought, as he took out the bowl of bloody water and went to scout round the kitchen. He found the cook and the bootboy fizzing with speculation, and told them to send up a plate of sandwiches and some wine, as quickly as they could.

When he got back upstairs, they were discussing Becky, so he chipped in.

"Can I suggest, sir, that you go now, with Her Royal Highness and the countess, to Rebecca's mother, Frau Winter? It's vital that she comes—I agree with Ad—with the princess—but she's only sixteen, and her mother will need to be reassured of the, er, the—"

"*Die Richtigkeit*," said the countess.

"*Ja*. The propriety," agreed the ambassador. "Very true. *Ja*."

They were both still dazed. Jim sympathized, but his hand was beginning to hurt like damnation, and when the gaping bootboy brought up the wine, he sank three glasses to dull the pain. Then the prince stood up to leave with Adelaide and the countess to astound Frau Winter, leaving Jim with the ambassador.

Count Thalgau slapped a fist into his palm several times, and fixed Jim with an eye that would have unseated a hussar.

"Do you speak German?" he said in English.

"Not perfectly, but I can manage," said Jim in German.

"Very well," the Count continued in his own language. "I want you to tell me the truth. How are you involved in this? And who has been spying, that you find yourself shedding blood to keep him away? Be warned, Mr. Taylor. I have been shocked this evening, but I love my country, I revere my prince, and now," he took a deep breath, "I am the most faithful servant of—of the princess. There is a great deal in this that I find mysterious. Tell me everything, or you will regret it."

So Jim began.

4
The Alhambra Theater

Becky was deep in an Italian grammar, her book at the edge of the pool of light in which her mother's hand was patiently drawing Deadwood Dick in the act of firing two pistols at a huge bearded outlaw six feet away from him, who was firing two pistols back. Perhaps the bullets had met in the air between them, because neither had come to any harm. One more dip of the pen, one more curl of the outlaw's beard filled in; and then Mama wiped the nib, put her hands in the small of her back, and stretched.

"Enough for now," she said, yawning.

"Cocoa?" said Becky, putting a marker in the grammar. The kettle was hissing gently on the hob, and the little wooden clock from Elpenbach was about to strike ten.

But before she could get up, there came a knocking at the outside door. Becky and her mother looked at each other: this lodging house was a staid, respectable place, where calls were seldom paid after six o'clock in the evening. They listened as Mrs. Page the landlady hobbled down the hall and opened the door.

A murmur of voices; several footsteps; and then a knock at their own sitting room door.

Becky ran to open it, her mother standing anxiously behind her. Mrs. Page's puzzled old face said, "A gentleman and, er, two ladies—come to see you, dear—I couldn't make out the name," she finished in a whisper.

Becky's eyes took in Adelaide, in cloak and hat; the prince; and a lady so grand and cold and monumental that she might have been made of marble.

"Oh! Ad—the prince—Your Highness—ma'am—Mama, it's—please come in," she said in utter confusion.

Mama was puzzled, but anxious to be polite, and simultaneously embarrassed by the shabbiness of everything. Why, they only had four chairs! But Mrs. Page had seen, and was bringing in another from the parlor.

Becky was trying to work out who should be introduced to whom, and whether she was supposed to know who the prince was, and whether she should have told her mother, as of course she had; but Adelaide spoke first.

"Rudolf," she said, "you know Miss Winter, and her mother. Becky, I think your mother knows that Herr Strauss is Prince Rudolf."

Mama curtsied to the prince, flushing deep red. Becky curtsied too, rather abruptly, and then Adelaide turned to the other lady.

"Countess," she said, "may I introduce Frau and—*und* Fräulein Winter. This is the Countess Thalgau. She's the wife of the Razkavian ambassador."

More curtsies; a frigid handshake. The countess looked around and closed her eyes in silent eloquence.

When Mrs. Page had come in with the other chair, and when they were all seated, the prince began to speak. He told them first about the assassination of the crown prince, and then about his own marriage. At first he spoke in English, in which he was accurate but not comfortable, but then he turned to Adelaide and said, "Excuse me, my dear; I must speak in German now; I cannot be precise otherwise."

His dreamer's face pale in the lamplight, he said to Becky's mother, "Frau Winter, when my wife told me that the tutor I had engaged was herself a native of our country, I felt the hand of fate guiding my affairs. Then I learned who her father was, and I was certain. I once had the privilege of meeting your late husband. He came to the palace to talk to me about the development of our laws, a visit arranged as part of my education. Believe me, I bitterly regret his death. One of the things I most wish to bring about is a change in our constitution to allow democratic parties to organize in the way your husband wanted.

"But as with everything else I want to do, I shall rely on the judgment and sensibility of my wife. Her experience of the world has given her a wisdom beyond her years, and a strength and perception of character on which I hope to rely greatly."

Becky noticed the countess turn and look at Adelaide with cold eyes. Adelaide herself was sitting quietly with her hands in her lap, watching the prince, and didn't notice.

"But my wife will need help," the prince went on. "She will need guidance and companionship. She will need instruction. And she has told me that Fräulein Winter can fulfill those needs in a way that no one else can.

"Frau Winter, I have spoken at length, for which I apologize. If you cannot allow Fräulein Winter to accompany the princess to Razkavia as her companion, I shall understand and respect your decision, and bid you good-day. In any case, madam, I truly beg your pardon for having disturbed you."

Mama looked at Becky, and took a deep breath. She put her hands together as if she were praying, and then clapped them very lightly as if she'd made up her mind.

"Your Highness," she said, "I want to say first how honored we are. And how much I wish we could receive you more comfortably. I well remember my husband's visit to the palace. He told me how attentively you had listened to him and questioned him. If he had lived, you would have found no wiser or more loyal counselor.

"And I am honored that you have confided in us. But your request is a great one...I am a widow in a strange country; I have to struggle to make a living. My only family is my aged mother, whom I cannot leave, and my daughter, whom I love dearly. If anything should happen to her, it would be the end of my life.

"However, she is a young woman of great strength and honesty, and many gifts. I have tried to raise her to be good, to be modest, to work hard, and to be charitable. I am proud of her. I think your princess will need a good friend. Well, she will find no friend truer or more valuable than my Rebecca. Sir, we are honored by your request. But you must allow me to say that Princess Adelaide will be even more honored by the friendship of my daughter.

"So my answer is yes, she may go, with my blessing. But I warn you, if anyone harms one hair of her head there is nowhere he can hide, for I will follow him to the ends of the earth and tear out his heart as he will have torn out mine. Rebecca, *liebchen...*"

And she blindly turned to Becky, her voice breaking, her arms out. Mother and daughter clung so close that Becky heard bones crack, and didn't know whether it was her ribs or Mama's corset; but it didn't matter, for she was howling too.

What a declaration to make to the crown prince!

When they were a little more composed, Prince Rudolf said, "We shall be leaving in thirty-six hours. You will need some clothes, Fräulein—mourning, and so on. Countess Thalgau will advise you. Frau Winter, I shall leave you some money to cover any expenses. Please let the countess know if you need any more..."

And there was gold on the table, more than the household had seen for years. Adelaide caught Becky's eye, and a little anxious smile flickered for a moment, and was answered with another. Becky wondered which of them would need the other most.

The Irish Guards had pursued the spy down into Marylebone, along the length of Baker Street, gathering reinforcements all the way, until there were a hundred or more yelling urchins chasing behind him. At the corner of Oxford Street, though, he leapt into a cab. Liam and Charlie were close enough to hear the address he gasped to the driver, and as the cab swung down into Mayfair they yelled, "This way! Follow us!" and raced along the length of Oxford Street before plunging down into Soho.

Breathless, they pelted through the back-doubles and arrived in Leicester Square just as a cab drew up by the stage door of the Alhambra Theater.

"Is that him?" said Liam, and "There he is!" shrieked Charlie, and "After him, lads!" cried Dermot.

The stage door-keeper had no chance: they poured in like maddened wasps. The evening's music-hall bill was just coming to an end, and the area backstage, the corridors, and the dressing rooms were thronged with artistes, carpenters, lighting men, and scene-shifters already; but within a minute there wasn't a corner of the theater, from the foyer to the flies, that wasn't infested with urchins.

"There he is!"

"I seen him—up there on the ladder!"

"He's gone down that trapdoor! After him!"

"He's along the corridor—there he goes!"

Five different men—acrobats, stage managers, or waiters—were pursued into corners, interrogated, and abandoned, before Liam, Charlie, and Dermot spotted their quarry in a corridor near the Green Room.

Determined, they raced along after him, just too late to prevent him from slipping into a dressing room. They heard a key turn, and hammered mercilessly on the paneled door.

"Come out, ye thieving toe-rag! Ye cowardly spy! Come out and fight, ye dirty devil!"

Silence from within; but the shouting and the clamor from behind them was getting louder.

"We'll have to break the door down, lads," said Liam, and they stood back across the narrow corridor, preparing to shoulder-charge. "One—two—"

And the door opened.

Off balance, they stumbled and gathered themselves to look up at the face of a woman: a beautiful, dark-eyed, bare-shouldered, raven-tressed, Spanish-looking actress in a scarlet gown. She was frightened; she could hardly speak for the rapid beating of her heart.

"Where's the man?" demanded Liam. "Where's he gone?"

She gestured helplessly at the open window.

"This way!" Liam yelled, just as the remaining swarm of urchins reached the door of the dressing room. Led by him, they poured through the room and out of the window, dropping darkly down the wall and scrambling through the clutter of new building works in Castle Street, bricks, planks, piles of rubble: gadflies after a maddened bull.

An imaginary bull.

The actress shut the window and with a long shuddering sigh let out the breath she'd been holding. She was exhausted; barely able to stand. Her breast heaving, she locked the door again, drew the curtains, and then put up her hand to take off the wig. She lifted up her dress, unhitched a fastening at the waist, stepped out of the trousers concealed beneath the skirt, and threw them over to join the hastily discarded jacket and waistcoat and shirt behind the door. Then she sat down heavily at the dressing table. Gradually her breathing became calmer. She loosed her tightly drawn black hair, and took out the bloodied knife from the sheath tied to her calf before wiping it on a silk handkerchief. She smiled faintly, and studied her reflection from this side and that.

Jim's unbelieving suspicion was right.

"A woman? What's her name?"

"Carmen Isabella Ruiz y Soler, sir. An actress."

"Reliable?"

"I believe I know how to control her, sir."

"Do you, by God? Well, you haven't failed me yet, I must admit, though this is one of the craziest schemes I ever heard of. Carry on, Bleichröder. And keep me informed."

We are six hundred miles away, in Berlin. The speaker is a ferocious-looking elderly man: round-headed, bald, with protuberant eyes and a sweeping mustache. He glares around, nods briefly, and leaves the room to go to his carriage. Officials in the antechamber bow—attendants open doors—functionaries hurry after him bearing documents, all moving with an air of edgy fear, for this is the great chancellor, Prince Otto von Bismarck.

The man in the office puts his hands on the arms of his chair and sits down carefully. He is a banker, the same age as Bismarck, but entirely without the commanding energy of the chancellor. Bleichröder has an air of studious abstraction: a noble, balding head, heavy whiskers, half-shut eyes, a thin curving nose. He waits until his secretary has closed the door.

"Well, Julius?" he says. "How do you interpret the meaning of that?"

This is a game they play. The young secretary draws on the knowledge he has, guesses the connections he doesn't know, and tries to divine the workings of his employer's fathomless and subtle mind.

"Razkavia...Isn't that the place where the crown prince was assassinated today, sir? I saw something in the midday telegrams...Little kingdom on the Bohemian border. Picturesque ceremony—something to do with a flag..."

"Yes. Right so far."

"Ah. It's coming back. Don't they mine something there? Tin or something?"

"Nickel. Very good, Julius."

"But I don't see why a Spanish actress is involved. Too deep for me, sir."

"Then I shall tell you. Go to the blue cabinet, if you please, and take out the file marked *Thalgau.*"

While the secretary unlocks the cabinet, the banker's hands move gently over the surface of his desk, rearranging a pen here, straightening the blotter, brushing off imagined specks of dust, lingering caressingly on a heavy little glass globe.

The secretary returns with the file, and Bleichröder leans back once more, hands behind his head, eyes half shut.

"Begin, then," he says, composing his mind.

5
Etiquette

The next day passed for Becky in a whirl of shopping. There wasn't time to have dresses made: they had to be bought ready-made and altered there and then. The countess watched through half-closed eyes, occasionally giving a curt order to Frau Winter, who relayed it in English to the milliners, the drapers, the dressmakers. Then there were valises to be bought, and a trunk; and Becky, remembering why she was going in the first place, insisted on buying copybooks and dictionaries for Adelaide. What could she teach her to read with? There wasn't time to look far: the two *Alice* books, *Black Beauty*...and a new game called Go as You Please, a chessboard and a set of checkers and chess pieces, and a handful of penny dreadfuls from Mama's worktable. That would have to do.

Her grandmother, bedridden and forgetful, knew something was happening, and fretted until Becky sat and talked to her in the evening light. The old lady couldn't understand much, but her papery hand lay contentedly in her granddaughter's until she fell asleep. And then there was more packing, more last-

that he was in love with Adelaide; still one more thing to worry about. But she didn't mention that in her letter, either.

As the light was fading on their second day of travel, the landscape began to change. The train was steaming (even more slowly now) through mountains, and the farther south they went, the higher the mountains became, until they had to look up from the carriage windows to see the tops of them, jagged edges of limestone pink in the evening light, swathed with scraps of cloud that were apricot and orange and pastel yellow. Farther down the slopes, dark green pines covered everything; and once in a clearing they saw a hunter, with his musket, his horn, and a frisking dog. He raised his feathered hat as they waved to him. Becky felt her spirits lifting: this was her country, her landscape, this was where she belonged. She was coming home.

Drifts of steam in the nighttime station, a red carpet, bowing officials doffing top hats, servants hastening to unload trunks and valises into a pair of carriages. Mourning: everyone in black, flags at half-mast for the dead crown prince. But from the public squares and gardens, from the Rose Labyrinth in the Spanish Gardens at the bend in the river, came the sound of jolly music as the bands (paid for by a music tax on tourists) oompahed their way through Weber and Strauss and Suppé; and the great cathedral bell tolling, tolling endlessly, and more bells striking the hour from the ancient churches in the little streets and squares. Cigar smoke in the air, and the scent of spring flowers, and the aroma of spicy stews and sauerkraut and grilling meat. The vastly overhanging eaves of the old buildings they passed under; balconies overflowing with scarlet geraniums; the lighted windows of beer cellars and cafés, replete with antlers and stuffed badgers and every kind of hunting trophy. The river, dark and swift, with the Rock of Eschtenburg on the far side, and the Red Eagle, the *Adlerfahne,* flying over the city as it had done for six hundred years.

Then the palace: icing-sugar columns in the moonlight, fountains tinkling in the formal gardens.

Servants bowing; marble stairs; statues, pictures, tapestries, carpets, porcelain. Adelaide beside Becky, grim, nervous, but bearing herself with tense dignity.

And a long wait in an anteroom where two dozen candles burned on gilt sconces in front of dark old looking glasses, while the prince explained things to his father the king. Adelaide, Becky, and the countess sat there for an hour—Becky timed it by the ormolu clock on the mantelpiece. Finally, at a quarter to midnight, the door opened and a majordomo or chamberlain of some kind bowed stiffly and said, "His Majesty will receive you now. When you enter the room you must curtsy once, inside the doorway, advance to the king and curtsy again. If you leave the room before he does you should walk backward, following the line of the carpet until you come level with where I shall be standing. Then you curtsy again and turn and leave. Please follow me."

Becky translated for Adelaide, who went first, with Becky and the countess following. They came to a large, brightly lit drawing room, where the prince was standing nervously by a blazing fire. The count was there too, looking solemn, and on a sofa sat an old, stern man dressed in deep mourning, with long gray side-whiskers, a bald head, and an expression of fathomless melancholy. His right hand lay along the arm of the sofa, and Becky noticed that his fingers never ceased to tremble. One foot was propped on a stool.

They curtsied, advanced to the sofa, curtsied again. The majordomo left silently.

"Countess," said the king in a hoarse, wheezing voice. "I trust this journey has not tired you?"

"Not at all, I thank Your Majesty."

"These are difficult times. How is your cousin, Lady Godstow?"

Like many monarchs, the old king had a prodigious memory for kinship; and he knew that the countess had a cousin three or four times removed, an English lady who was married to one of the lords in waiting at Queen Victoria's court. The countess actually flushed with pleasure, and they spoke about her cousin, and the rest of her family, for quite ten minutes before the king turned to Becky.

But not to Adelaide yet. They were all still standing, and Adelaide was desperately tired; but the king ignored her completely and turned to Becky.

"Fräulein Winter," he said. "You are very young to have developed all the talents I have been hearing about. The education of young women must be highly advanced in England. Here in Razkavia we are more old-fashioned. There is nothing we prize more in a girl than modesty; perhaps you will find us slow to appreciate you."

It took Becky a few moments to realize what he was saying, and then she hated him at once. She couldn't help remembering that this was the man who'd been responsible, however indirectly, for her father's death; and she hated him, too, for his deliberate snub to Adelaide, in not deigning to speak to her until last, after a mere interpreter. And she was tired and hungry, and she knew she shouldn't be doing it as soon as she began, but she couldn't help it.

She said, "Your Majesty is very gracious. But I am Razkavian myself, and my mother always told me that however poor our country might be in some things, it was rich in courtesy and kindness. I am glad to have the chance of learning about those qualities from the example of Your Majesty."

And she swept the deepest curtsy she could manage, until her nose nearly touched the carpet. She was aware of the countess frozen by her side, of the count bristling with anger, of the prince trembling, but mainly of Adelaide standing alert and puzzled beside her; and she looked up to see an ancient coldness in the eyes of the king.

It was a long stare, which she returned; and then he waved her aside and turned to Adelaide. He looked her up and down once or twice and then spoke, and Becky translated as the countess had told her, in a quiet voice and as swiftly and unobtrusively as she could, keeping close to their own words.

He said: "So this is the bride my son has chosen."

Adelaide replied, "I am honored to meet Your Majesty."

"Your family name was Bevan, I believe. Tell me about your family."

"My mother was a seamstress, Your Majesty. She died in the workhouse at Wapping. My father was a recruiting sergeant, but I never saw him. That's all I know."

She spoke plainly. The king's face, as Becky translated, was stony; only his fingers, fluttering more freely than ever, betrayed what he was feeling.

Then he went on: "They tell me you have become a princess."

"I have become the wife of a prince. But that's all I can choose to do. If it's someone else's wish to make me a princess, I shall try to be a good one, for his sake."

A long pause then, filled with the crackle of wood in the hearth and the chime of midnight from the mantel clock. The king's fingers fluttered more intensely once, twice, three times, as he tried to lift his right arm and failed. Becky realized that he must have suffered some kind of apoplectic seizure, and that in fact he was very old, and very ill.

But he managed to move his left arm and pat the cushion next to him. Looking at Adelaide, he said gently, "Come and sit beside me," and for a confusing second he reminded Becky of her own dear grandfather, and she had to struggle to control her voice as she translated. So Adelaide sat next to the king, and he sent for wine. When it was poured the king took a glass and with enormous effort handed it to Adelaide in his shaking hand, without spilling a drop, and then took another himself.

"Adelaide," he said. "That is a good name. It is like our eagle, our *Adler.* Did you see the Red Eagle flying over the Rock? I thought that in time my son Wilhelm would have carried the banner from the cathedral to the Rock, but our Heavenly Father decided otherwise. So be it. Rudolf is worthy. Make sure he does not slip, Adelaide."

He took only a sip of wine, and then sat silently beside her for a minute or so, holding her hand. Then he heaved a sigh which seemed to rack him painfully, and flicked a glance at his son.

The prince understood, and took away the stool from under the old man's foot and helped him to stand up.

Adelaide stood as well, and the king stooped to kiss her gently.

"Good-night, Adelaide," he said.

He said good-night to the prince and to the count and countess, and the majordomo took his arm to help him away. Becky was conscious of a deep, deep blush spreading up from her neck to the roots of her hair, but she knew she had to speak to him.

"Your Majesty," she began, and he stopped, and she curtsied once more. "I'm extremely sorry, sir. I was very rude to you, and I beg your pardon."

She couldn't face him. After a short pause he said, "Good-night, child. When you see your mother again, give her my thanks."

Then step by tiny shaking step he left the room. A servant closed the door.

6
Eagles and Birdlime

Becky was right about Jim, in one respect at least: he considered himself the equal of anyone, in a rough-and-ready democratic way. The company of stableboys and pickpockets was familiar to him, and so was the company of artists, actors, and earls; but he'd never seen a royal court before, and he was fascinated.

Early in the morning of their first full day in Razkavia, he was summoned to the office of the Chamberlain. Baron Gödel was the head of the royal household, the man responsible for the smooth running of all the ceremonies and receptions, for making all the household appointments, for administering the royal accounts. Jim entered his office with curiosity.

The baron was in his fifties, pale, with a face whose skin was loose and pouchy, pale eyes that bulged, and teeth that sloped backward like a rat's. He was so strikingly ugly that Jim instantly felt sorry for him. Then he noticed the look in Gödel's eye: the man was well aware of the effect his appearance had, and was watching to see how he'd react. A little ripple of triumph seemed to flick itself like a fish and dart away into the glaucous moistness of his eyes. Then Jim saw the fastidious care with which the man was dressed: the faultless cut of his coat, the spotless white of his collar, the glossy black of his hair, brushed so tightly that it seemed pasted to his skull. The baron was vain as well as ugly; well, that was interesting.

"Herr Taylor," the Chamberlain said, without asking him to sit down. "I understand that His Royal Highness has appointed you to his service in a private capacity. Of course, I should not wish to interfere with his arrangements. But I must inform you that you have no position whatsoever in the royal household. His Royal Highness's office is fully staffed; there is a full complement of domestic servants; his safety is carefully watched night and day by the palace guard. You understand what I am saying? There is no job for you here, no position for you to fill; there will be no salary. His Royal Highness has informed my office that he wishes you to be accommodated with the upper servants. The room you slept in last night is required by one of my secretaries. No doubt they will find you somewhere else if you ask in the steward's office. Your duties and your reimbursement are a matter for His Royal Highness to settle himself; all I require is that you conduct yourself in an appropriate manner while you are in the palace, and that you do not impede any of the work of the household. Good-day to you."

"Good-day," said Jim, and left.

So that was how the land lay. Still, it might have been worse; Gödel could have tied him down with a hundred petty duties, leaving him no time to do what he was really there for.

Which was what, exactly?

The prince didn't know. Like a child, he'd trustingly attached himself to the nearest friendly presence, just as he'd married Adelaide because she was kind to him. He expected Jim to protect him, but he also expected Jim to know what to protect him from, and how to go about it. It wasn't entirely for

Adelaide's sake that Jim felt obliged to do it, for he liked the prince; the fellow was no more than a bewildered child, but one who wanted to do his duty, whatever that was. He was like Pierrot in the Harlequinade: moonstruck, innocent, a tender lover too simple for the world. Which left Jim as the crafty servant, with the task of extracting him from danger.

Not a bad role to play, all things considered. But it meant that Jim would have to get the measure of the place first: this wasn't home territory. So after a long day spent arguing with the steward's office and installing himself in a narrow little room in the servants' attic, above Becky's more comfortable room on the floor below, Jim decided to look around; and early in the evening, he put on a snappy tweed suit, his ratcatcher's cap, and a dark green necktie, and sauntered off toward the center of the city.

It was a curious place, Eschtenburg: half German and half Bohemian, half medieval and half baroque, half up-to-date and rational and half plain barmy. On the western side of the river were the palace, the government buildings, the banks and embassies and hotels, the university and the cathedral. On the eastern side, clustered around the rock where the Red Eagle flew, was the Old Town, and a more insanitary, creaking, tottering stew of a place Jim hadn't seen anywhere in Europe—at least, not since they'd knocked down the slums around Seven Dials to make room for Charing Cross Road. In the oldest parts there weren't even any streets: the buildings were all jumbled together. According to one tale, the houses would give themselves a shake overnight and turn up somewhere quite different in the morning. According to another, the mists from the river played tricks with the appearance of things: they dissolved statues, altered house names, etched new designs into doorposts and window frames.

Jim, intrigued, intended to stroll across one of the handsome old bridges and see if he got lost, but before he got that far he was tempted into a cellar in the university quarter by the richest smell of grilled sausages and beer that he'd ever met. There was music in there, too: trombones in a hearty polka. It was too much to resist, so he pushed open the door and went down the steps.

The cellar was a narrow, smoky little place, and most of the customers were students. They wore a uniform, a semimilitary tunic and narrow trousers, with shoulder flashes and ribbons in their lapels to indicate which fraternity they belonged to. There were about eighty or ninety of them in a space that would have been snug with thirty. A brass band with fat red faces gleamed and oompahed on a tiny platform at the end of the room, and through the fog of cigar smoke Jim saw on the walls enough antlers and stuffed animals to populate a small forest.

He wedged himself into a corner, ordered some wurst and sauerkraut and a mug of beer, and found he'd picked about the best spot in Eschtenburg to learn about politics, for no more than six feet away there was a furious quarrel going on.

The subject seemed to be the royal family and their attitude to the German question. One student, in a uniform with red-and-black shoulder flashes, was banging the table and ranting in a harsh monotone above all the rest of the noise. His eyes were wild, his face was white, and there were unpleasant flecks of foam at the corners of his mouth—never the sign of a fellow Jim would want to pass the time with.

He was being yelled on by the red-and-blacks, and trying to shout them down was a smaller number of students in green and yellow. Jim was trying to make out what the speaker was saying when the serving girl brought his beer, about half a gallon by the look of it, in a handsome earthenware mug with a pewter lid. He lifted it to drink and suddenly got a shove in the back that sent about a pint of froth onto the sawdust floor.

"*Ach! Mein Herr!* I beg your pardon—damn you, Reiner! Make room, can't you? Allow me to buy you some more beer, sir—"

Jim turned to see a stocky, curly-haired student with bright blue eyes, who was struggling to heave his way in and sit down. He was one of the green-and-yellow brigade.

"Nothing spilled," said Jim, "except foam."

"Then I shall buy you some more foam. You are English?"

"Jim Taylor," he said, offering a hand. "And who are you?"

"Karl von Gaisberg, student of philosophy. I am sorry you have to suffer the ranting of those mystical Hegelians—like Glatz over there," and he pointed to the speechmaker.

"What's he saying?" said Jim. "Did I hear the phrase *blood and iron?* That's Prince von Bismarck's line, isn't it?"

Karl von Gaisberg made an expression of disgust. "Moonshine. There's a group of students who worship Bismarck and all things German. Race and blood and the holy destiny of Greater Razkavia. Contemptible rubbish, if you ask me."

"So you're on the side of Prince Rudolf and democracy, eh?"

"Absolutely!" said von Gaisberg. "He's not perfect, but our only chance lies with him. These people would rush us into the arms of Bismarck; fatal. Even Franz-Josef would be better than that."

Since that was roughly Daniel Goldberg's angle, and since Karl von Gaisberg seemed the kind of cheerful, noisy, careless, honest fellow Jim liked anyway, he called for two more beers; and while Jim ate his sausages and sauerkraut, Karl told him a little more about the background to the argument.

"Who's this Leopold he's mentioned once or twice?" Jim asked.

"Prince Leopold. The king's eldest son..."

"I thought that was Wilhelm, the crown prince who was assassinated?"

"Leopold was his elder brother. Dead too, many years ago. But there was something strange about his death—there was a scandal that was hushed up. You don't hear him mentioned now; it's as if they wanted to forget him. Glatz and his crew have seized on the idea of Leopold as a sort of lost leader, you know, betrayed by cowards and traitors...It's a good ploy; they don't have to face reality at all."

The foam-flecked orator had reached a pitch of frenzy by now that was holding most of the crowd. Jim listened closely, and tried to make out what he was saying, but his harsh scream made it difficult.

Then someone shouted, "But you don't want a Razkavian king! You want a German puppet!"

"It's a lie!" shrieked Glatz. "I want a pure Razkavian royalty! A royalty worthy of Walter von Eschten—not this mincing clown of a prince and his English whore!"

Those words fell into a silence. Even the band had wheezed to a halt. Everyone was still; and then Jim pushed his plate away and stood up.

He began to remove his jacket. Karl von Gaisberg whispered, "Down, you crazy Englishman! Glatz is a good swordsman—he'll run you through." Jim felt a little twitch of triumph as all eyes turned to him, and simultaneously cursed himself for a zany; he'd come out to spy, not to play D'Artagnan.

"What are you doing?" sneered Glatz. "This is nothing to do

with you. You are a foreigner. Keep out of Razkavia's quarrels."

"You're wrong," said Jim. "In the first place, you've just said something about an English lady which demands an answer. In the second place, even if I am a foreigner, I'm Prince Rudolf's man through and through. So if these other gentlemen will accept my help, I'm happy to offer it."

And he rolled up his sleeves, to cheers and the banging of tables from the green-and-yellows, to whistles and catcalls from the red-and-blacks. Out of the corner of his eye he could see the band hastily packing their instruments away, and knew the fun was about to begin. And then Glatz leaned across the table and slapped his face with an open palm.

In the next fraction of a second Jim could see the whole sequence that was meant to follow: the formal challenge, the seconds, the choice of weapons, the medical attendants—and Jim carried away with a fatal puncture. Not for the first time in his life, he thanked the gods he wasn't born a gentleman. He shot out a fist and punched Glatz squarely on the nose.

The man fell like a log, and then there began the best melee Jim had seen since the night he was thrown out of the Rose and Crown after a dispute over the Two Thousand Guineas. Tables overturned, benches crashed, pots of beer flew like cannonballs. These Razkavians were hearty fighters, and Jim could see from the fury in the narrow cellar that an ugly quantity of passion had been building up for a long time. It might have been tricky, but in a wild scrap like that, a natural street-hardened hoodlum had the advantage over the most scientifically trained gentleman; and he left the first three red-and-blacks stunned and dazed after only half a minute or so, then stood back to look for the next batch.

Then he saw Glatz, nose bleeding like a standpipe, belaboring a fallen green-and-yellow. Jim kicked Glatz's legs away, and was about to attend to him more closely when he heard a noise he recognized. Policemen sounded the same the world over: heavy feet in boots, whistles, a banging on the door; and the best way to deal with them was to vanish at once. He grabbed his jacket, seized von Gaisberg's arm, and hauled him toward the kitchen. The stout serving girl hopped out of the way like a flea, and then they were in a dark little yard, then an alley, and then a kind of park with ornamental cherry trees, where they collapsed on a bench. Karl was laughing helplessly.

"Did you see Glatz's face when you hit him? He couldn't believe it! And Scheiber—when he jumped on the bench and the other end flew up and hit Vranitzky on the jaw—marvelous! Well, Mr. Taylor," he went on, "you're a good fighter, whatever else you do. But who are you? And what's your interest in Prince Rudolf?"

Jim mopped the wound in his hand, which had opened up again. The moon was shining brightly enough to show him the student's tousled curls and bright eyes, the rents in his tunic, the loose shoulder flash. There was a rumble of traffic from the streets of the capital all around them, and across the river, which gleamed like pewter, the great Rock loomed high with the *Adlerfahne* hanging still under the stars. Jim made up his mind.

"All right, I'll tell you," he said. "It began in London, ten years ago..."

He told von Gaisberg everything, from Adelaide's first appearance as a little haunted shadow of a thing with the fragrance of Holland's Lodgings about her, to the old king's acceptance of her the night before, of which he'd had a full account from Becky.

The student sat astounded. When Jim had finished, Karl

slapped his knee, leaned back on the bench, and gave a long whistle.

"I don't need to tell you I've taken a risk," Jim said, "telling you all this. But I've seen the way you fight, and I don't think it'll harm the prince's interest for you to know the whole truth. There are going to be all kinds of rumors—Glatz has got hold of one already—and the damnable thing is, some of them are true. She does come from the lowest slums in London; she *was* a...well, she was no better than she should be. She can barely read or write. At the same time she's as tough as you like, she's warm and shrewd and clever, and she'll fight for the prince till she drops.

"So there you are. That's your princess, and that's what I'm doing here in her service. Can I count on you?"

Without a second's hesitation, Karl von Gaisberg was pumping his hand, and vowing to bring all the Richterbund, as the green-and-yellow faction was called, to the defense of the prince and princess.

"I'll hold you to that," said Jim, as the cathedral clock struck midnight. It was then that he realized that most of the excellent sausages and almost all the beer had been used as missiles before he'd consumed them, and he was damnably hungry. A scrap always had that effect on him. In London he'd have found a coffee stall or strolled along to Smithfield, where the chophouses did a roaring trade in the small hours for the meat porters. But he wasn't so familiar with Eschtenburg, and when he asked Karl about somewhere to eat, the student shook his head.

"We go to bed early here," he said. "Never mind. Come back to my room—I've got some bread and cheese and a bottle of something..."

So they climbed four flights of stairs to Karl's room high over the University Square, where, Karl assured him, if you hung out of the window and leaned to the left while standing tiptoe in the gutter, you had a fine view of the forested hills to the north. Jim took his word for it. There by the light of a candle they supped on dry bread, drier cheese, and plum brandy, while Karl told him about Razkavian politics, and dueling, and drinking, and the serious business of being a student, and they began to like each other a great deal.

Next day Jim spoke to the prince privately, and told him about the fight in the beer cellar.

"The point is, sir, the people are aware of your marriage, but they need to see the princess publicly acknowledged. The longer she's kept out of sight, the more rumors will grow and the worse your position will get. Can't you speak to His Majesty and suggest some kind of announcement? Perhaps even a service in the cathedral?"

"It is very difficult at the moment...The court is still in mourning for my brother and his wife...Taylor, who is killing us all?"

"That's what I'm trying to find out, sir. I don't think Glatz and his slavering mob of students are anything to worry about. But they're a symptom, you see. I'm more interested in the woman."

"Woman? What woman?"

"The spy in the garden that night, remember?"

"A *woman?*"

"I wasn't sure. But when the Irish Guards told me how they'd followed the spy to a theater, and an actress had put them off the track, I began to see how she could have done it...I haven't asked you before, sir, and I shan't do again: but have you been involved with a woman like that? One who might want to avenge herself on you for some reason?"

The prince was so obviously bewildered that Jim believed his denial at once.

"But you must make some announcement soon about your marriage," he said. "Mourning or no, that's the only way to get the people on your side."

Another thing was nagging at Jim's mind, and that was the dead prince, Leopold. There were endless tributes to the murdered Crown Prince Wilhelm and his princess, articles in the papers praising his diligence and her beauty; photographic portraits and engravings on sale, complete with black borders; reports of the search for the cowardly assassins, who had been traced, according to which paper you read, to Brussels, or St. Petersburg, or Budapest, but then invariably lost. There was a surfeit of Prince Wilhelm; but of his elder brother, the king's first son, not a word. It was as if he'd been expunged from history.

Furthermore, Jim found that when he asked about him, he met a frosty response: frowns, indrawn breaths. Even Count Thalgau was reluctant to speak about him.

"That's all a long time ago," he said. "No point in raking up old scandals. That prince is dead; our job's to protect this one. Where'd you get that black eye, my boy?"

Jim told the count about the fight in the cellar, and the old man chortled with delight, smacking a fist into his palm.

"By God!" he said. "I'd love to have been there! That's the kind of spirit we need around the palace, young rascals like your von Gaisberg. I knew his father, you know. Got drunk with him more than once."

"I had the notion," Jim said, "of setting up a kind of private guard, with the help of the Richterbund. A kind of unofficial, plain-clothes bodyguard for the prince and princess."

"Excellent idea. But don't tell Gödel, whatever you do; he'd ban it at once. I wish I was young again, Taylor. I'd come and join your private guard like a shot..."

Jim was becoming very attached to this loud old warrior; there was shrewdness under the bluster, and a warm heart under the ferocity. The count was a poor man, or so he'd gathered; old family estates had been dwindling, and, most unusually, he'd had to live on his ambassador's salary. He had remained with the prince since Rudolf had returned not only because the countess was guiding Adelaide through the manners of the court, but because Rudolf had given him a position on his personal staff.

However, the count clearly wasn't going to tell him about Prince Leopold. Jim went in search of information elsewhere, and later that week, he found himself in a part of the palace he hadn't yet seen: the picture gallery.

There he spent half an hour gazing at the representations of forgotten battles and incomprehensible scenes from mythology, plump nudes, and muscle-bound heroes gesturing in exaggerated ways that would have gone down well in the Victoria Theater, in Lambeth, where they liked their emotions undiluted. There were portraits of past monarchs, too: there was one of poor mad King Michael with his swan bride that made Jim goggle; and high up in the darkest corner of the gallery, a young man in a hussar colonel's uniform who looked very like Rudolf. So like, in fact, that Jim uttered a muffled exclamation of surprise, which was heard by the elderly curator, who was sorting aquatints at a table farther down the gallery.

The old man came up to see where he was looking.

"The late Prince Leopold," he said in a hushed voice. "It is a not insignificant example of the work of the great Winterhalter. Would you like to examine it more closely?"

He pulled some mahogany steps from an alcove, and Jim

climbed to peer at the likeness of Rudolf's dead brother. They weren't all that alike, at a second look; where Rudolf's expression was dreamy, Leopold's had been weak, and probably weaker in real life, for no doubt the great Winterhalter had been flattering his paymaster anyway. There was a hint of gnawing petulance in the curve of the lips, and a curious droop to one eyelid that made him look on the verge of delivering a furtive wink. But he was handsome, after a fashion, and no doubt he'd been complimented on the dimple in his chin.

"What happened to Prince Leopold?" Jim asked.

The old curator drew in a judicious breath and flicked a little glance over his shoulder. Perhaps no one had spoken to him for months, or perhaps he was an old gossip anyway; Jim came to the foot of the steps to enable him to speak confidentially.

"The fact is that he contracted a most *unfortunate* marriage. An actress, I believe; Spanish; most unsuitable. King Wilhelm was *beside* himself with fury. The woman was banished at once—treated, I gather, with some contempt. Even cruelty, some would say. What would have happened next, I don't know; Leopold was the crown prince, you understand; but there was a hunting accident, and he died. The affair was forgotten. His younger brother was a *much* more steady character—poor Prince Wilhelm, you understand. So when Prince Rudolf...but I don't need to labor the point."

Jim felt as if a door had opened in his mind. Everyone at court, from the king down to the scullery maid, must have seen the parallel at once: first Leopold, and then Rudolf, had married profoundly beneath himself.

And then came another little revelation: the spy! The woman in the Alhambra Theater...

"Well, well, well. Thank you for telling me this; I'm greatly obliged."

He took a last look at Leopold, fixing that handsome weakness in his memory. It was hardly surprising that no one wanted to talk about him; but what other secrets were hidden in the palace?

The old king spent a great deal of time in Adelaide's company. Becky, shadowing her everywhere, watched and wondered as the king walked along the terrace holding her arm in the morning sunshine, or sat with her as she drove a little dogcart along the graveled paths. It was as if he were making amends to Adelaide for his hostility to Prince Leopold's wife; or perhaps he was simply becoming fond of her. At all events, he was keeping her to himself.

However, in Adelaide's second week in Razkavia, he agreed that the time had come to make a formal announcement.

He invited the leading politicians, churchmen, and landowners—all the prominent citizens of Razkavia, together with the most important ambassadors—to a reception at the palace the following evening.

The city was now full of rumors, as Jim had foreseen. Everyone's interest was enormous, and when the evening arrived, the palace ballroom was thronged. Jim, in formal evening dress, watched from the edge of the room, with a pistol in his pocket. It was a strange occasion; the court was still in mourning, but there was an undercurrent of excitement and expectancy, and when the royal party entered the room, every pair of eyes focused at once on the pale slender figure of Adelaide, elegant in black, next to the prince and just behind the king.

Becky, only a foot or two away, saw those eyes turn, a sea of them; and felt stage fright on Adelaide's behalf.

The old king was walking without help, though everyone

nearby could see how much effort it took. He stood on a carpeted dais and spoke loudly and clearly, but he couldn't disguise the tremor in his voice:

"Dear Razkavians! Dear guests! At a time of mourning, such a gathering as this might be thought unusual, not to say improper; but these are far from usual times. We live in an anxious world; great changes are happening abroad; swift and mighty developments in science and industry are taking place beyond our ancient frontiers. Among these changes three things remain steadfast: the Rock of Eschtenburg, the Red Eagle, and the sacred unity of the family.

"My dear son Wilhelm has been taken from us. But my son Rudolf steps at once into the position he vacates. And he has brought me, in the middle of our common sorrow, a great joy that I want to share with you as soon as possible. We are in the modern age now, and circumstances change so rapidly that we have to move swiftly to keep up with them. We have to fly like an eagle. Like a Red Eagle!

"So, my people, my friends, here is an announcement to bring you joy. My son Rudolf has married. It was a quiet marriage, and our sad loss has made any public celebration inappropriate, but our private joy, which is now a public one, is unbounded. Adelaide..."

Becky was standing just behind Adelaide, interpreting in a quiet voice. So far it had been straightforward, but then there came a difficult part, because the old man was making a complicated pun on her name. *Adel* in German means nobility, and Becky had to explain that to her:

"He's saying that birth doesn't matter when you have *Adel des Herzens*—that's nobility of the heart—and now he's talking about the Eagle again, the *Adler*, and saying that you're *adlig*, that's noble—and—quick! Go forward!"

For the king was holding out his trembling hand. Adelaide gave Becky one quick look that mingled alarm and impatience with Becky's helplessness, and then looked up at the old man with such open affection that they saw it from the far end of the room. She stepped up beside him, and an aide handed the king a decoration on a ribbon.

"Princess Adelaide," he said, placing it around her neck.

So there it was; she was officially a princess, recognized as such by the king himself; and no one could argue with that. A few minutes later she and the prince (and Becky) were at the center of a circle of well-wishers, and Becky was busily interpreting their words and Adelaide's replies.

One of the first to greet her was the British Ambassador, Sir Charles Dawson, a gray-whiskered drudge who spoke to her in German. When she replied in cockney English, he nearly swallowed his eyeglass.

"I'm a Londoner, Sir Charles. I can talk English same as what you can. Pleased to meet you."

"I—bless my soul, I—upon my word—I—good gracious me! An English la—er—Englishwo—um—English, by Jove! Ha! Hrrumph! Yes, indeed!"

The silly old buffer must have been the only person in Eschtenburg not to have heard the rumors about her, thought Becky. So much for the efficiency of the British Diplomatic Service.

He harrumphed away in a daze, and a little after that, a giant appeared in front of them, clicked his heels, bowed, and kissed Adelaide's hand.

His black hair was brushed straight upwards, and his mustache was so sharply waxed that Becky thought he ought to put corks on the ends before kissing people with it. His black eyes glittered.

"Count Otto von Schwartzberg," murmured an aide.

The famous huntsman! Becky's first feeling was simply pity for any animal, wolf, elk, or mastodon that found itself within range. Intrigued, she looked at his bear-slaughtering hands. They were the biggest she'd ever seen, and covered in scars.

"Cousin!" he barked to Adelaide. "I am pleased to welcome you to Razkavia."

He ignored the prince entirely. Adelaide coolly took back her hand and said, "Thank you, Count Otto. I have heard of your exploits in the hunt. I look forward to learning about the birds and the beasts in the forest. If there's any left," she added to Becky, saying, "Don't translate that."

Count Otto glared down at her and then burst into laughter.

"A little English goldfinch!" he roared, and whereas in anyone less immense that volume of noise would have been insupportable, in him it seemed only natural. He wasn't made to be indoors, that was the problem; Becky thought that he would have been delightful company if he were on the other side of a valley. The prince looked uncomfortable, but Adelaide hadn't finished.

"Have you ever killed a goldfinch with your crossbow, Count Otto?"

"Oh, you don't shoot goldfinches! You catch them with birdlime and keep them in pretty cages!"

"Then you must be thinking of some other bird," she said. "English birds don't go in cages. And you don't catch eagles with birdlime, neither."

As Becky translated this, Adelaide watched the count arrogantly. The prince was looking elsewhere, talking to the archbishop, but Jim was nearby, and so was the king, listening intently, and when Becky had finished translating, the old man laughed so loudly that she thought he'd choke.

Count Otto smiled piratically. White teeth flashed beneath his mustache.

"You have many people to talk to," he said. "Good-night, cousin."

He bowed again and turned his back.

And so the evening wore on, with a continual stream of people to be introduced to, to find polite phrases for, to smile at. When all the nobles and foreign ambassadors had been introduced, there came the turn of those further down the scale: the officials and politicians who actually ran the country. One by one they came forward, bowed, said some polite words, and went. Becky was getting dizzy; her head was ringing, her feet hurt, her throat was dry—for while everyone else had to contribute just half the conversation, she had to relay the whole of it, in both directions. In the end she had to suppress a silly hysteria that began to bubble in her breast as the shiny stoutnesses beamed and clicked and bowed, one after the other: Herr Schnickenbinder, the Mayor of Andersbad; Herr Rumpelwurst, the Inspector of Water Purity; Herr Knorpelsack, the Director of Postal Services...

Surely those names weren't real? She must be making them up. There'd be a diplomatic incident. She'd be dismissed, imprisoned, shot. She had to blink, shake her head, concentrate hard.

Supervising everything, making the most important introductions, seeming to float at the edge of every conversation, was the Chamberlain, the Baron von Gödel. Becky knew who he was, and feared him without knowing why. Toward the end of the evening, at a moment when Becky wasn't needed because Adelaide was talking quietly with Rudolf, Gödel beckoned her with a finger. Becky felt her heart beat faster.

He drew her to the edge of the room and leaned close. She could smell his eau de cologne, the grease on his hair, the violet-scented sugar drops he sucked to sweeten his breath.

"You are speaking too loudly," he said in his smooth, purring voice. "That is not the way for an interpreter to behave. You must speak more modestly. What is more, you should not stare rudely at the speakers' faces. There is an insolence in you that is most unpleasing. You are in danger of forgetting your place. If that happens, you will lose it."

Becky had to look at people's faces to be sure of the shade of meaning they were intending to convey; and Adelaide herself had asked her to speak up. But there was no point in arguing with the Chamberlain: all Becky wanted was to get away from him.

"Very good, sir," she said, and smiled sweetly when he dismissed her. Jim, who had seen, winked at her swiftly and moved on.

And so the evening passed, and so Adelaide was formally acknowledged as a princess.

That night, the king died.

7 Whirlpool

Within ten minutes of the king's manservant bringing in his silver pot of coffee at seven, all the palace knew that King Wilhelm was dead. Jim, ravenous for breakfast, was shaving and dressing when a footman knocked at his door and told him that he was wanted at once in the count's room.

He hurried downstairs and found the count being helped into his black cravat, and as soon as he saw the expression in the old man's face, he knew what had happened.

"His Majesty is dead?"

"His Majesty is alive," the count said, glaring at Jim over his bristling mustache as the valet fiddled at his neck. "King Wilhelm died peacefully in his sleep. We have now to consider quickly how best to advise and protect King Rudolf. *Ach*, enough, man, be on your way, I'll finish it myself," he snapped at the valet, who bowed and scuttled out.

Jim had been going to face the count with his discovery about Prince Leopold, and ask for more information about the Spanish actress, but this wasn't the time. The old man was stretching his chin up in the mirror, fiddling the cravat into place.

"That'll do," he said after a final twist, and reached for his silver-backed hairbrushes. "Now listen. His Majesty isn't in charge yet, not by a long way. He's going to have a mighty struggle before he overcomes Gödel and makes his own arrangements in the palace. He can't dismiss the man—it's a hereditary position. And frankly he's not grown-up enough to know his own mind, so we'll have to help him. He wants to see me in five minutes, and you in ten. In the Green Office. I'll encourage him to offer you a more responsible position, and Gödel will object, but if the king stands firm he'll have to go along with it. Your job is to be patient and hold your tongue until it's decided, you understand?"

"Yes. Count, was Baron Gödel behind the assassination of Prince Wilhelm?"

"What?"

"Was he?"

"Certainly not! The idea is absurd. He's a confounded nuisance, but he's a loyal servant of the crown. Don't waste your time with speculation like that, for God's sake, or you'll make me distrust my own judgment about you. Ten minutes—eight minutes, now. Don't be late."

Jim tapped a finger against his teeth, thoughtfully, and sauntered along the garden corridor toward the Green Office, where household business was transacted.

Precisely on time, the outer door opened and a somber official let him in. The office was heavy with plush upholstery and deep fringes; there was an air of stuffy grandeur in the very way the lines of the desk bulged and the chair legs swelled and narrowed.

King Rudolf sat behind the desk, wearing the uniform of what must have been the only sober-suited regiment in the country. Jim bowed. Standing to the king's right was the count, and on his other side was Baron Gödel.

"Thank you for coming, Taylor," said the new king. He

looked pale and lost, and his voice was quiet, as if he could hardly summon breath.

Gödel said smoothly, "Herr Taylor, His Majesty has informed me that he had it in mind to offer you a higher position on his staff. I shall be quite frank with you; I advise him against it. We know nothing of you beyond the facts that you are extremely young, you have a taste for unorthodox companions, and you have no connection with our country. You are here, it seems to me, as a mercenary. If an enemy should offer you a higher sum to betray His Majesty, how could we trust you to resist? A Razkavian, born under the Red Eagle, we would trust without question. A foreigner..."

Rudolf shrank; it was his judgment being questioned. Count Thalgau was bristling warningly, but Jim felt his heart leap with anger.

"It's true," he said, "I'm a foreigner. I plead guilty to other faults as well: yes, I'm young. I'm not high-born. I enjoy the company of rogues and artists and vagabonds. As for the mercenary charge, I admit that when I first came across His Majesty—or His Royal Highness, as he was then—I offered my services as a private detective. We shook hands, and that handshake was my guarantee of honor, because I'm not just any foreigner, I'm an Englishman, by God, and I'll thank you to remember it. I'm not bribed by treaties or bullied by threats, and I won't be bought by gold. My loyalty is freely and wholeheartedly given to the king and queen, given for life, and God help the man or woman who doubts it."

The count was bursting to say something, and the king looked anxious, but a smile of gratitude passed over his face for a moment. Then he flicked a nervous glance at Gödel.

The Chamberlain bowed very slightly.

"Of course, I can only advise, sir," he said to Rudolf. "If it is your wish, no doubt we can arrange a post of some kind for

Herr Taylor; something ceremonial, perhaps, would be suitable. Now you are king, sir, your private office and staff come under the management of the Chamberlain's office, so Herr Taylor would be answerable directly to me like all your other servants. If you command, sir, I shall arrange something."

"Very well," said Rudolf wearily. "See to it, Baron."

Gödel smiled; it was like oil spreading on a puddle of water. Jim ignored him and bowed to the king.

"My condolences on His late Majesty's death, sir," he said. "I shall serve you and Her Majesty as well as I can."

"I know you will, Taylor. Thank you."

Jim left. Outside the office he stopped and shook his head.

Damn fool, he thought. *You walked right into it, you clown.* Because now he'd have even less freedom than before: Gödel would pin him down in some poodle-faking routine when he ought to be out hunting this Spanish mummer—if she really did exist, and if it really was her.

He snarled, and aimed a vicious kick at an imaginary football, sending it crashing through the windows with an imaginary explosion of broken glass. Then he went down to breakfast.

He spent the rest of the morning watching the various dignitaries who arrived to give their condolences to the king and queen. The archbishop was one of the first: a cadaverous old coot, Jim thought him, with a gray skull-face under the black skullcap. Then came the ambassadors, the German and the Austro-Hungarian arriving at precisely the same moment and giving the Chamberlain a nice little problem in protocol: whom should he announce first? But Chamberlains are paid to solve problems like that, and the two ambassadors were talking amiably enough when they left, though that, Jim supposed, was what *they* were paid to do. In the visitors came, out they went, and meanwhile the work of the palace went on: silver had to be polished, horses had to be watered and fed, the guard had to be changed, luncheon had to be served.

At half-past two, Jim was sent for: the queen requested his attendance. He found Her Majesty in the drawing room overlooking the terrace where she'd walked arm in arm with the old king. She was in black, of course; standing by the window, fiddling with a fan, her little face pale and those great smoke-dark eyes damp with tears...

Jim collected himself and bowed just in time.

"Thank you, countess," Adelaide said. "Please leave us for five minutes."

Countess Thalgau curtsied—she had to, now—and sailed out like an iceberg. Becky was about to go, but Adelaide shook her head, and she stayed. She was more tired than Adelaide; pale, with a hint of pink about the nose, she looked as if she were coming down with a cold.

"You gotta stay," Adelaide said tonelessly. "Gawd knows what they'd say if I was left on me own with a bloke. Unless he was the bloody archbishop. Great moldy skellinton he is. Where you been, Jim?"

Her voice was hoarse, her patience frayed and sore. Jim knew the signs: he'd seen them in little Harriet, Sally's child, when she had a fever and couldn't sleep.

"If Your Majesty will permit," he said, "I'll tell you. I think I know who might be behind the assassination. Has the king ever spoken to you about his older brother Prince Leopold?"

Her eyes narrowed. But she looked bewildered, not angry, and she shook her head.

"No. I know who he was, but that's all. They don't speak about him much. Why?"

Jim told them what he'd found out.

"And now I've been a bloody fool," he finished, "and got myself under the thumb of the Chamberlain. Baron Gargoyle.

What I need to do is get out in the city and snoop around with Karl von Gaisberg and the Richterbund. Are we going to talk normally, Your Majesty? Because if not—"

"Of *course,*" she said, but softly. "I couldn't bear it otherwise. But only when it's the three of us. Else it'd get back to...to *them,* to people like your crazy student Glatz. Then they'd have another accusation to throw at King Rudolf, see? Poor man, he's in a daze. He was never meant to be king. But I gotta help him. And that means you gotta help me, see. I can't survive this without a bit of normal gossip every so often."

She slumped into a chair. She had two different manners, Jim knew: one serene and gracious, the other coarse and lazy and affectionate. He loved them both, but especially the second one, because she kept it private. But as he thought about it now, he found it more and more difficult to hit it exactly. In the grace and charm of her royal manner there was always a hint of a pouting challenge; and at her coarsest she could never conceal a winning tenderness...He could think about her forever.

"I'll just have to do my detecting on the sly," he said. "I won't give it up. There's something going on underneath all this that I can't quite make out...So what's the drill from now on?"

"Funeral on Tuesday," said Adelaide. "Then there's two weeks of mourning; then the coronation. I can manage all that. The countess tells me what to do and where to stand and I goes and does it. But it's the politics as I can't make out..."

"Well?" he said. "Leave it to the king. It's a man's job, politics."

He said it to provoke, but it was Becky who answered. Her voice was hoarse.

"Don't be an idiot," she said. "His Majesty is relying on Adelaide, can't you see that? King Wilhelm had never let him see the state documents. He'd only been crown prince for a short time, don't forget, and all he's really interested in anyway is poetry. So he's as ignorant as any of us, and he's getting so much contradictory advice that his head's spinning. Adelaide's got to be his best adviser. He relies on her absolutely. So she's got to know what to advise. So you've got to find out, and tell her."

Her voice gave out entirely.

"See?" said Her Majesty. "It's Germany or the other lot, and if they don't get an answer soon they'll fight, and if they *do* get an answer there'll be a war anyway, cause the loser'll object. And in the meantime there's a flaming assassin creeping about. So what the bloody hell am I going to do, Jim?"

He scratched his head. Then he said, "I think I'd ask Dan Goldberg, and I think I know what he'd say. He'd say get the people on your side. Get out and show yourself as often as you can. They don't know you yet, and they're not sure about Ru—about His Majesty, I mean. I'm sure they'll take to you, but you've got to give them the chance. Then, if it comes to a struggle, you'll have their goodwill, and that could tip the balance."

He stopped and looked at Becky somberly.

"The thing I won't disguise from you," he went on, "is that it might be dangerous. But what I can promise is that the Richterbund—that's the student fraternity with the green-and-yellow shoulder flashes, remember—will be nearby wherever you go. You might not see them, but they'll be there. So get out and meet the people, but be prepared for danger. And that's my advice, for what it's worth."

Adelaide nodded.

"Thanks, Jim," she said.

He left Becky wearily getting out the Halma board.

Becky, writing twice weekly to her mother, was leaving out more and more. She put in the first part of Jim's advice, but left out the second; and she filled her letters with detailed accounts of their daily life. There was plenty to write about, for she was discovering that being the closest friend of a queen was several degrees more difficult than being the language tutor and games-player-in-chief to a princess. There was much less time, for one thing; every moment of the day seemed to have been booked up in advance by a vast anonymous planning-machine, and lessons—never mind Ludo, or chess—had to be fitted into the gaps.

Adelaide's day began at seven, when her maid brought her a tray of coffee and some sweet rolls and filled a bath for her. Then she dressed in the clothes arranged by her mistress of the wardrobe (a plump French lady who had turned pale when she saw what Adelaide had brought with her, and had ordered a *couturier* from Paris to attend forthwith, bearing more). Then a secretary would attend at half-past nine, with notes of acknowledgment to the letters of condolence for her to sign (she could manage an *A*, and said majestically that that was enough). Then there'd be a visitor or two: a delegation from the Ladies' Charity Committee of Andersbad, or the wives of the chancellor and senate of the university, come to pay their respects.

Then there was luncheon, invariably with some stuffy guest, invariably with Countess Thalgau watching closely nearby; then in the afternoon a session with the countess: the demeanor that would be expected of the queen during the late king's funeral; how to greet foreign heads of state; which knife and fork to use when sturgeon was on the menu...Adelaide submitted to it all with a stubborn patience.

All this time, of course, the whole city was itching to look at her. Curiosity was immense, which was why it was worth seeing every visitor who called, and striving to be polite; so with Jim's advice in mind, Adelaide asked Countess Thalgau to arrange a number of public visits—to the cathedral to inspect the arrangements for the late king's funeral; to the Rose Labyrinth in the Spanish Gardens by the river to unveil a statue; to the Fever

Hospital to open a new wing. One or two of the papers criticized her for this; it was unseemly, they said, to move out in public so much during a period of mourning. But the criticism was outweighed by the respect Adelaide was gaining. Every time she stopped her carriage to buy some roses from an old flower-seller and thank her with a smile, every time she walked along a hospital ward and shook hands with the patients, every time she brought little presents for the children in an orphanage, she won more hearts.

More so than the king, in fact. She radiated a natural sweetness that was simple and unaffected, whereas Rudolf was stiff and self-conscious in public. Becky watched sympathetically, but the harder he tried, the more clumsy he looked.

And everywhere that Adelaide went, Becky went with her. She sat behind her at table, she sat opposite her in her carriage, she stood behind her chair when she received visitors; and every word that Adelaide heard or spoke, except those in private with her husband, came to her through Becky. Quite often, when Adelaide's tact ran thin or her patience failed, Becky was able to say what the queen should have said, and then her Englishing of the visitors' words would include the odd extra sentence or two, such as (in the most diplomatic murmur), "Stop pouting, for God's sake," or "Mind your manners, you rude little strumpet," or "Can't you think of anything to say? Tell them what a good job they're doing."

Becky was never sure whether Countess Thalgau noticed, because the countess was always there as well, quite close enough to hear, and she spoke English after a fashion; but she never showed a flicker of response.

However, one morning, she found out. Becky was sitting as usual beside Adelaide in the morning room while Countess Thalgau gave her a lesson on the connections between Razkavian royalty and other European noble families. They had developed a pattern of working by this time: the countess was cold and pedantic, Adelaide was cold and accurate, and questions and answers were conveyed from one to the other through Becky, who felt like one of the pneumatic tubes in large emporiums through which bills and receipts whooshed and thudded, for all the human contact she was bringing from one to the other.

There came a knock on the door, and the footman announced a visitor: the Chamberlain himself. He was elaborately, fulsomely apologetic for the interruption, and then he said, in English, ignoring Becky:

"Tomorrow, Your Majesty, we should like to present to you your new interpreter, Dr. Unger. He is a scholar of the university, a graduate of Heidelberg and the Sorbonne, and a valued consultant to the Razkavian Foreign Ministry. He will take the place of Fräulein Winter, who will be able to return to her family and her studies in London."

Becky's eyes widened; Countess Thalgau's eyes narrowed. Adelaide's blazed.

"What?" she said.

"Now that Your Majesty is the queen rather than a princess, it would naturally be appropriate for a more highly qualified man to be at your service. In the circumstances you would, of course, wish to reward Fräulein Winter for her services, and no doubt a small decoration would be in order. But—"

"Whose idea is this?" said Adelaide. Her nostrils were flared; a dusky red suffused her cheeks.

"It is felt that it would be more proper. I am sure that Fräulein Winter is highly talented, but—"

"*Felt?* Who feels that? I don't. Are you telling me it's the king's idea?"

"His Majesty is naturally anxious to ensure that you have the very best advice and assistance. Dr. Unger is a man of great—"

Adelaide stood. Becky and the countess had to stand as well, but it wasn't their sudden getting to their feet so much as the fury and contempt that blazed from Adelaide's slender form that made the Chamberlain take a step backward.

"I wish Dr. Unger every success in his career," Adelaide said icily. "But Fräulein Winter is my interpreter. Her and no one else. And what's more, *I'll* decide who I want advising me. Do you understand?"

"I—naturally, I—"

"Good morning to you."

"Possibly Dr. Unger could work alongside Fräulein Winter, in some kind of advisory—"

Adelaide drew breath, but before she could say anything, Countess Thalgau broke in.

To Becky's utter astonishment she snapped in rapid German, "Baron von Gödel! I should not have to remind you that you are speaking to the queen! You have heard her answer. How dare you persist with this impertinence? Fräulein Winter discharges her duties—and more than her duties—with the utmost skill, tact, and promptness. I cannot imagine any man doing it better. Now you are taking up Her Majesty's time; please be on your way."

Becky was silently astounded. The Chamberlain bowed smoothly and left, and a few moments later the lesson resumed as if nothing had happened. The countess's manner was exactly the same as before: cold, formal, and brusque; but Becky looked at her with a new, wary respect.

Jim saw Karl von Gaisberg and the rest of the Richterbund as often as he could manage to get away from the palace. They usually gathered in the Café Florestan, a little coffeehouse by the Matthias Bridge, where the proprietor was both discreet and generous with credit. A couple of days before the coronation, Jim took Becky with him. She seldom had any time away from the formality of the court, and she enjoyed being able to walk unnoticed down the busy streets, as if she were a normal citizen.

But once she was in the café, with a glass of chocolate and a slice of torte in front of her, she found herself the object of all eyes. The students of the Richterbund vied with each other in paying her compliments and then in trying not to blush, which was charming, and disconcerting, and embarrassing, in that order; and then Karl von Gaisberg arrived. Jim introduced them, and it was Becky's turn to blush. It was because he bowed over her hand and kissed it formally, and because she thought he was making fun of her but realized almost at once that he was being very serious and very polite, mastering his obvious shyness in order to do so. And she'd nearly laughed at him! No wonder she blushed.

"Any luck, boys?" Jim said.

"I've been round all the hotels," said one of the students. "Lot of journalists about. I've managed to find five women traveling alone, but three of them are over seventy and the other two are invalid sisters, in Andersbad for the cure. They've come here to see the coronation and then they're back to the waters."

"Keep looking. What about you, Gustav?"

"I've been through the newspaper files. There isn't much about Prince Leopold's marriage there, but the censor would have stopped them printing it anyway. I did find an account of his death, though. Apparently he was killed by a boar near the hunting lodge at Ritterwald. The only witness was the huntsman who was with him—an old family retainer called Busch. I suppose we could go and talk to him, if he's still alive."

"It's worth a try. Hans?"

"Friedrich and I have scuppered Glatz! We heard he was

going to disrupt the queen's visit to the School of Mines tomorrow, and we told him that they'd changed the plans and she was going to the Conservatoire instead. So he'll be hanging around with a gang of malcontents, and they'll have no one to jeer at."

"Excellent! Now, what about the plans for the coronation itself? Karl?"

Karl cleared his throat and cast a quick shy glance at Becky before describing the way they intended to guard the route. After a minute or so he forgot the shyness and spoke clearly and forcefully, and Becky saw another leader in him, quieter, less mercurial than Jim, perhaps, and certainly less experienced, but equally strong.

"The problem is our numbers," he finished by saying. "We can muster sixty fellows, sixty-three at a pinch, but no more. And of course our only weapons are swords. We're allowed to carry them by the rules of the fraternity, but we haven't got a pistol between us."

"I wish I could join you!" Becky said.

"Can you shoot?" said someone.

"I bet I could if I tried."

"I'll teach you," offered someone else. "They make little dainty pistols you can carry in a handbag. I've seen them."

Becky looked at him curiously. "What makes you think I want to be dainty about it?" she said. "I'd just as soon be a pirate, and fire a cannon. In any case, I've got to be with the queen; she needs me. I'll watch out for you all."

"I hope you won't need us," said Karl. "If we come into it at all, then things will have gone badly wrong."

"Enough," said Jim. "You've done all you can. Let's have some beer. But keep an eye on the hotels, and especially on the railway station..."

Later, as they were walking back across the bridge, Becky said, "Do you really expect trouble at the coronation?"

"Yes. I wish I didn't. You sound as if you're looking forward to it."

"Do I?"

"All this talk of cannons and so forth. You're a bloodthirsty character, aren't you?"

"I don't know," she said honestly. "I've never had the chance to find out. I'm pretty sure I would fight if I had to, though. I wouldn't give in, or flinch and cry and faint. People don't think girls are brave, but I'd love the chance to try...just once, perhaps; just once, so I could know what it was like to risk my life and fight to the death. It's not that I want to kill people, it's that I want to find out about *me*. I'll never completely know about myself unless I try."

"*I* don't think girls are less brave than men, but then I know Sally—Mrs. Goldberg. I think I'd trust you in a fight, though."

"Why?"

"Just a guess. You made an impression on Karl von Gaisberg, you know."

"Oh, really? Oh. Mmm. They...they seem very competent. The Richterbund..."

"I couldn't have found a better bunch. Karl especially...Makes me wonder what I've missed, Becky, never having been a student. It's a nice life at university, fighting and singing and drinking and so on. When this is over I might take up philosophy—if I thought I could stand the pace."

Later, when Becky had returned to her room, Jim wandered out in the grounds of the palace. It was a fine clear night without a moon, and the formal garden lay still and scented under the myriad stars. Jim walked the light gravel path between the dark little hedges, half-sleepy, half-intoxicated with the beauty of the night, entirely in love with Adelaide, whose window he could see above the stone terrace with its marble urns. He stood and watched for a while, and then left the garden for the wilder park, where a great sweep of grass, dotted with trees, undulated toward the distant forest.

He wandered aimlessly over the grass for twenty minutes or so, moving in a wide curve away from the palace. The silence was profound. He might have been the only human being in the world.

Suddenly there came a sound that turned him to ice. It was a man's voice, screaming. It came without warning out of the dark and died away.

Jim had never been so afraid. His muscles seemed to have melted; he was nearly sick with fright. It was more than a scream—it was a howl of horrible anguish—a rising, falling wail that spoke of infinite pain. He gripped the stick he was carrying and forced himself to stand still and remember which way the sound had come from: over there? Toward the forest? Was it some night animal, or an owl, which he could safely ignore?

No, it wasn't. Swallowing hard, he set off quietly in the direction it had come from, toward a group of oak trees at the edge of a little dip in the ground. Crouching low and feeling better for the activity, he moved closer, listening with every nerve he had, prepared for something vile to spring at him: but nothing did. He reached the first tree, stood with his hand on the trunk, listening still, and heard nothing.

He tapped the trunk with his stick. Nothing responded.

He moved under the trees, eyes wide, staring at every shadow. Nothing moved; the shadows were only shadows; there was nothing there to harm him, nothing there that had screamed.

Cautiously he left the oak trees and looked further around. Nothing; starlight, silence, shadows.

He gave a long soft shaky whistle and went to bed.

On the night before the coronation, the palace and the city were alive with bustle and preparation. In the palace kitchens, the pastry cooks were completing the towers of icing and pastry that would decorate the table at the state banquet, and in the icehouse, a sculptor was busy chipping and shaving away at a huge block of ice brought there from St. Petersburg and kept intact since the winter. It was going to represent the cathedral, though if the day turned out to be hot and too much melted, the sculptor would transform it speedily into a rugged simulacrum of the Eschtenburg Rock, complete with funicular railway and tiny flag.

In the stables, the horses were being fed and watered, their tails plaited, their manes combed. The coach had been polished and oiled and buffed and regilded, new tires put on the wheels, the seats stuffed with fresh horsehair. Outside in the city, the streets were being swept and cleaned, the flowers in the window boxes watered and trimmed, every window pane along the route polished until it sparkled. Beside the Nenuphar Lake in Stralitzky Park, a team of Neapolitan pyrotechnicians were setting the fuses and the revolving wheels for the fireworks display. The choir was being rehearsed in the cathedral. The opera house orchestra was going through the program for the coronation ball, including, of course, Johann Strauss the Younger's Andersbad Waltz. The sentries on duty outside the palace were stamping and wheeling and saluting and presenting arms with even more vigor than usual, while the Razkavian police were patrolling the streets, twirling their whiskers and frowning officially. In every hotel, inn, and beer cellar, restaurateurs and chefs and landlords were checking their casks of beer, their cellars of wine, their sides of venison. In bars and cafés, journalists and correspondents from all over Europe—and one or two from America—were gathering local color and essential background information in the usual way, namely by talking to one another over glasses of strong drink.

In the cathedral vestry, where the flag had rested since the death of the old king (the period between a royal death and a coronation was the only time it wasn't flying), the nuns of St. Agatha, the seamstresses who tended to it, were going over it with fine needles and finer thread, mending every rent and patching every thin spot and strengthening every seam, and outlining the ancient eagle in fresh scarlet silk, and attaching new golden tassels to the border.

And the focus of all this activity, the new king and his young queen, sat across a little table playing a child's game and clapping and laughing and groaning, and Becky sat with them, like a nursemaid with two charges.

It was a game called Whirlpool. Adelaide (who was sharpening her reading on a book of chess openings) had wanted to play chess, but not with Becky, who wasn't a strong enough opponent, so they had played Whirlpool instead. The object was to be the last to be sucked down into the vortex, so you needed low scores on the dice instead of high ones, and Adelaide had been cheating outrageously. Despite accidentally knocking the dice on the floor and then pretending they only showed two, and despite wrongly counting the number of squares she had to move, and despite elaborately talking about something else just after Becky had her move and then insisting that she'd moved last and it was Becky's turn again, she finally had to accept that her little tin ship was going to plunge into the maelstrom long before Becky's; and at that point she had the nerve to say that Becky must be cheating. Becky had laughed at her.

Adelaide was about to flare into a tantrum—Becky knew the signs—when there came a gentle knock on the door, and the king came in.

Becky curtsied. Adelaide jumped up and greeted him with a kiss. She was genuinely fond of him, Becky thought; she had a great capacity for fondness. She'd called Becky sister once or twice, surprising herself as much as Becky, and doing her best to cancel the little revelation with a flourish of petulance. So Becky was never surprised to see how affectionate she was with Rudolf, though she felt that it was the sort of love you might show a favorite brother—not, perhaps, a husband.

Becky had prepared to leave, but King Rudolf said, "No, Miss Winter, please stay with us. You are playing a game? Which one is this?"

"We've nearly finished this," Adelaide said. "Play chess with me, Rudi. Becky can watch and learn a new opening."

"No, no. I like these games best. May I join you?"

A little smirk of triumph from Her Majesty: she could start again, unvortexed. She swept the pieces off the board, and the king sat down with them in that comfortable, rather overfurnished room, at the table with its crimson cloth. Darkness was gathering outside, and the lamps were lit, casting their yellow warmth over the table and the brightly colored board, and the ivory dice, and the little metal ships, and their hands: the king's a-glitter with the ring of state, and Adelaide's a delicate rose-pink as she shook the dice between her cupped palms before rolling double ones.

"Snake's eyes!" she said, clapping with delight. "It's going to be all right this time."

She moved her ship two squares and the game began.

In one of the handsome tall old buildings in St. Stephen's Square, overlooking the cathedral steps, a woman stood ringing the doorbell of an apartment on the fourth floor. The man who stood behind her was carrying a long, leather-bound box and what might have been a tripod in a green felt bag.

A manservant opened the door. The householder, a bachelor cigar merchant called Alois Egger, didn't know the lady, who gave her name as Señora Menendez, a representative of the leading fashion journal in Madrid. Her associate was a photographer. Was Herr Egger aware of the enormous interest aroused throughout Europe by the accession of this young and beautiful queen? If Señora Menendez could obtain early details—and photographs—of the coronation gown...And this apartment overlooked the cathedral steps, did it not?

Indeed it did. The balcony gave one of the finest views in the city.

Herr Egger was no provincial stick-in-the-mud; he was a cosmopolitan businessman; he traveled to Amsterdam several times a year; he had even been to Havana once. What a pleasure, to do business with a modern woman as agreeable and charming as Señora Menendez! Why, it put him in mind of a certain evening in Cuba—the moon behind the palm trees—the soft notes of a guitar—red rose, black hair...

And the price she offered was really quite generous. They agreed: he would vacate the apartment early in the morning and let her and the photographer have the exclusive use of it throughout the coronation. He would be in pocket, the ladies of Madrid would have their fashion picture-story, and perhaps—next evening—who could tell? A little dinner, a stroll in the Spanish Gardens, the city *en fête*...It might be Havana once again.

So everything was ready for the coronation.

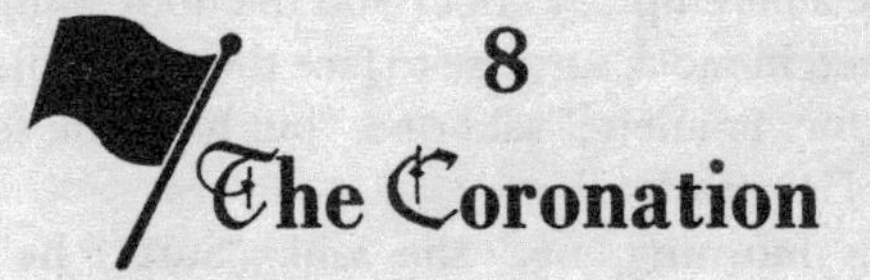

8
The Coronation

Becky's maid woke her at six. She couldn't lie a moment in bed; she jumped out and stood at her window, gazing out at the park, the red-brown roofs of the city below, and the dark sap green of the distant hills, as the sun touched everything with a pearly fresh clarity that Frau Winter's acquaintance Monsieur Pissarro might have been able to depict, but which Becky could only wonder at.

Then wash, dress, eat, hurry back to room, maid to do hair, looking glass, shoes, hat, brooch, reticule...oh, where *was* it? And purse: money...would there be a collection? Did they pass the plate around at a coronation? Surely not; but here was a coin or two just in case...What's the time? It *can't* be; hurry, hurry.

She hastened downstairs, nearly tripped on the carpet in the West Corridor, and ran full tilt into someone.

It was Jim. He had an expression of baffled fury, but not at her. He drew her into the little anteroom beyond the library.

"Listen," he said, "there's not much time—"

"I know! I've got to be at the West Door in *three minutes!*"

"Shut your trap and listen. Gödel's concocted some ridiculous charge and ordered me confined to the palace, damn his eyes. I've given the sergeant at arms the slip once, but if he finds me again it'll be lock and key. I'm going to try and get out in a minute and join Karl and the others. Something's up, Becky. By God, if I could—"

He froze, and listened, and then darted behind the heavy curtain. Becky pretended to be fiddling with her gloves as there came a peremptory knock and the door swung open.

She turned in mock surprise to face the two soldiers.

"Excuse me, Fräulein," said one, "but have you seen the Englishman? Herr Taylor?"

"Not this morning, no," she said. "Surely he's with His Majesty?"

"No, he's missing, Fräulein. Excuse me for disturbing you."

He saluted and withdrew. It was time for Becky to be at the West Door, or she'd make everyone late; she was going to travel to the cathedral with the count and countess, because Adelaide had insisted that she was to be close by.

"Jim?" she whispered desperately. "I *must* go!"

"See if they're still in the corridor," he said, coming out from behind the curtain. "Give me a nod if it's clear. Remember—green-and-yellow's safe."

She opened the door. The red-carpeted corridor stretched empty to left and right, and she looked back and whispered, "All clear," before darting out. She tore along to the entrance and reached it just in time, stumbling past the surprised footman and out onto the steps like a low comedian in a farce. In the open carriage below, the count was glaring at her like a hand grenade. Becky saw that there was a fourth passenger, and groaned inwardly.

"I do beg your pardon," she said, scrambling up in the least unladylike fashion she could manage. "I caught my heel in the carpet and tripped as I came out."

There was a frosty silence. She took her seat beside the count, facing backwards. The groom swung the door shut, the coachman shook the reins, and they trundled slowly away to join the state coach, which was already moving through the gates. Becky longed to turn her head and look at the crowd, but it would have been ill-mannered, because the count was introducing her to the old gentleman opposite, a duke of some kind whose name she didn't catch. Not knowing how to curtsy sitting down, but feeling that some kind of gesture was due, she gave a sort of ugly squirm and he very politely lifted his top hat. The carriage slowed as it caught up with the state coach, and then another two carriages swung in behind them; and then a troop of hussars or uhlans or lancers trotted up from somewhere, jingling and snorting and monstrously pleased with themselves as they eyed Adelaide squintwise from beneath their black fur helmets.

And then they were off, a huge cheer shaking the rooftops and scattering pigeons, and a thousand flags waving from windows and doorways and balconies. The actual distance to the cathedral was not very great, but the drive took the best part of half an hour, since they went down the Cesky Boulevard and under the Arch of Remembrance, and then into Stralitzky Park and along the Nenuphar Lake past the grotto-pavilion that King Michael had built in 1765 for his swan bride.

All along the route, citizens waved flags and tourists raised their hats and policemen stood stiffly saluting. Here and there Becky saw a young figure move through the throng, and caught a glimpse of a green-and-yellow flash at his shoulder; or hoped she did, anyway.

Jim slipped along to the end of the West Corridor and looked around the corner across the saloon and into the banqueting hall. At the other end of that, a long way off, there was a serving room with a steam cupboard for keeping the plates and dishes hot, and beyond that, a short passage to the kitchen; but could he get to the other end of the banqueting hall without being seen? Servants were coming in and out every few minutes to arrange flowers, to position chairs, to set out glasses...

Voices behind him. Nothing for it; have to go. He crouched and darted across the saloon, into the banqueting hall—empty—thank God!—a clatter of plates: someone was in the serving room—dive under the table.

The cloth came halfway down to the floor all around. Provided he kept quiet, he should be able to get from this end to the other, because the floor was carpeted; nothing to scrape or knock on; but it was a long way. The table was as long as a cricket pitch: Jim had paced it out once, twenty-two yards from end to end. And it was supported by several massive central legs, over whose radiating feet, like smoothly polished roots, he'd have to clamber.

He set off. It took him far longer than he hoped, because when he was halfway down, a squad of footmen came in to set out the cutlery with geometrical precision. All he could see was white stockings and black patent-leather buckled shoes on either side of him, moving slowly from one setting to the next. He could hear a hiss of steam from the serving room, the soft light knocks of cutlery set down on the tablecloth, the murmur of conversation—which stopped when the steward (dark trousers) came in to stroll the length of the table, stop to criticize, and move on.

Then came another silence, and feet and legs turned to the door through which Jim had come in. Uniformed legs at the end of the table: the tight maroon trousers with black stripe of the palace guard.

"Have you seen His Majesty's secretary? The Englishman Taylor?"

"No, Sergeant," from the steward.

"If you do, ring the alarm at once, you understand?"

"The alarm, Sergeant? But—"

"It's a matter of vital importance. There may be a plot against the king."

"And the Englishman is—"

"Exactly. Keep your eyes open. Right, Corporal, you take the ballroom. I'll go upstairs to the gallery..."

They left. Jim swore silently. It was worse than he'd guessed; for when the blow did fall—as he was sure it would, now—they'd pin the blame on him. All the more urgent to get out...How much longer could they *take,* these flunkies?

Nearly half an hour, it turned out. By the time the last spoon had been set in place, the last chair set exactly parallel with the table, the last speck of dust flicked off the last glass, Jim was nearly weeping with rage and frustration.

But finally all the footmen had left the banqueting hall. Jim counted to one hundred to give himself a bit of space, crawled out, and sprinted to the serving room. A servant with an armful of dishes watched openmouthed as Jim swung around the corner and down the passage. He banged through the kitchen door and dashed among the squads of under-cooks and scullions busy trimming joints of meat and chopping vegetables, and found himself in a flagstoned yard. He paused to see where he was. Someone was shouting, and he could hear the pounding of running feet, so he ran at the far wall, took a leap up from a convenient barrel, and, scrambling over, found himself in the stable yard.

It was about time he had some luck, he thought, and there she was: a magnificent bay mare, all saddled up for the colonel of dragoons, who was ticking off a groom in the corner of the yard. Jim wasn't much of a hand with horses, but he knew how to tell them to go and ask them to stop, and roughly how to stay on in between, so he leapt up into the saddle, found the stirrups, and grabbed the reins; and before the colonel could draw breath, let alone his saber, Jim was out of the stable yard and down the gravel toward the main gate.

The procession had started off some time before, and the crowd following it had left the district near the palace fairly empty; but before long Jim had to slow down, because the nearer he came to the center, the more people filled the streets. He changed to a trot, then a walk, and then the crowd was so thick that it was quicker to abandon the horse altogether. He left her in the charge of a man with a vast mustache and a Hungarian waistcoat, promising to pay twenty crowns if he was still there that afternoon; and privately guessing that the man would have got fifty for her and vanished before half an hour was up. *Good luck to him,* Jim thought.

Then it was onward on foot, running through the crowd, dodging around slow-moving pedestrians and swinging around corners and leaping up steps, on fire to reach the cathedral and prevent—what? He couldn't guess, or rather he could; which made it all the more imperative to get there in time.

As the procession turned into St. Stephen's Square in front of the cathedral, Becky gasped at the size of the crowd and the great cheer that arose, but mainly at the beauty of the place on this brilliant summer morning. The fine old houses with their baroque rooflines and their carved window frames shone ocher and gold and cream in the clear sunlight. Figures waved from the iron balconies; on the other side of the square, the ancient Gothic blackness of the cathedral loomed high against the blue. Through a gap between the houses, Becky could see the gray Rock of Eschtenburg across the river, without its banner, waiting.

Inside the cathedral everything seemed dark until her eyes adjusted to the shafts of color slanting through the stained-glass windows. The aisles on either side were crowded with people standing, and every place was taken, or seemed to be; Becky wondered for a moment if they'd have to perch on the font. But there were seats at the front for the party from the palace, and she felt both proud and self-conscious as she walked up the aisle with the count and countess. The organ was playing all the time, and they had hardly reached their seats when there was a great fanfare of trumpets, almost loud enough to stir the folds of the flag in its bracket by the great door, and everyone stood as the frail old figure of the archbishop led the king and queen slowly up the aisle.

The king wore the uniform of colonel in chief of the Eschtenburger Guards, the smartest of all the regiments: snowy white, with a row of medals on his chest, gold epaulettes, and a long curved sword with a scarlet tassel. Naturally, he was bareheaded, and as they went past Becky she could see that the poor man was going gray.

Adelaide, beside him, was wearing a dress of rich cream silk. She had her hand on his arm, though Becky could see who was steadying whom.

The choir began to sing, and then there was a Mass, and finally, at fifteen minutes past eleven, the actual coronation took place. It was a simple ceremony: a prayer, an oath sworn by Rudolf that he would faithfully bear the Red Eagle, and then the archbishop anointed him with holy oil. Becky watched Rudolf and Adelaide kneeling side by side on the raised cushion, looking like little children in a play, and felt a lump in her throat that wasn't entirely patriotism.

There was another prayer, for long life and fruitfulness, and then the archbishop turned to the pageboy who'd been standing nearby and took the crown from the cushion he held. It was nothing much to look at: simply a hoop of black iron, set with a single huge irregular yellow topaz; but it had been forged from the very sword with which Walter von Eschten had defended the Rock and beaten Ottokar the Second at the Battle of Wendelstein, and the topaz was the dowry of Erszebet Cséhak, the Hungarian countess who'd married Walter's son Karl. So the Crown of Razkavia was more precious than any golden bauble.

Rudolf stood to face the congregation, and the archbishop held the crown high and placed it gently on the king's head. A sort of collective sigh went round the cathedral, and the ancient archbishop knelt to kiss the king's hand. Becky was sure she could hear his knees creaking.

Then Adelaide also kissed Rudolf's hand, and the trumpets blazed a great chord as the organ thundered below them. The archbishop led the way down the aisle toward the door where the *Adlerfahne* hung, and as they passed everyone gazed at them, staring openly: congregations, like cats, may look at kings.

The door had been opened wide. The archbishop waited for the congregation to regroup itself around them, which meant a great deal of polite jostling. Becky caught Adelaide's eye, and the queen seemed to see her interpreter with relief, for a quick bright smile flashed into her eyes before the impassivity descended again.

Eventually everything was ready. Below them in the square four thousand or more—who could tell how many?—pairs of eyes looked upward. Soldiers and policemen stood ready to clear the route toward the ancient bridge.

Then the archbishop turned to the *Adlerfahne*. The flag itself was about eight feet long and six deep, made of gold-yellow silk, with the red eagle embroidered in scarlet and crimson. Around the edge was a fringe of golden tassels. It was fastened to a flagpole about twelve feet long, and it was very heavy; but then, it was to be carried by a king.

The archbishop said a prayer, and sprinkled the flag with holy water; then Rudolf took hold of the flagpole and lifted it from the bracket, and walked the three or four yards out onto the cathedral steps.

As he appeared, a great cheer rang out. Hats were waved, the crowd swirled to make way as the soldiers and police began to organize the path for him, and the trumpeters, lined up on the steps, raised the golden instruments and sounded the Eagle Fanfare.

Adelaide joined the king, a little behind him on his right, and Becky wasn't sure she didn't hear an extra shout or cheer of greeting. For the moment, anyway, Razkavians had put all their doubts about King Rudolf aside. Aesthete, dandy, mooncalf he might have been, but he was their king, the *Adlerträger,* the Eagle-bearer, and they loved him for that. This was the moment when the nation remade itself: this carrying of the flag, this renewal. Becky felt her heart surge with pride, and sorrow too, for her father. He should have been here to see this. But there was joy in her too, and she knew that many and many a citizen felt as she did: their king, their flag, their freedom, their nationhood. They would have died for him.

But it was he who died for them. As he took the first step down toward the square, a shot rang out, shockingly, horribly loud even above the cheers and the fanfare, and Rudolf stumbled. The tumult and the music stopped in a moment, faltering into a hideous silence as the great silken flag drooped and sagged down, down, downward, as if the Eagle itself had been shot, and Becky heard the whole square, four thousand people, hold their breath as one.

The first to move was Adelaide, and her first move was toward her husband. A great red rose seemed to be blooming on the snow of his uniformed breast, and her hands went out to him, but with the last of his strength he held up the flag and whispered, "*Der Adler...*"

A dozen hands reached up around him, but stopped; every man, woman, and child in the square reached up involuntarily; but they held back, because the flag was firm in the hands of the queen, Adelaide, and she was holding it.

The archbishop was on his knees beside the dying king. Already the crowd below was surging forward and then parting, inviting her down, urging her on.

She had to struggle to get the flagpole upright, and then inelegantly rested it on her hip while she moved one hand for a more comfortable grip; and then with one passionate, devastated glance at Rudolf (which the crowd saw, and noted), began to move down the steps and into the square.

The count was at her side on the left, Becky at her right. Out of the corner of her eye, Becky could see Karl von Gaisberg and half a dozen other green-and-yellows shove through the crowd and stand like a guard of honor for Adelaide to walk between. They closed ranks to keep the crowd back and give her space to move into, and she took the first steps across the cobbles toward the old houses at the corner of the square, and the bridge beyond.

The issue was clear: if Adelaide managed to carry the *Adlerfahne* to the Rock, Razkavia would remain free. But against her was the possibility at any moment of another assassin, or the same one still at large with another bullet; and there was the weight of the ancient flag, the sheer difficulty of managing a twelve-foot pole with forty-eight square feet of heavy multi-layered silk hanging from it—and Rudolf had been practiced and drilled, and she had not; and there was the natural anguish she felt at seeing her husband shot down beside her…

The count had drawn his revolver. Karl von Gaisberg came close to Becky and said quietly, "Where's Jim?"

"They tried to arrest him in the palace. I don't know if he managed to get out."

He whistled softly. "Will she make it?"

"Who can tell? But she'll die trying."

"Let's hope not…"

He took his place again at the head of the phalanx, and Becky moved up beside Adelaide, who saw, and cast a proud, anguished look at her.

"Rudi?" she said, in a strained voice.

Becky could only shake her head.

"I can't do it, Becky," Adelaide muttered. "I *can't*…"

"Yes, you can," Becky said back. "Rest if you want to. Take as long as you like. But you can, you *can*."

Adelaide stopped, but only to shift the weight from one side of her body to the other, propping the foot of the flagpole on her hip. A hundred anxious faces pressed close, eyes wide, mouths gaping, and then a voice cried, *"Ein hoch dem Königin!"*

"Hoch! Hoch für Adelaide!" More voices joined in, and the cheer strengthened her, for she hoisted the flag once more and they moved on.

Jim reached the square just as the procession came out through the cathedral door; in time to hear the fanfare, to hear the fatal shot, to see Rudolf fall. A bitter lump of pity came to his throat; Rudolf had never asked for this, he'd never sought the crown, but he'd done his best, he'd shouldered the burden, and through Jim's mind there ran the knowledge that if the king had seen what was coming, he'd have gone ahead and done his duty all the same. Adelaide had seen something in him, poor zany, and Jim had always felt the deepest kind of admiration for the way men who weren't naturally brave could face danger without flinching.

He saw Adelaide field the flag; a professional cricketer couldn't have done it better, he thought. Then he remembered something else, and foreseeing the arguments later if things weren't done properly, he forced his way up the cathedral steps, said a word to the archbishop, and picked up the crown. No one had noticed it; the iron hoop had rolled off Rudolf's head and was lying in the gutter.

There was no point in trying to jostle their way over the bridge, so he tugged the archbishop's arm and beckoned to a captain of hussars, holding up the crown. The man's eyes narrowed, he reached for his sword—then he understood, and joined them. Together he and Jim hurried the archbishop down the steps, around the side of the cathedral, and down to the ferry at the water's edge.

It was a leaky old flat-bottomed barge that was hauled from one side to the other by means of a wire rope suspended over the water. Jim had watched the old ferryman a dozen times, and it looked easy, but it took all his strength, and the captain's, and the archbishop's prayers, and still the boat swung wildly this way and that.

Jim looked upstream, saw the commotion along the parapet of the bridge, and wondered grimly if she'd get there first after all.

"Heave!" he shouted. "Pull harder!"

• • •

Above the heads of the crowd, Becky could see the statues that lined the parapet of the bridge. Each one was covered in a heavy crop of small boys waving their caps and cheering. Like the square, the road across the bridge was cobbled, and she tensely watched Adelaide's delicate satin shoes feeling for balance.

Step by slow step they moved on, up the crown of the bridge to the very center, and so thick was the crowd—standing, clinging together, even along the stone coping of the balustrade—that Becky feared that if one missed his footing, he'd take another dozen down into the water with him. Adelaide was crying silently. Her teeth were clenched, her face was white, her arms were trembling.

"We're over halfway there," Becky said. "Just keep going!"

"It's all bloody uphill now, innit?" Adelaide muttered back through the tears, but she didn't stop.

At the other end of the bridge the road passed under a great Gothic archway and gatehouse, every window of which was thronged. The road narrowed, and it was getting harder to force a way through the crowd. Karl shouted, "Make way! Make way for the queen to get through! Make way there!"

The count had replaced his revolver, and was watching her intently from only a foot or so away, tensed to hold her if she faltered. His fierce old face was full of anxiety and pride.

As they reached the gatehouse under which they had to pass, Adelaide was shaking so much that Becky thought for a moment that she'd drop the flag; and *What then? What then?* pounded through her head. But Adelaide didn't drop it; she paused again to rest it on her hip, and looked up at the count before leaning momentarily on his broad chest; and then she moved on again, under the gatehouse, and the crowd on the left parted, shoving and pushing and clambering onto every window ledge, every minute projection, and opening the way to the flight of steps that led up to the summit of the Rock.

"Pull, Captain, pull!"

How did the old ferryman do it? Jim had marveled before at the way some doddering old clot who could hardly spoon gruel into his face would dig a trench or cut down a tree in a quarter the time it would take a hearty youth with bulging muscles; and here was the proof of it again. He and the captain were sweating and trembling, and the barge was yawing wildly, and they still hadn't reached the shore.

"Ja—hau ruck! Hau ruck!"

Damn it, Jim thought, what was he doing this for? Well, it wasn't only for Adelaide. It was for Rudolf too, and the count; and for Becky; and for Karl von Gaisberg; and for the whole of this rickety little country, with its pride and its history and its honor. He felt as Razkavian as the good captain just then, so he swung into the heaving with a will, and before long they were out of the main current and making easier progress toward the wooden jetty on the far bank.

And then they were clambering ashore.

"Where now? The funicular?" said the captain.

"It's the only way. Come on!"

They hustled the man of God up the lane around the base of the Rock toward the little station, where they banged on the door of the stationmaster's cottage until someone heard and came running.

"No—forbidden—the funicular is not functioning—"

But then he saw the archbishop, who indicated the crown Jim was holding; and he took it all in. At once he began to throw levers and uncock taps, for the funicular was weight-driven. A tank of water at the top (fed by the very spring that had kept Walter von Eschten and his knights alive centuries before) filled a tank in the empty carriage at the top, which, now being heavier than the one below, duly trundled down, pulling the lower one up. It was neat, simple, and silent, but achingly slow; so while the archbishop sat in the carriage and waited, the captain and Jim set off to run up the rough slope beside the track.

Adelaide looked up at the path, closed her eyes, and bit her lip before looking again at the ground to be sure of her footing. The path was narrow—no more than two people could walk abreast—with a railing on the left and stone-walled houses, which after a short distance gave way to the naked rock itself, on the right. From every window, faces looked down as first Karl and two other students stepped upward, then Adelaide and the count. Becky was nearly blocked, but Adelaide called desperately, "Becky! Stay with me!" and she twisted and heaved her way through to the step behind her.

"I'm here," she said. "I'm with you."

More students fell in behind, and the crowd surged up ahead, stumbling, clambering, making room. Adelaide's feet in their soft shoes (torn now, ragged and dusty, never intended for this) fumbled uncertainly as they lifted her from step to step.

A low, constant moan was coming from her throat. Her teeth were gritted, Becky could see as she looked back, and her eyes were drenched in tears. Adelaide halted, and Becky couldn't see what she wanted, and then the count said hoarsely—"Her dress—she'll trip—" and stood aside for Becky to dart up beside her and lift the heavy embroidered silk up a little so her feet could find the next step without stumbling.

She could feel Adelaide's whole body shaking, and let the

queen lean on her for a few seconds; then heard the whisper, "Get out the way—I'm going on—" and stood back to let her take a few steps more.

Onward and upward, a step at a time, and ever and ever more slowly. The crowd below and those waiting at the summit, as well as all the people perched on ledges or clinging to the bushes that grew from the side of the Rock, were silent now. The cheers had died; all those close to her could see the strain in her chalk-white face, and share the anguish as she bit so hard into her lip that she was drawing blood.

"Just around the next bend," Becky said. "Not far now. Just keep going. Lean on me. Stop if you want to. Rest. Take as long as you like. But it's not far now..."

All Adelaide's strength was used up. She couldn't answer; she could barely see; a perpetual whimper shook her chest, and Becky could even see a line of blood appearing, a frightful thing, at the tip of each fingernail. The perspiration shone on her face, and the carefully coiffed hair was stuck in damp streaks to her forehead and across her eyes. Becky reached up to wipe it away, and felt the trembling in her very skull.

At the top of the steps, just around the next bend, was the little parade ground with the flagpole at the center, with the platform for the funicular railway at the far side. Nearly there, nearly there... But as they rounded the bend and Adelaide's poor blistered feet fumbled for the last six steps, a shadow fell across them.

Becky looked up at the giant form, the dark brooding eyes, of Otto von Schwartzberg.

And Adelaide faltered. She stopped. "I can't," she whispered. "I'm finished, Becky, I want to die, I can't do it..."

Otto von Schwartzberg's expression was inscrutable; he might have been planning to strike her dead or to lift her in his arms to the summit, and no one could guess which; and such was his colossal presence that no one—not even the count—knew what to do, for a second or so. And the flag was drooping, drooping...

Then, into that stillness, a figure leapt from the summit of the Rock, and landed lightly in front of Otto von Schwartzberg. Fair-haired, disheveled, bleeding, with torn jacket, he stood tensely in front of the giant. He was clasping something in his left hand.

"Move," he said. "You're in the queen's way. Move at once."

No one had spoken to Otto von Schwartzberg like that before, in any language. He stepped aside, and Adelaide took the last steps onto the platform, and the whole city saw the flag appear, and the whole city cheered.

The Eagle Guard—the sentries who patrolled the Rock day and night—sprang forward as the count barked at them, and took the *Adlerfahne* from their queen's hands just as she sank into Becky's arms, unconscious.

All around there were scenes of extraordinary jubilation. Hats were thrown into the air, as the flag rose proudly up the flagpole, the rooftops and the Rock echoed with cheers and the little explosions of firecrackers and a fanfare from the trumpets of the Eagle Guard. Where Otto von Schwartzberg had gone, no one knew. The count was concerned about Adelaide, but in Becky's reticule there was a bottle of smelling salts. She waved it under Adelaide's nose, and the stinging shock made the girl draw away and shake her head. She opened her eyes—they fluttered, they blinked—she looked up, and saw the Red Eagle flying in the blue air.

"I done it," she whispered.

Then there was a wheeze and clank of machinery, and the pretty wooden carriage of the funicular railway rose into view.

Out of it stepped the archbishop, frail and anxious and stained with the blood of the king, and then Jim handed him what he'd been carrying: the iron crown of Razkavia.

Becky helped Adelaide up, and under the flag she'd carried to the Rock the new queen stood, pale and trembling, and was crowned, and everyone on the summit knelt to pay her homage.

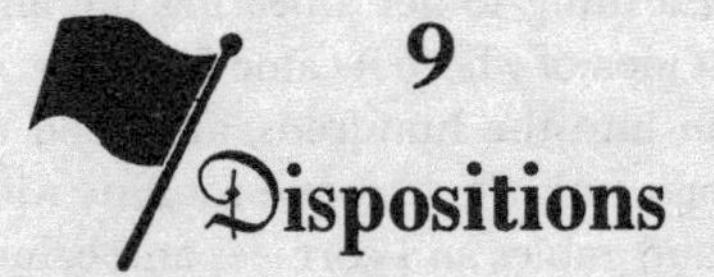

9 Dispositions

For an hour or two after Adelaide was crowned, there was a wild confusion of excitement and grief throughout the city. Thousands of people had seen it happen, but it was still scarcely believable; it wasn't until Adelaide had recovered enough to ride down the Rock in the funicular railway that it began to sink in. The open barouche that had been going to take Rudolf back to the palace as king now had to take her alone as queen, and she sat in it, pale and shivering now that the shock of it was reaching her, with the iron crown on her dark hair and an expression that was indomitable. She was ravaged; she could never hide the play of thoughts over her face; and that, as Jim was coming to see, was her strongest hold over the people—over her subjects. She could hide nothing, so they believed her.

But the situation was full of peril. Jim commandeered another horse and rode beside the carriage all the way to the palace, more than half expecting another bullet, with the count riding at the other side. Garlands, cheers, shouts of support rose all around, and through it all she sat with exactly the right expression: a cheerful grin wasn't in order, but neither was misery. She looked grim, proud, determined, sorrowful, fearless. Jim caught the count's eye, and knew they were thinking the same thought: by some miraculous fluke, Razkavia had found itself exactly the right ruler. Little Adelaide from Hangman's Wharf was a queen, every inch of her.

Meanwhile, soldiers and police were combing the area of St. Stephen's Square for any trace of the assassin. But a single shot is too startling a thing to get a bearing on, and each witness had a different idea of where it came from; the number of windows alone ran into the hundreds, and then there were balconies, doorways, and the baroque roofline with its profusion of pediments and gables and cornices and balustrades...not to mention the multitude of tiny crooked alleys, no more than half-known even by those who lived in the square, and never mapped. The search went on, but without any real expectation of success.

At the palace, there was an immense flurry. Everything had been set up for a king, for the formal reception, and guests were arriving (prominent citizens for luncheon, important foreigners that evening) and suddenly there was no one in charge. As the carriage and escort clattered in under the portico, Jim's enemy the Chamberlain, the Baron von Gödel, appeared at the door, bowing suavely, but with a pallor of nervousness as he looked at Jim. The count leaned over to say something quietly to Adelaide, but as Becky wasn't there to translate she had to half-guess his meaning and nod; and turning back to Gödel, the count said, "Her Majesty will go to her private apartments. The reception will take place as planned. I shall see you in the Green Office in fifteen minutes."

Jim dismounted, handed his horse to a groom, and followed the count inside just as the second coach, with the countess and Becky, turned in; and, reassured that Adelaide would have someone friendly with her, he walked after the count to the Green Office.

As soon as the door was shut, the count swept off his plumed hat and dashed it to the floor.

"Schwartzberg!" he roared in a voice that shook the glass in the window frames and rippled the ink in the crystal inkwell.

"You think so?"

"Who else? The murdering wolf...But he didn't reckon on our little English eagle, eh? You don't catch eagles with birdlime!"

"No, count. I'm sure it wasn't him. Anyway, if he's as clever as that, there won't be any proof left. I've got another idea—"

But the count was preoccupied, slapping his thigh, tapping a thumb on his chin, strolling restlessly between the desk and the window.

"Taylor, she's good, she's tough—but I'm afraid, my boy, I'm shaking in my boots. What's going to become of us? We'd better prepare a speech for her to make at the reception—or should we cancel it? Her husband's just been shot dead in front of her—who could expect a woman to—?"

"You'd expect a queen to," Jim pointed out. "And a queen's what you've got. If you want my advice, you won't tell her what to say, either. Let her find the words herself. You've seen her touch with the people; trust her."

"H'mm," said the count, rubbing his jaw. "I wonder."

"And we ought to think urgently about the Baron von Gödel. Did you know I'd been forbidden to leave the palace this morning? They sent the sergeant at arms to search the place for me, and put me under arrest. Did you see Gödel's face when he ushered us in just now?"

"But—" The count was astounded. He sat down heavily. "But you were..."

"I got out, of course. Count, there's danger very close—maybe in the palace itself. I don't trust that man an inch. Couldn't we move him out?"

The count spread his hands wearily. "The post of Chamberlain is hereditary. There's nothing to be done about Gödel...I suppose we could set up some alternative chain of command...But these things have to be done in the proper way. Let me think about it."

Jim would have said more, but there came a knock on the door. The Baron von Gödel came in, pallid but unflustered.

"Her Majesty has just appointed me her private secretary," boomed the count: a barefaced lie, but Gödel was in no position to challenge it. "Until she makes further appointments, the work of the palace will go on as before. Mr. Taylor is my personal representative; you will give him every assistance. You understand that? He is not to be impeded in any way. What has happened to the arrangements for the reception?"

Gödel swallowed hard and said, "Everything is in place, Count Thalgau. In view of the tragic circumstances, I have ordered that the band of the Eagle Guard should not play during the reception. Her Majesty will receive her guests in the Great Hall. I think they will all respond to the situation by paying their respects and leaving swiftly."

"See to that, then. As soon as the reception is over, Her Majesty will receive Mr. Taylor and myself in her private office. You will hold yourself in readiness for whatever dispositions she makes."

"Certainly, Count."

He clicked heels, bowed smoothly, and left.

"Will he obey?" said Jim.

"At first, yes. He can see which way the wind's blowing

...Damn it, this is a perilous time. I think we've got a week to establish control. If by this time on Monday next we haven't got a firm grip on the country, it'll fall. Now go on, Taylor, change your clothes and be quick about it."

Twenty minutes later, in full fig, Jim joined the guests in the Great Hall. They were representatives of every distinguished branch of Razkavian life: practically the whole of the aristocracy, mayors, senators, the speaker of the Upper House, councillors of state, eminent lawyers and bankers and churchmen and professors and even a poet or artist or two. Their mood was subdued, solemn, restrained, but every single one of them was itching for a glimpse of the new queen.

Only fifteen minutes late, there was a fanfare, and Adelaide's slender figure, graceful in black, came down the stairs. The countess was there at her side, and Becky only a step or two behind. Jim caught her eye and winked.

The plan had been for her and the king to stand at the foot of the steps and greet the guests as they came past in order of precedence. But she halted a step or two above, so that she could be seen by everyone, and said in hesitant but clear German:

"Welcome to the palace. My dear husband would have wished me to greet you each personally, and so I will, but please allow me to say something to you all. When my husband was a prince, I vowed before God to be a good princess. When he became king, I vowed to serve and honor him faithfully. Now that the burden and the great honor of reigning has fallen to me alone, I vow before you all to serve Razkavia to the utmost limit of my strength. Let there be no doubt in anyone's heart: Razkavia has a queen, and that queen will defend and love her country till the day she dies. Long live the Red Eagle! Long live Razkavia!"

Then they knew she was theirs.

That evening, when the excitement of the day had subsided a little, Jim went out to find Karl von Gaisberg. There were several things worrying him, not all of which he wanted to confide to the count.

He found Karl in the Café Florestan, sitting with four or five others. They greeted Jim with avid curiosity: What had happened at the palace? He answered all their questions, and then said:

"Now as far as I know, the police haven't arrested anyone yet. Frankly, I don't expect them to. But I'm pretty certain it wasn't Otto von Schwartzberg behind this; it's not his style."

"What was he doing on the Rock, then?" said Gustav. "I thought he was going to knock her down and swipe the flag!"

"I think he was taking her measure. He didn't actually threaten her. Let's think harder about what actually happened this morning. Were you close enough to see the king as he came down the steps?"

Karl nodded. "I was at the foot of them, Anton here was further along near the bridge...I saw it all."

"I was in the middle of the crowd," said Gustav. "I saw it too."

"But *what* did you see?"

"Well..." said Gustav. "I heard the shot, I saw him fall."

"Which way?"

"Backward. No—wait..."

"No!" said Karl. "He was turning to the left—isn't that right?"

"He *did* fall backward," said Anton. "But it was after he'd turned to the left, I thought."

"I think that's what I saw, too," said Jim. "The bullet caught him full in the breast as he was turning, and it knocked him away from it. Otherwise Ad—Her Majesty—wouldn't have been able to catch the flag."

"By God, that's right!" said Gustav. "She was behind him on that side—he fell back toward her!"

"So," said Jim, "doesn't that give us a clue about where the bullet came from?"

They were silent. Then Karl pulled one of the Florestan's tattered menus toward him and got out a pencil. He roughly sketched a plan of the square, showing the cathedral steps and a cross where Rudolf had fallen.

"How far had he turned? He was a few steps down—"

"Higher than that, surely?" said Anton. "I could see him clearly from all the way across the square. I think he must have been only a step or two from the top. And he hadn't turned completely."

"About a quarter turn?" said Gustav.

"About that," said Karl. "Did he fall directly backward, though?"

"No. Up a bit. Like this..."

Gustav took the pencil and sketched in the angle. Jim, watching, nodded.

"I was to one side. She was directly between me and the king, but I saw the flag begin to fall back toward me. I think that angle's right. Draw a line out from it..."

Karl did so.

"Well, what's there?" said Gustav.

Karl shrugged. "A block of apartments? I can't remember."

"My uncle lives there," said Anton hesitantly. "At least, in one of the houses along that side..."

"What are we waiting for? Let's go and pay a call on him," said Jim.

Anton's uncle, a prosperous dentist called Weill, was delighted to receive his nephew's friends. Like their neighbors, he and his wife had been on their bunting-draped balcony when the shot had been fired, and had gazed horrified as the king died below them.

"Well, the shot was very loud, wouldn't you say, Mathilde?" he said. "I thought it came from higher up."

Their flat was on the third floor. Frau Weill wasn't sure.

"It was so sudden—it seemed to come from all around. Like thunder," she said. "Anyway, upstairs—who is there? Madame Czerny is too old—eighty-nine, would you believe that?—I can't see her shooting anyone. And Herr Egger wasn't there anyway."

"Who is Herr Egger?" said Jim.

"He's a cigar merchant," said Herr Weill. "Very friendly man. Always gives me a fine Havana at Christmas. And I always offer to pull a tooth out for him in exchange, and he always says, No, no, I insist, it's more blessed to give than to receive. But he wasn't there today, I happen to know, because I saw him late last night in the bar of the Hotel Europa, and he told me he'd rented his apartment for the day to a journalist..."

Herr Weill realized what this could have meant a second after everyone else. He looked upward, appalled.

"Surely..." his wife said. "They would have had papers, identification...Wouldn't they?"

"Have the police been here?" asked Jim.

"Yes, they came to all the apartments, obviously, and we told them what we'd heard...You don't think...?"

"We'll go and speak to Herr Egger, if he's in," said Jim, getting up. "In the meantime, please don't say anything about this. What I think you might do is write an account of everything you know, just as you told it to us, and deposit it with your lawyer."

"Yes—yes—good idea—I'll do that at once," said the ashen-faced dentist, hurrying across to a bureau.

"Herr Egger won't get into trouble, will he?" said Frau Weill. "Such a friendly man! I couldn't bear it—"

"I don't know," said Jim. "But thank you very much for your help. Which number is his flat?"

Herr Egger was at home, and a little put out. He'd brought home a big bunch of roses to present to the lady journalist from Madrid, and she'd gone, without even leaving a card. Well, no doubt her colleague had snapped a fine picture of the king's death; but that was small consolation.

He received Jim and the students in the sitting room, with the doors open onto the balcony from which, by now, Jim was certain the shot had come. Herr Egger's pomaded hair and waxed mustache, together with the powerful aroma of eau de cologne and Parma violets he exuded, disclosed a man whose vanity was stronger than his sense of the ridiculous, and Jim quickly realized that they'd better not give him any clue about what they really suspected.

"I'm looking for a journalist," he said. "I work for an English paper myself, and I believe you rented your flat to one of my colleagues. The thing is, he's got some information for me and I can't find him. You don't happen to know where he's gone?"

"Ah, you're out of luck, my boy! You've come to the wrong place. I know it wasn't your colleague who rented my flat—and d'you know how I know that?"

"No," said Jim politely.

"Because it wasn't a *he,* it was a *she.* There! What d'you think of that?"

"Remarkable," said Jim, feeling his stomach tighten. "A lady journalist, eh? Did you tell the police?"

"The police?"

"They called at every household, apparently. Looking for the assassin, I suppose."

"I don't know if they called here or not; I gave my servants the day off."

"Very generous of you. Your lady journalist—what did she look like?"

"Oh, a stunner!" said Herr Egger roguishly. "Spanish, you know. Dark hair, black eyes, fine..." He gestured to indicate what it was that was fine. "You know. Name of Menendez. Course, I'm familiar with Spanish women. Speak the language a little. Travel to Havana, oh, every year on business. Cigars."

"Did she leave an address? What paper did she work for?"

"No address, no. Some periodical dealing with fashion, I believe. Madrid. Had a photographer with her—long case—tripod thing, I suppose. Fine-looking woman. Bit—er—*ripe,* I'd have said, for a young chap like you."

"Did she speak German? Or did you speak Spanish?"

"Oh, German. Strong accent. Fine voice, though. Like a cello at dusk...You'll take a cigarillo? Try these. New line. Come from Las Palmas. Glass of wine?"

10
The Map Room

During the next few days, a whirlwind seemed to possess Adelaide. She hardly slept. She confirmed the count in his private secretaryship, she created the position of interpreter-in-chief for Becky, she made Countess Thalgau a lady-in-waiting; she summoned the chief of police and demanded to know exactly what his plans were for catching the assassin, and ordered him to report daily to Count Thalgau on the progress; she oversaw the arrangements for King Rudolf's funeral; she saw all the palace domestic staff, from the steward down to the scullery maids, and told them what she expected of them; she planned a series of luncheons to which, after the first period of mourning, she intended to invite leading citizens; she walked bareheaded behind the gun carriage that took Rudolf's body to the cathedral; she took two hours of furiously hard instruction in German every day, and made really extraordinary progress; she asked the British Embassy for their copy of the Army and Navy Stores catalog, seized on it with glee, and ordered every single game, from Animal Misfitz to Zelo, by way of Blinking Dandy, Puffette, Tipple-Topple, El Teb, Guessodor, Cape to Cairo, Wibley Wob, and so on. Following that, she came down with what the royal physician called nervous prostration, and slept for twenty-four hours without waking.

Very soon, the new structure of the royal household began to take shape. The Chamberlain, Jim's enemy Baron von Gödel, couldn't be moved; but he could be bypassed. All Adelaide's decisions were relayed to the palace and the world outside through Count Thalgau instead. Her personal circle was very small: it was limited to Becky and the countess, who, if she wasn't the liveliest of companions, was at least safe, as Adelaide said. Becky tried her hardest to learn chess, and made some progress; and, more successfully, made the acquaintance of a chambermaid who'd heard that the stable cat had recently produced kittens. They were sent for; one was chosen, and presented to Adelaide as her kitten-in-waiting. It was pitch black, and hence lucky. Adelaide called it Saucepan.

As Adelaide's German improved, Becky became less of an interpreter and more of a counselor, and began to learn alongside the queen. Adelaide's reading was still uncertain, so they practiced on official memoranda, learning together about the output of nickel from the Karlstein mines, about the customs negotiations with Germany, about the projected tax revenues.

Before long, Adelaide decided to speak to the Chancellor. He was the leader of the senate, the holder of the highest political office in the country: not that that meant very much, since he hadn't been elected democratically, but appointed by King Wilhelm. He was an elderly man called the Baron von Stahl, and when he met Adelaide, it was educational for both of them. He didn't know how to treat her at first, and patronized her flirtatiously. She soon put a stop to that.

"I understand that Queen Victoria used to enjoy being flattered by Mr. Disraeli," she said to him severely. "That's because she was an old woman. When I'm an old woman you can do the same to me. In the meantime I'm not in the mood, because I'm in mourning, and in any case there are plenty of young men about who'd flatter me better than you're doing. If you want me to respect you, tell me honestly about the senate, and leave out the soft soap."

Becky had to render that accurately, because Adelaide's German was quite good enough to follow what she was saying, and with the queen's narrowed eyes on one side and the Chancellor's pop-eyed amazement on the other, she had an uncomfortable couple of minutes. The old man wasn't a bad sort; he soon gathered his wits and spoke more respectfully, and gave the queen a full and fair report.

And it soon became clear what the most pressing problem was, as if they hadn't suspected already. Both Germany and Austria-Hungary wanted to swallow Razkavia whole, not for a few vineyards, a dozen castles, and some sulfur springs, but for the nickel in the mines: the devil's copper. The mighty steelworks at Essen were hungry for it, and Emperor Franz-Josef didn't want them to have it in case it gave Bismarck and Emperor Wilhelm an advantage. The need to find a settlement was so urgent that it outweighed every internal question, such as the vine blight in Neustadt, the falling revenues from the casino in Andersbad, and the need to find new investment capital for the railway company.

Adelaide listened carefully and thanked him. As soon as he'd gone, she decided to visit the nickel mines and see what all the fuss was about. Brushing aside Count Thalgau's objection that it was unseemly, that mourning made such visits inappropriate, and so on, she ordered the royal train made ready for a visit to Karlstein, and one bright autumn morning, off they chugged the forty miles or so toward Andersbad at the other end of the country, and then up the branch line to Karlstein.

All the miners and their families were at the station to greet them. The red carpet and the speech of welcome were familiar to her by this time, and the speech she made in reply was very prettily delivered. It was curious, Becky thought, how she'd never managed (never tried) to alter the broad cockney of her native language; when she spoke English, her whole nature seemed to relax into a salty coarseness; but when she spoke German, she stood a little straighter, she carried herself more gracefully, she seemed to radiate a quality for which the only word Becky could find was not German but French: *chic*. She was very *chic* that morning in Karlstein, and the crowd admired her greatly.

The chief engineer who showed them around was a curly-haired young man called Herr Küpke, who soon found that her interest was genuine, and that he could explain things without having to simplify as for a half-wit. When she insisted on going underground, though, he was nonplussed.

"But, Your Majesty, we had not prepared for an underground visit—the conditions are hardly those which—"

She flashed her eyes at him. "If the mine is safe, I shall come to no harm. If it isn't, I want to see what my subjects have to put up with."

Her answer was all round Karlstein within the hour, and she got a bigger cheer as she waved good-bye later than the one that had greeted her appearance on the Rock of Eschtenburg.

Becky didn't see a thing. Unknown to herself, she'd been claustrophobic all her life, and as soon as the little line of trucks they sat in moved out of the sunshine and into the mountain she felt herself gripped with terror, and shut her eyes tight. Once they were out in the daylight again, Adelaide looked at her severely.

"I hope you was making notes of all that," she said. "Sulking about in a mood. You ought to show some interest and encourage people."

The chief engineer bowed very low and kissed her hand when they left, and Adelaide gave him a long, sultry look that made him blush; so Becky had something to tell her off about, too.

Before they left that part of the country to go back to Eschtenburg, Adelaide wanted to visit the castle of Wendelstein, where Walter von Eschten had finally defeated Ottokar the Second. The castle lay about a mile from Andersbad, up a path through the forest. Count Otto's estate was not far away, and courtesy would normally have required that he appear and pay his respects, but he was thought to be out of the country, on his way to hunt big game in East Africa.

The old castle of Wendelstein was a ruin now; only the tower was still intact, but the entrance was choked with rubble. Adelaide wandered over the grass, listening to the count explain how Walter had enticed the Bohemians onto the broad meadow between the castle and the edge of the forest and then charged them repeatedly with the knights he'd kept in reserve; and then how the Bohemians, their morale broken by months of Walter's guerrilla tactics, broke and fled. Becky looked over the peaceful scene with powerful emotions. Her country; her history...

The warm autumn sun laid gold over it all. Insects buzzed in the grass; a man was swinging a scythe in the distance; from the railway line through the forest some way below, a train whistled. It was time to go.

As Becky told her mother in the twice-weekly letter, this was the strangest time she'd ever known. She and Adelaide had to live through the accreditation of every new official, the speeches in honor of that retiring general or this visiting princeling, the dedications, the openings, the receptions, the services of memorial and thanksgiving...There were times when Adelaide wept tears of exhaustion and rebellious fury, and turned on Becky as if it were all her fault. Then Becky had to remind herself that she was a loyal citizen of Razkavia, and that this was her queen speaking. Mostly, it worked.

And all the time there was the contrast between Adelaide the cockney strumpet and the noblemen who treated her with such profound respect; there was the charm with which she inveigled every guest into a game of chess, and the urgent passion with which she played it, the increasing skill and mastery of tactics she showed; there was the gradual growth in her of decision, authority, knowledge. How could Becky help but be fascinated?

Finally, the diplomacy began; Adelaide invited the Great Powers to send representatives to Razkavia for talks. The officials were appalled.

"Your Majesty, it is unthinkable—" said the foreign secretary.

"Too late. I've thought it."

"But there are protocols—"

"Good. You deal with the protocols and I'll deal with the business."

"But the official channels—"

"Official channels are for keeping officials in."

She wouldn't be told, and still the objections came fluttering up. Finally she lost her temper, and threw an inkwell, shrieking in a way that didn't need translating even if Becky had known the German for "pernicated procrastinators" and "gotch-gutted Goths." The officials bowed hastily and hurried out, and invitations were sent that very afternoon.

• • •

Meanwhile, Jim and the Richterbund were spending every moment they had in the search for the Spanish actress. He had told the count about the woman journalist and Herr Egger's flat, and the count had relayed that to the chief of police at their next daily meeting; but Jim had little faith in the police, who lacked a detective branch entirely. Spiked helmets, gold epaulettes, and maroon uniforms showed that the Razkavian police mind was focused more on splendor than efficiency.

Jim had little doubt that the Spanish actress was still in the city, though he couldn't have said why he was so sure. Karl, Gustav, Heinrich, and the others frequented the cafés and beer cellars of the Old Town, they talked to the porters at the railway station, they hung about the stage doors of the opera house and the two theaters, they pestered the hall-porters of every hotel, and got nowhere.

In the end it was Jim who got the first clue, and that was indirect. He found it, of all places, in the steward's pantry in the palace, which formed a sort of common room for the upper servants. Jim found servants well worth cultivating, and they liked him, too, for his lack of airs and his salty conversation.

He was in the steward's pantry one evening when the under-steward came in shaking his head.

"What's the matter?" someone asked.

"That Gödel. He wants a maid especially detailed to look after some old girl he's brought in and put in that empty room in the attic corridor, number fourteen. I can't spare a maid just for that! And if I say we'll need more money to pay the wages of a new girl, he'll take it out of ours, damn his eyes."

"Who is she?"

"God knows. Some old biddy from Schloss Neustadt, I think. No, I'm wrong: Ritterwald..."

These were royal family estates, Jim knew. Why would Gödel be taking such a close interest in an old retainer? He pricked up his ears.

The under-steward was saying to a footman, "Look, I know it's late, and I know you're off duty, but I'm telling you to do it. She hasn't got much—just a trunk and a couple of boxes—take 'em up there and don't argue."

"Is this for the old biddy?" said Jim. "Let me do it. I always wanted to be a footman."

The servant was only too pleased to let him, and the under-steward merely shrugged and hastened out to arrange for a supper tray to be sent up. Jim slipped on the footman's coat and waistcoat and arranged a napkin hastily into a stock around his neck.

"Never mind the breeches," he said, "I'll say they're in the wash. She'll have to see my lovely legs another time. Where do I go?"

The servant told him, and he hastened along the bare lower corridor to the stable entrance, where an impatient carrier was unloading a wicker trunk from the back of a carriage, and handing down a battered dressing case to the old woman on the step.

"Hello, Granny," Jim said. "Let me give you a hand with that trunk. What you got in here? Lead weights?"

In fact it was very light; the old woman evidently had few possessions. He took the trunk up to the room the under-steward had mentioned, where someone had already laid a small fire and left a candle.

"Here we are," he said. "There'll be a bit of food coming up in a minute, as soon as they've stirred the maids up. All right for you in here?"

The old woman looked around and gave a little nod. She was

a thin, straight-backed old person, with a brisk birdlike manner and bright red cheeks.

"Thank you, dear," she said. "Very nice. I shall be comfortable in here."

"What's your name?" said Jim. "I like to be respectful to my elders."

"Yes, I can see," she said. "My name is Frau Busch. Who are you?"

Jim had felt a little shock, like that of electricity.

He thought swiftly. "Jakob," he said. "That's my name. Anything you want, Frau Busch, you just ask for me. Here's the maid coming. Enjoy your supper!"

He left the room and lingered for some time on the stairs, trying to think what it was that had given him that little electric jolt. Where had he heard her name before?

Then he had it. Gustav, on the night before the coronation, telling what he'd discovered in the newspaper files about Prince Leopold: the one witness to his death had been a huntsman called Busch.

And it had happened at Ritterwald, where this old lady had come from.

Next day, Becky made a discovery too.

Whenever she had a spare hour or so, she liked to go to the map room. Old King Wilhelm had been keenly interested in geography—had traveled widely in his youth—and he'd collected with a passion. The map room held drawer upon drawer—wide, shallow mahogany drawers with bright brass handles—of maps and charts from all over the world, and a vast table for examining them on, together with various globes, both terrestrial and celestial, a little Gregorian telescope on an equatorial mounting, and sundry items of navigational equipment in baize-lined rosewood boxes.

The room was dusted and polished, but hardly anyone went there anymore. Becky used it as a retreat, liking the quiet, the smell of beeswax polish, the precision of the maps and instruments.

On the afternoon of the day before the talks began, she spent a few minutes looking through the telescope, but couldn't get it to focus. Then, idly, she thought she'd look for a map of London, to see if it showed the street she lived in; but it occurred to her that there wasn't a catalog. How did the old king look for a map of West Africa, say, if he wanted one?

Her tidy mind fretted at the question, and then she remembered that in the little office that led off the map room, there was a cabinet she hadn't examined. Perhaps that was it.

She opened the door and went in. Unlike most other doors in the palace, this one wasn't hung very well, and swung shut slowly behind her, so that when (after a few minutes' searching through the index cards that were indeed in the cabinet) Becky heard voices in the map room, she realized that whoever had come in didn't know she was there.

She had no intention of hiding, but it hardly seemed necessary to cough or stamp or drop a book on the floor and let them know she was there, for surely their purpose was as innocent as her own. Indeed, one of the voices, she soon made out, was the count's. But it had a tone in it she'd never heard before: a sort of half-curt, half-anxious urgency. The other man spoke in the precise pedantic way of a narrow schoolmaster. By the time Becky had heard a little of what they were saying, it was too late to stop listening.

"I understand, Herr Bangemann, that you have a rare talent," the count said. "I'd like to see it displayed, if you wouldn't mind. I have a document here." The sound of a drawer being opened, a stiff paper being unfolded. "How long do you need for the first page?"

"Only as long as to read it through. Shall we say a minute?"

"Very well. I'll time you."

Silence, in which Becky couldn't help counting. Evidently she went more slowly than the count's watch; she had reached fifty-five when the count said, "Time's up."

The paper rustled again, and Herr Bangemann cleared his throat daintily, and began to speak.

"A Report on the Expedition to the Headwaters of the Orinoco and Rio Bravo Rivers, carried out under the auspices of the Royal Geographical Society of Razkavia, 1843-44..."

It went on for some time. It was clear that he was reciting it from memory.

"Remarkable," said the count. "Word for word. Now, how much can you carry in your memory?"

"Some not inconsiderable amount," said Herr Bangemann modestly. "I have not had occasion to commit more than sixty pages of foolscap to memory, but I am tolerably certain that I could, if required, carry more than that."

"And you need just one look at it?"

"That is correct. I had a blow on the head when a child, and the gift arrived, as I suppose, in recompense."

"Extraordinary...Now, I gather you're a family man."

"I have five daughters, Your Excellency. All good, clever girls. But, ah, undeniably, they are a strain on the purse. The salary of a clerk..."

"Quite so. Well now, Herr Bangemann: I need someone with your particular talent. This is of the nature of a private, not to say secret, commission..."

He broke off. Becky's heart leapt; had he heard her? But she heard the sound of the outer door opening and closing again, and the count went on more quietly:

"As I say, a highly discreet commission. No one is to know of this, you understand."

"You may rely on me entirely, Count Thalgau."

Their voices had sunk to a murmur. Becky found herself straining to hear, and then blushed: she'd never eavesdropped before, and wasn't enjoying it. The men in the map room spoke for a further minute or two, but she heard nothing clearly except, at one point, the clink of coins.

Eventually, the outer door closed, and there was silence. Becky stayed where she was for some time before coming out cautiously. It was disturbing, because she'd seen the count as being as strong and steadfast as the Rock of Eschtenburg itself; and yet what he'd sounded like in the map room was furtive.

She couldn't tell Adelaide: Her Majesty had quite enough to think about. Jim was the person to confide in, if she could only track him down. Becky left a message in his room, and crossed her fingers.

That evening, in the drawing room, Becky set out the board for a new game, the Continental Railway Race. The board was a map of Europe, and Adelaide took one look at it and sniffed with disdain, because Razkavia was too small to be shown.

"Some map this is," she said, and flicked a fingernail at the little tin trains that were going to race from London to Constantinople, or Brindisi to Stockholm. "Tin trains, tin ships going down the whirlpool—you know what I am, Becky? I'm a tin princess. Like chess: I come all the way across the board and turned into a queen. Still only tin, though...Want a game of chess? No, I don't either, tonight. Let's go out on the terrace and get some fresh air. It's so blooming stuffy in here..."

Becky opened the French windows, and they went out to lean

on the stone balustrade and look out over the evening parkland. The air was still and close. The line of forest was vague already; individual trees were lost in a blur of gloom, and the sky above was darker than ever, steel-dark with a touch of Prussian blue. The grass of the park, stretching out to the distant woodland, was swept here and there by little cats'-paws of turbulence that stroked the surface for a moment and vanished again. Suddenly a rent appeared in the clouds and the last of the sun struck through, making the grass and the trees ring out at once with a green so intense Becky could almost hear it. A fretful breeze flattened the grass like an invisible spirit, swirling toward them and brushing their cheeks with coolness.

"Becky," said Adelaide, turning to face the dark line of trees across the glowing grass.

"Yes?"

"I suppose this is my home now, innit?"

"I suppose it is."

"I never thought I'd ever have a home. I thought I'd die on the streets, or in the workhouse. Or in jail. I thought it was bound to end like that...Or disease. I thought I'd get, you know, one of those diseases...or consumption, maybe...and waste away or go mad and die in a lunatic asylum. I was sure of it."

"Well, you won't, will you?"

She said nothing for a minute. Then Adelaide sighed so deeply she almost shook. She gazed at the forest as the breeze played with the dark ringlets around her face.

"Poor Rudi," she said gently. "I never...I never *loved* him, Becky...I was fond of him, I really was, but...I think when you've done what I've done, when you've been with men for money, I think you stop being able to *love*...I dunno. It's funny. There's three men I might have loved. One was an old boy called Mr. Molloy. He looked after me when I first met Jim and Miss Lockhart. He was like a father to me, he was kind and gentle...Then there was the old king. That's odd, isn't it, I only knew him a month and he had every reason to hate me, but I got that fond of him..."

Her voice faltered. The sunlight had all gone, the sky was bruise-black-purple; the wind from the forest was stronger now, and cool gusts made Becky pull her shawl closer around her shoulders.

"I think he loved you too," she said.

"Becky, am I doing all right as queen?"

"What a funny question! I don't think anyone in the world could do better."

"I think Miss Lockhart could. Mrs. Goldberg, I mean. When these talks are over, d'you think she'd come and visit us?"

"I'm sure she would. We'll write and ask."

"I think..." Adelaide said quietly, her hands on the stone coping and her head turned away, "I think if she...I'd love to feel that she was proud of me...I think if *she* approved, I wouldn't mind what anyone else thought."

"Who's the third man?" Becky asked after a few moments.

"The third man?"

"After Mr. Molloy and the king."

"Oh, that. I dunno. I probably made a mistake, it's probably only two. I'm going in now; it's getting chilly. I'm going to have a cup of chocolate and then go to bed. Don't hang about here catching cold. You've got a lot of talking to do tomorrow."

After Adelaide had gone to bed, Becky sat and read for a while, but she couldn't settle. She went to knock on Jim's door, but he was never in; she tried to play chess by herself, left hand against right, and then forgot whose move it was; she tried the Continental Railway Race, and gave up when her little tin train reached Vienna; she tried to read again, but the only books were either tedious or frivolous, and she was too tired for the one and too much on edge for the other.

Finally, she wrapped her shawl around her shoulders and went out on the terrace again. The evening was wild now; she could hear the lashing of the trees even from where she was, and felt a strange apprehension as if spirits were abroad in the wind, tossed and swept like dead leaves from one spot to another, never resting, never giving back their goodness to the earth, never fully dead but in some vast limbo between life and extinction, tossing and tumbling without end...

She stood at the end of the terrace gripping the balustrade, and closed her eyes to the blustery darkness to feel the wind more fully.

Suddenly, with a vivid apprehension of fear, she opened them again; and a moment later, an arm encircled her throat, a hand was pressed over her mouth, and someone bore her roughly to the ground.

11
Inside the Grotto

And a voice whispered in her ear: "Becky—it's Jim—hush—keep still—there's danger—"

She felt herself pass from one kind of tension to another. He took his hand away from her mouth and twisted up into a crouch, peering through the balustrade.

Moving as quietly as she could, she sat up too, looked where he was looking, and saw against the pale stone of the palace wall below them the dark figure of a woman moving slowly out from underneath the terrace.

"Who is it?" she whispered.

"It's an old servant called Frau Busch. She's the widow of the huntsman who was with Prince Leopold when he died..."

Becky was suddenly aware that Jim had a pistol in his hand, though she hadn't seen him draw it. The fitful moonlight glittered in his eyes. The woman had stopped no more than twenty yards away from them, in the shadow of a dark bush.

"What's happening?" Becky whispered. "What's she doing?"

"Sssh," was all the reply she got. Jim was watching intently.

After a minute she saw his expression change, for something was happening farther along, and as she peered between the fat stone balusters she saw another figure moving silently around the corner of the building to join the woman waiting by the wall.

"Another woman," Becky whispered. "Or is it?"

She sensed a tension in Jim like that of a cat waiting to spring on a mouse. He didn't need to put a finger to his lips: she knew she had to be quiet. They watched as the second woman joined Frau Busch. There was a whispered exchange, and the two figures left the shelter of the palace to tiptoe across the gravel walk, and then they were on the grass, moving away toward the distant trees.

"I'm going to follow them," Jim whispered. "You stay here."

"Not a bit of it! I'm coming with you!"

"No, you're not," he said. "That other woman is *dangerous.* She's the one I've been looking for all this time—the assassin. How could I face your mother if anything happened to you? And as if that wasn't enough, Adelaide needs you in good form tomorrow, don't forget. That's your job. This is mine."

Becky chewed her lip. He was right. Then she gasped and put her hand to her mouth. "Oh! Did you get my message about the map room? I left it in your room."

"I haven't been there for a couple of nights." Jim turned back to the grass. The two figures were nearly out of sight. "Look, there's no time now—I'll lose them. Tell me later."

He ran to the steps at the center of the terrace, where he paused to check the direction the two figures had taken, and then darted out lightly across the gravel walk and onto the grass beyond. Becky watched, gathering her dark shawl around her, until his shape was lost in the blur of night.

• • •

Keeping low, Jim hurried over the tussocky grass after the two women. There was no point in trying to keep quiet, for the wind was wilder now, driving squadrons and flotillas of battered clouds past the glaring beacon of the moon and lashing the distant trees into a frenzy. Jim loped onward without taking his eyes off the two dark figures ahead—one tense and urgent, the other trim and birdlike, stepping delicately over the rough ground.

He found, to his disquiet, that they were heading for that part of the grounds where he'd heard the hideous scream. It was hard to be sure; one clump of trees was very like another, and the ground rose and dipped deceivingly; but it was lighter tonight because of the moon, and presently there was no doubt.

However, Frau Busch, who seemed to be leading the way, moved leftward a little, changing direction to head for a Palladian bridge that spanned the end of a lake. Jim knew that the water from the lake flowed over an artificial cascade and down into a romantic chasm: a miniature one, set about with cedar trees and a ruined chapel, and ending in a grotto. The two women moved down into the little valley and along beside the stream toward the entrance of the grotto itself.

The place looked bizarre under the moon. It was bizarre enough in daylight, as Jim knew, having wandered here one afternoon, looking for the source of that scream; he didn't like grottoes at the best of times, finding their shells and grotesqueries ugly and their climate damp, but this one was especially villainous. The entrance to the grotto was formed by the gaping mouth of a weed-fringed giant stone face whose eyes bulged leeringly above, and the rock all around it was studded with distorted images of snakes, frogs, lizards, toads, seemingly extruded from the stone itself. A gap in the clouds let the inconstant moonlight flare down again, the blacks and grays and smudged shadows giving the scene the appearance of a picture from a penny dreadful: *The Fatal Grotto, or The Murderers' Quest.*

He crouched in the shadow of the ivy-covered wall of the fake ruin, watching as the two women stopped on the path beside the stream.

Frau Busch bent among the reeds to pull at a rope. A narrow, punt-like craft, shiny with damp, emerged at the end of it. The old woman clambered stiffly into the boat, the actress stepping after her and sitting down as Frau Busch took the oars. There was the little flare of a match, which settled into the glow of a lantern in the actress's hand; and then they pushed off, and after only a moment or two the current took them, and the boat began to drift in toward the cave.

Jim cursed and leapt down the slope. When he reached the bank there was no sign of the boat. The great dark mouth of the grotto yawned mockingly as the black water swept silently into it, reflecting the moon in oily swirls and loops of silver. Now what should he do?

Well, he'd have to follow; but he hadn't thought of a boat, damn it. He moved along the weedy path beside the stream and into the mouth of the grotto itself. The first chamber was dimly visible in the moonlight from outside, but where the path led under an arch it became pitch black. The sound of the wind was fainter in there, the sound of the water louder as it echoed from the rocky roof and walls. The ground underfoot was wet and irregular, certainly muddy and possibly dangerous, for the stream was flowing past only inches away.

He moved on into the darkness. He would have lit a match, but he didn't want to give himself away. Of all the crazy things to do, plunging into this loathsome hole must rank among the barmiest; if he got lost—if the tunnel forked and he didn't realize...

Keep your hand on the wall, he thought. It was slimy and cold, and once to his disgust it *moved*...and turned into a toad, making him step back with an exclamation and nearly fall into the stream; but if he kept his hand on the wall all the way in and all the way back, surely he'd find his way out —

Then a cascade of ice-cold fear fell the length of his spine. From the intense darkness ahead, there came that scream again.

It was the cry of an imprisoned ghoul; something abominably tortured, in an extremity of pain and despair. It was distorted by the echoing passages it came through, and muffled by the splashing of the water, and he couldn't tell how far away it was, but it was enough to drench him in terror. It put him in mind of the Minotaur, waiting in the pitchy blackness for the next victim to feel his trembling way in to the heart of the maze...

How long he stood there, with his heart pounding and his skin crawling, he couldn't have told. Eventually, faintly, he gathered his wits, and not a moment too soon: for there was a glimmer on the rocky walls ahead. The boat was returning.

He looked around quickly for a place to conceal himself. Shadows, darkness everywhere, but there was a deeper shadow than the rest, where a little alcove had been cut out of the rock. It was so shallow that he hadn't even noticed it when he'd felt his way past, but if he pressed himself into it...

He heard the splash of the oars. There was no time to find anywhere else. He turned his collar up, pulled his cap down to conceal the paleness of his face, put his hand on the pistol in his pocket.

The splashing came closer. So did the light, and soon it was shining clearly on the water, the wavering flame in the lantern enough to illuminate the whole of the tunnel. Surely they'd see him?

He held his breath, watching through half-closed eyes from under the brim of his cap as the boat moved past him. But neither of the occupants noticed him, for each of them was preoccupied with some intense private emotion. The old woman's face was full of sorrow; the actress's face was hidden by a hood. Once a bitter sob shook her whole body.

And then they were past. Darkness filled the tunnel again; the sound of the oars diminished.

"Well, what are you going to do *now*, you silly bastard?" Jim said to himself softly, though he knew the answer.

He took a deep breath, let it out slowly, and felt for his matches. It didn't matter if he showed a light now; they wouldn't be back. He struck one, took several steps forward, shielding it carefully until it went out, and repeated the process a dozen times or more. Once he heard a splash in the water behind him, and nearly dropped the match in fear, but turned to see the head of a rat swimming away; and once a low, anguished moan that seemed to come from everywhere at once shook him horribly.

But it told him he was closer, and it was a human voice now, not a ghoul or a demon; and furthermore, he was becoming convinced with every step he took that he knew whose voice it was.

Presently he rounded a corner in the tunnel. The water still swirled slowly along on his left, and the path broadened a foot or two. Set into the wall on the right was an iron grating. Bars as thick as Jim's thumb were set securely into the rock itself, and the door in the center of them was secured by a massive padlock.

Beyond the grating lay a cell little more than eight feet by eight. Lying on a mattress in the corner, wide awake and terrified, was a ragged figure who looked like an emaciated version of Prince Rudolf; but when he sat up and came closer to the bars, as if drawn by the flare of the match, Jim saw that his guess had been right. There, under the stubble and the dirt but as clearly as in the portrait in the gallery, were the drooping eyelid and the dimpled chin of Rudolf's eldest brother, Prince Leopold, alive.

"Your Highness," Jim whispered in German, holding up a match.

The man didn't react. His eyes, bright and feverish, had no understanding in them; it was like looking at an animal.

"Prince Leopold? It is you, isn't it? Listen, I'm Taylor, you understand? Taylor. I'm going to get you out. Let's have a look at that padlock—"

But the match went out, and the prince whimpered and scrambled away in the darkness. There were only three matches left. Jim cursed quietly, and was about to strike the next when there came a sound from farther down the tunnel: an echoing noise as of a great iron gate being drawn back, and then the sound of heavy boots. Someone was coming.

The prince had heard, and was uttering little inarticulate cries. Jim whispered, "Listen! Your Highness! I'm going now, but I'll be back! I'll get you out of here—you understand?"

Then, with his left hand on the wall of the tunnel, he moved away as quietly as he could. When he'd gone around the first bend he stopped for a moment and looked back. There was a faint gleam on the rough wet wall, but it wasn't moving, and the footsteps had stopped.

Instead, he heard a man's voice saying, not unkindly: "There, there, stop your crying now, old boy. Lutz is back. See? I went up top to stretch my legs and get a breath of air. What's that you're saying? Flame? Fire? No, no, that's the lantern, it won't burn you. Put your head down and go to sleep, go on. You don't want to be awake when Kraus comes on duty..."

A faint cry of fear; a coarse laugh.

Jim listened for a little longer, but heard no more. He turned and left the tunnel.

Half an hour later, as the palace clock struck one, he was opening the door of his room. His hands and face were filthy, his boots and trousers splashed with mud, his shirt and trousers were clammy and cold, and before he woke the count he wanted to clean himself up a bit.

As he shut the door quietly he saw a folded note on the floor. He opened it and read:

> **Dear Jim, I felt I must tell you what I heard this afternoon. I don't know what it means, but it worried me; I think it was the *furtiveness* as much as what they actually said...**

It was Becky's note from the day before, with an account of her unintended eavesdropping in the map room. As he read it, Jim sat down slowly; there was no point in calling on the count after all. Was there no solid ground anywhere? The whole filthy palace was riddled and rotten with plots and secrecies; it would serve them right if it all came crashing down around their cowardly ears. Except that Adelaide...

Adelaide was trying to *save* the lousy place, damn it to hell!

Jim lit the last of his matches and burned the note; nothing was safe anymore. But if he couldn't go to the count, he could go to Frau Busch. She'd be back in her room by now.

He washed his face and changed quickly into dry clothes, put on some rubber-soled shoes, and left his room. The corridor was dark, but he knew his way well enough: along to the stairs at the end, up to the attic floor, and count the doors along to number fourteen.

He paused, listening carefully. There was a faint line of light under the door, and slight sounds of movement came from inside, as if of someone folding back bedclothes. He knocked softly and heard a sharp intake of breath.

"Who's that?"

He turned the handle and went in, shutting the door silently behind him.

"Jakob," he said. "Remember me? I carried your trunk up for you."

"What do you want? You're not a servant, I can tell. Who are you?"

The old woman was standing by the bed, her white nightdress voluminous around her, a lacy nightcap on her gray hair. The candle on the bedside table flickered in the draft.

Jim said, "I'm Count Thalgau's private secretary. And you're in trouble, Frau Busch. I followed you to the grotto this evening, and I saw the man who's in there. Why is Prince Leopold being kept prisoner? And why are you helping his wife?"

She gave a helpless little gasp and sat down on the bed. Her mouth opened once or twice and then set in a trembling line.

"You'd better tell me," he said. "You know that woman is the one who killed King Rudolf. See this scar on my hand? She did that with a knife. I wouldn't be at all surprised if she was behind the deaths of Prince Wilhelm and Princess Anna, too. Your husband was with Prince Leopold when he was reported killed—and now you're mixed up in this. You're in trouble.

Wake up and realize it. What's going on?"

She put a hand to her breast and closed her eyes. A sigh shook her, and then she began to cry softly.

"I didn't mean to do anything wrong! All I ever did was out of love! What are you going to do? Are you going to give me away to Baron Gödel? He would have me shot! And how would *that* help anyone?"

"You tell me," said Jim. "I'll sit here and listen. We're all alone; we've got plenty of time. Tell me everything."

The old woman got into bed and pulled the blankets up high, shivering as if with cold.

"I was his nurse," she said. "I was nurse to all of them, but I loved him best. When he married, I was the first person he told; he brought his wife to see me, secretly. He wanted *me* to approve, you see. He was closer to me than to anyone. She wasn't what I would have chosen, but it wasn't my place to choose his wife for him, and she loved him, in her way; she was fierce and passionate; I could see she would be loyal, and he needed that so much; he was frightened of his father, frightened of Baron Gödel, frightened of his duty, almost.

"So I kept their secret, but of course it wasn't a secret for long. They found out and banished her, and then took him to Ritterwald. My husband was the chief huntsman. They told him what to do: he was to take Prince Leopold out into the forest, and find a boar, and then say that the prince had been killed in the hunt. Some men met them in the forest and took the prince away to Neustadt, to the asylum there, where he was kept prisoner. I know, because Baron Gödel paid me to go and look after him."

"It was Gödel's plan, then?"

"Oh, yes."

"Did the king know about it?"

"That was no concern of mine. In the king's eyes, Prince Leopold died when he married that woman."

"So it was Gödel's doing, keeping him alive...But he's mad, poor man."

"Wouldn't you be? Locked away underground, no one to know you're alive, forbidden to speak to anyone? Of course he went mad, poor dear soul. I did my best to look after him, but I could see it happen, little by little; the madness crept over him like...like cobwebs creeping over an empty room. Oh, I cursed myself many and many a time! I prayed that some power would take us all back ten years, before it had happened! My husband, poor man, he knew, and he couldn't face what he'd done; he shot himself soon afterward. I've looked after Prince Leopold all his life, baby, boy, young man, prisoner, madman. I looked after him in Neustadt, and when they moved him here a little while ago, they brought me here to be close to him..."

"Why did Gödel bring him here?"

"I don't know. No concern of mine. I suppose he's going to overturn that English girl...Are you English?"

"Yes."

"I thought so. One of her servants?"

"Yes. So are you, Frau Busch. She's the monarch. Gödel isn't. What he's doing is treason, and if you're doing anything to help him, you're a traitor too. Tell me about the actress. What's her name?"

"Carmen Ruiz is her stage name. She uses other names as well."

"Why did you take her there tonight? Is that part of Gödel's plan as well?"

"No! God forbid! He doesn't know the first thing about her. I kept in touch with her, for his sake, for the prince. Prince! Ha!

He's king, rightfully, and she is the queen! That English—"

"Don't you know your own history? Queen Adelaide is the *Adlerträger,* and rightfully so. Do you think that poor man would be capable of ruling? He'll be fit for nothing for the rest of his life. What did you think would happen when you involved his wife? Did you know she was responsible for killing the other two princes?"

"Nothing to do with me."

She sat there defiantly, her lips set, her cheeks flushed, her bright eyes red-rimmed and hard. He stared her out. Finally her gaze faltered and dropped, and tears spilled onto the sheet.

"It's no concern of mine!" she sobbed. "I wrote to her because she loved him! And I took her there tonight because she wanted to see that he was still alive! All I do is for him, my poor baby Leo, my little prince..."

"Do you want to see him out of that filthy hole?"

"Yes!"

"So do I. He needs to be set free and cared for properly. But listen to me, Frau Busch."

"I'm listening..." Her eyes were bloodshot, her breathing was labored.

"You've already gone behind Gödel's back. If he finds out what you've done, he'll punish you, he'll send you away, you'll never see Prince Leopold again. And if he doesn't punish you, I will. If you're sent away, that'll be the end of the prince. Now where can I find Carmen Ruiz?"

"What are you going to do?"

"What's that phrase you keep using? It's no concern of yours. If you want the prince to stay alive, and if you want the chance to keep on looking after him, tell me where that woman is."

She gulped, or choked. Her breast heaved laboriously, and

she said "In Para...Parasol...Paracelsus..."

Then her head fell forward. A light high moan came from her throat, and a thread of saliva trailed from her chin onto the sheet. Jim leapt up, looking around for the bellpull, and remembering a second later that there wouldn't be one in a servant's room anyway. Frau Busch was having some kind of apoplectic seizure: what should he do? He laid her down, made sure she wasn't choking, and ran to bang on the door of the next room along.

He opened it without waiting for a reply, and said to the sleepy maid who looked up astonished from her bed, "Frau Busch, next door to you. She's ill—didn't you hear her cry out? She woke me up! Run and get help, and hurry now."

Leaving the girl to scramble up, Jim ran back down to his own room, put his revolver in his pocket, and set off again.

12 Statecraft

Forty-five minutes later, Jim was climbing the dusty stairs to the attic where Karl von Gaisberg lived. He tapped on the door, opened it, and by the light of a match saw that Karl was fast asleep. A half-eaten meal still occupied part of the table, and a fat mouse slouched resentfully away to eye Jim from a hole in the wainscoting. Beside the dirty plate a volume of Schopenhauer had its place marked with the blade of a fencing foil; a candle had guttered to extinguishment between the horns of a goat's skull, whose eye sockets wore a pair of broken spectacles; a champagne cork stopped the mouth of a crusted inkpot; a broken chair, meant for fuel, lay beside the iron stove; a photograph of the actress Sarah Bernhardt was pinned to the wall above Karl's bed, surrounded by hearts drawn on the crumbling plaster. On the floor all around lay at least two dozen sheets of paper covered with blots, scrawls, crossings-out, diagrams, and closely written Gothic script. It was headed, "An Examination of the Idealist Implications of Schopenhauer's Platonism." Halfway down the last sheet was the triumphant word FINIS.

Jim stepped over the papers, flung open the shutters, and rattled the poker in the stove to wake the embers.

Karl stirred and groaned.

"What're you doing? Who's that?"

"It's Jim. Where d'you keep the coffee?"

"Flower pot. Windowsill. What's the time? What are you doing up?"

Karl sat up shivering, and shrugged on the dressing gown Jim threw him. The cathedral clock a stone's throw away stirred itself in a shiver of cogs and springs and weights, and the ancient mechanism marched through its whirring pantomime before striking five. Karl rubbed his hair and yawned while Jim put some water on the stove to boil.

"Listen, my boy," Jim said, "we've got trouble..."

He thrust the last chair leg into the stove, and then sat down to tell Karl about the night's events. By the time he'd finished, the water in the little copper pot was boiling, and Karl padded across the cold floor to find two cups.

"Leopold?" he said. "Are you sure? It's impossible."

"I saw him, and I saw the Spanish actress, and I heard it from the mouth of the old woman. It's true."

"But...why? *Cui bono?* Who gains by keeping him prisoner all this time? Not the royal family, surely."

"No. I don't think the old king even knew about it. This was a scheme of Gödel's from beginning to end. He kept Leopold up his sleeve so that he could bring him back as ruler one day. You remember the fight in the beer cellar on the night we met? That fellow Glatz was going on about Leopold. I think there's a strong current of blood-loyalty in this place, especially in the old dark corners of it. Gödel's been planning some trouble, and that's why he brought Leopold to the grotto from the asylum at Neustadt, ready to bring him out. But he didn't reckon that Leopold's old nurse would contact the Spanish woman..."

"Have you told Count Thalgau?"

"No, damn it. He's up to something of his own." Jim told Karl about Becky's note, and went to the window to look out over the city. The wind of the night had scattered the clouds, and the air was fresh; and in the east the stars were fading as the dawn lightened the sky behind them. "So we've got to do two things," Jim went on. "We've got to rescue Prince Leopold, both for his own sake and to spike Gõdel's guns; and we've got to find the Spanish woman. And we've got to do them both without telling the count. Do you know anywhere in the Old Town with a name like Paracelsus?"

Adelaide was awake early. She lay tense and eager between the fine linen sheets, stroking the little sleeping black kitten with one hand, fretting for the moment when she would lay her plans before the German and Austrian negotiators. She felt herself at the very center of a multitude of life as the city woke around her. She could almost see them all, her subjects: the servants yawning and lighting fires in the cold kitchens, bakers sliding their flat paddles under crusty steaming loaves to take them out of hot ovens, farmers slapping the flanks of cows in the milking parlors, monks in the Abbey of St. Martin mumbling over the office of Prime. They were all waking one by one, and only little Saucepan was asleep.

As the sun rose and the traffic thickened in the streets, as the waiters in the cafés hurried from table to table with steaming coffee and hot rolls, the chief Austrian representative stood at the open window of the embassy breathing deeply and swinging a pair of Indian clubs to improve the vigor of his circulation, and the chief German representative lay in bed ponderingly snoozily whether to order an extra brioche for breakfast, to fortify him against the rigors of the day.

In an apartment on the third floor of a solid old building on the Glockengasse, one of the clerks from the Razkavian Ministry of Foreign Affairs dabbed at his neat mustache with a snowy napkin, pushed back his chair from the table, and, having smoothed down his already glossy hair, went into the hall to say good-bye to his family.

His wife was holding out his attaché case and his homburg hat; his five daughters stood in line, in order of size, ready to be kissed.

"Good-bye, Gretl...Inge...Bertha...Anna...Marlene. Be good girls. Work hard today, as Papa will. Good-bye, my dear. I shall be a little late this evening; we have a formidable task. A formidable task!"

They waited respectfully while he gave his mustache an extra twist in the looking glass and set the hat jauntily on his pomaded head, and then waved good-bye as he set off down the stairs.

"Good-bye, Papa! Good-bye, Papa!"

From all over the city, Herr Bangemann's colleagues—the clerks and secretaries and junior administrative assistants—were making for the palace, with an extra spring in their step, an extra shine on their shoes. And the ushers and the footmen of the palace staff were busily laying out the Council Chamber in preparation for the talks.

The Council Chamber was on the sunny side of the palace; the autumn light gilded everything inside it with a meticulous splendor. The table was spread with a green baize cloth, and in front of each place (there were sixteen: five each for Germany and Austria, five for Razkavia, and the queen's own chair at the center) there lay a blotting pad, a crystal inkwell with red and black ink, a little tray of pens and pencils, a carafe of water, a glass, and an ashtray.

Behind each of the principal chairs was a smaller, less comfortable one, on which a clerk or secretary was to sit. Behind

Adelaide's chair, of course, was Becky's, a little back and to the right.

As the delegates assembled in the anteroom, with secretaries clutching their bundles of papers and boxes of documents and volumes of legal argument, Adelaide the queen stood in her drawing room on the floor above and peered closely into a looking glass held by her maid.

"Very handsome," she said. "Oughter knock their eyes out. Here—tuck that bit of hair over me ear, come on, get it right. Becky! Stop yawning! That's the third time in two minutes. They haven't come here to look at your tonsils, girl. You been up all night? You look God's-own awful. You shouldn't fool about when we got important business to do. What's the time? How long they been waiting? Give 'em another minute. Five minutes late is royal; four's hasty. Six is languid. I don't want to be languid today, I'm going to make the buggers hop, see if I don't. All right, Marie-Hélène, stop fussing, you baggage, go and open the door. Where's the count? Ah, here he is..."

Frowning grimly to try and suppress another yawn, Becky followed. She hadn't slept properly; her dreams had been filled with a dark woman, armed with a knife, cloaked and faceless and climbing slowly up the stone side of the palace toward a window, but whether her window or Adelaide's, she couldn't say. And now her head ached and her eyes were red. Well, she'd have to concentrate harder than ever in her life if she was going to help Adelaide through these talks. This was what she'd become queen for, she'd said. It was the most important thing she'd ever do.

Her Majesty was pale, composed, beautiful. Only the set of her lips and the little flicking of a thumb against a finger showed her tension, as the footmen bowed and threw open the double doors that led into the Council Chamber.

Well, if she ever stops being queen, she could earn a handsome living on the stage, thought Becky, watching the thirty or so pairs of eyes turn and widen in admiration.

Adelaide went to her place and spoke. She had written the speech herself, letter by laborious letter, and Becky had translated it and rehearsed her thoroughly. Now teacher watched pupil proudly as the clear voice spoke the words in faultless German, pitched perfectly to the size of the room and the solemnity of the occasion.

"Good morning to you all. Welcome to the Council Chamber of my palace. At first I thought that we might hold these talks in the Great Hall of the castle, where Walter von Eschten signed the Treaty in 1257 that guaranteed the freedom of Razkavia.

"But then I decided that castles are for times of war, palaces for times of peace. Razkavia is not threatened now as it was then; our little country is established and safe and guaranteed."

She paused a moment, a slight expectant smile on her lips, and sure enough there came a murmur of agreement, a shuffle of feet, a few discreet nods. Who could disagree with something so innocently expressed? And it was exactly enough to establish an atmosphere of willingness, of good intentions, even of a certain sly humor.

Becky settled down to work, and soon forgot the ache in her head and the stiffness in her shoulders in the sheer fascination of watching history being made.

In the Café Florestan, the Richterbund were pooling their knowledge of the city. Paracelsus...what the hell did that mean?

"Paracelsus-Strasse?" suggested someone.

"Is there such a place?"

"No! You're thinking of Agrippa-Strasse, near the castle!"

"Well, another alchemist...Paracelsus-Garten, that's what she meant."

"It's not Paracelsus-Garten, it's Parasol-Garten! Where the Marionette Theater is!"

"Oh, yes. So it is. Well, there's a Paradies-Garten too. It might be that."

"Stick to Paracelsus, for God's sake. Paracelsus Platz? Is there a Paracelsus Platz?"

"It's a code. She was referring to gold, because of the alchemy. I reckon she meant the Goldener-gasse."

"There's a painting of Paracelsus somewhere. I'm sure I've seen it. In the museum..."

Jim looked at Karl, who blew out his cheeks. "Better start looking," he said. "We'll each take a section of the city and search it thoroughly. Anything you find, report back. Anton, stay here and keep a note of where everyone is and what they find..."

And so the search for Paracelsus began.

Adelaide played statecraft with all the guile and passion that she put into her other games, and Becky began to realize that perhaps she had been preparing for this with every throw of the dice, every move of a chess piece. As the morning went past, and the details of the negotiating positions became clearer, Becky, beside her at the heart of it, followed her moves with increasing admiration.

At midmorning, the German trade minister insisted on a large discount on the price of Razkavian nickel in order to compensate Germany for not being able to buy the whole of it. Adelaide called an adjournment, and while the rest of the delegates were walking on the terrace smoking their cigars, deep in discussion, she cast the German minister a smouldering look from her great dark eyes and invited him to come and see the last of the roses. Helplessly, he went, and Becky, interpreting from a step or two behind, watched like a ghost as the two of them walked along between the rose beds. Adelaide looked up at him and spoke fervently about the great affection and admiration Razkavia felt for Germany, and how a mystical bond of kinship united the two peoples in a spiritual union that was far above the demands of commerce. Before five minutes were up the poor man was half-convinced, firstly, that Adelaide was in love with him; secondly, that he was too noble to take advantage of it; but, thirdly, that an offer of help on his part would be worn in her heart forevermore. And when the talks resumed, the size of the discount agreed on was somehow much less than the Germans had originally asked for.

Then the Austrians raised a difficulty. Their chief negotiator insisted on raising the amount of nickel Razkavia sold to them from two hundred to three hundred and fifty tons per year. Becky saw the Germans bristle, but at that point they broke for luncheon. Adelaide gave a quiet order to Count Thalgau, who spoke to a footman, and when they went into the banqueting hall, who should be sitting next to Her Majesty but the Austrian minister of finance. He was very different from the impressionable German, and at first Adelaide seemed to find it hard to play him; in any case, the head of the table in full view of all the guests wasn't the place for outright flirting.

Eventually, with the *charlotte à la parisienne,* there came an opening. Adelaide had turned the conversation to the minister's life outside his profession. Was he fond of music, for example? Vienna was a great musical center...Rather stiffly he mentioned hunting. Becky saw Adelaide sit forward just a little, intently. Hunting? She *longed* to know about the hunt. What should she hunt first? How should she begin? Within a minute the minister had forgotten his luncheon and was speaking so lyrically about the joys of the chase that Becky felt she ought to set her translation to music and score it for horns. Adelaide listened, prompting with a question here, a comment there, and Becky knew she had him. Sure enough, during the afternoon session it emerged that the forests surrounding the nickel mines were exceptionally well supplied with game of all kinds, and that to increase the production of ore would involve driving a new road through the mountains and ruining the hunting forever.

That cast a new light on the prospects for expansion. There was plenty of ore left, but new methods of extracting it would need to be developed—perhaps with the advice of the Imperial Institute of Mining in Vienna...The Austrian minister was eager to help.

Becky marveled at the change that had come over the sullen, bored, overdressed, illiterate girl she'd met only a few months before. *That* Adelaide would have sneered and pouted and sulked; this one was patient, gracious, witty, and implacable. Becky, a genuinely modest person, did not think for one moment that any of the credit for that change was due to herself. By the end of the day, she sensed that a vast alteration had come about, not only in her view of Adelaide, but also in the history of Razkavia, for the Great Powers were discussing amicably something over which they might have gone to war; and there was not the slightest hint that Razkavia's future was anything but secure.

However, there remained the need to get that security guaranteed, and that was to be the subject of the next day's talks. Becky was nearly dead on her feet; she went straight to bed, her throat sore, her head drumming with exhaustion, and slept as she'd never slept before. She was doing a job, a complex and important job; she was needed; she was utterly happy.

• • •

Streets with no names, alleys with no ends, little squares that invited you in and then concealed the way out...The students of the Richterbund could trace a subtle argument through the dense pages of Hegelian philosophy, but live detection demanded a different kind of cunning. The search went on through the first day of the talks, fruitlessly. The command post in the Café Florestan was relieved three times, and a map of the city was spreading farther and farther over the table, one bit of paper pasted to the next as it was filled in and searched and found wanting. They turned up every conceivable variation on Paradise, Paris, Parallel, Paraguay, Parasol, Paralysis; on Cornelius Agrippa, Albertus Magnus, and anyone else vaguely connected with alchemy; on gold, and names with *gold* in them; on Theophrastus Philippus Aureolus Bombastus von Hohenheim, that being the full name of the great Paracelsus himself; and got nowhere.

As darkness fell, Jim and Karl wandered out onto the old bridge and leaned on the stone balustrade overlooking the river.

"Parapet," said Karl.

"Parakeet."

"Parabolic sections. What are we going to do when we find her, Jim? Arrest her?"

"No. The police would bungle it, and I'm not sure of Count Thalgau anymore. What I thought was that we might offer to help her."

"What?"

"Or pretend to. We go to her and say, Look, you want Leopold out, we'll help you rescue him. He's as good as helpless; he needs someone to look after him, and Frau Busch is out of action, so it'll have to be Carmen Ruiz. She knows what sort of state he's in, after all. And she knows where he is, and how well he's guarded. She couldn't spring him on her own. She might have one accomplice—that fellow Herr Egger thought was the photographer—but for a job like this, she needs a proper troop. She needs us."

"We use him as bait to catch her, you mean?"

"Exactly. And once we've got both of them, we can fix that bastard Gödel; we can put her under lock and key; we can find some proper care for Leopold; we can tie the whole thing up. So that's what we'll do. Have you got a better plan?"

"No, I haven't. Did you sleep last night, by the way?"

"No, come to think of it." Jim yawned widely.

"Hadn't you better go and get some rest? You won't be fit for anything, least of all fighting in a tunnel. We'll keep on looking. If we find her before the morning, I'll send a message."

Jim clapped him on the shoulder.

"Good lad," he said. "I'll give Fräulein Winter your regards, shall I? She took quite a shine to you the other day. I'll be back at the café first thing in the morning."

13
The Little Glass Globe

The weather was beginning to change. A depression over central Europe had brought cold winds in from Russia, with the first snow flurries of the winter. There was no pale sunlight shafting down through the Council Chamber windows on the second day of the Tripartite Talks.

Becky had woken after a deep and confusing sleep, in which she was being held prisoner by three identical Spanish women. Jim burst in like D'Artagnan with sword and plumed hat and a ridiculous false beard, which he claimed he wore to keep off the mosquitoes. She began to tell him crossly that he was confusing *mousquetaire* with *moustique,* but he wouldn't listen, so she shook him, and woke to find herself struggling with the maid. It felt as if only a minute had passed since she'd gone to bed.

Bath, breakfast, gargle, and back to the Council Chamber. Despite the gray sky outside, the good mood of the previous day was still intact; it was as if some enchantment had been laid over the participants, to make them jovial and forgiving, keen to accommodate one another's needs and search actively for ways to overcome their objections. Becky, at the center of everything, saw more closely than anyone how much of the enchantment was Adelaide's, hers the good humor diffused through the room, the mood of chivalry evoked and rewarded by her subtle grace. During luncheon Becky wondered whether a man could have done this, and answered her own question: No. But did that mean that Adelaide's achievement was due entirely to her charm? Could any beautiful woman bring about a treaty of this importance by simpering and flirting? Of course not. It wasn't her charm that was doing the work: it was her game-player's intelligence, her native stubbornness and wit. Her beauty was a card in her hand; it was right to use it. Becky, not beautiful herself, felt no envy, only admiration.

Late in the afternoon, a student entered the Café Florestan and came up to the three tables where the map was growing. Battered and crumpled and crinkled and blotched, it spread out in front of Anton and the two dispirited students with him like the dirtiest tablecloth in the world.

"I'm not sure..." began the student diffidently. "There's a little square with a fountain full of fallen leaves, and a marble statue, and I think the statue might be Paracelsus. It's like that picture of him in the museum, anyway. It doesn't say."

"Where is it?" said Anton, reaching wearily for his pen.

"Well, it's...kind of..." said the student, bending to try and make sense of the map. "There. Sort of. Down a little alley. It's called Hohenheim-Platz. I could take you there..."

"Hohenheim-Platz?"

"That was..." began one of the others.

"That was him!" said a second.

"I reckon you've got it! Have a rum! Have two rums! Karl and

Jim will be back in five minutes. You can drink two rums in five minutes, can't you?"

And thirty minutes after that, the student, only slightly fuddled, showed Jim and Karl the little square. It was so small it was almost a courtyard; the great plane tree arched over everything in it, including the little fountain, now choked with leaves, and the marble statue of a brooding, choleric-looking man wrapped in a robe and glowering at an open book.

There was only one house in the square, the other sides being formed by the wall of a cemetery, the side of a church, and the back of a law stationer's warehouse. Jim tapped his teeth with a thumbnail, thinking.

"Better make sure there's not a back way out," he said. "Don't stare at the house; sit on the edge of the fountain and sketch the statue or something. I'll be back in five minutes."

And he was, with a large bunch of roses. Karl raised his eyebrows.

"She's an actress," said Jim, "and I know actresses. They need attention and flattery. So do actors. I mean really *need* it, just as you and I need air to breathe. These flowers will get us inside, you'll see."

He scribbled a note, pinned it to the roses, and pulled the doorbell of the dark narrow house. After a minute a dingy housemaid opened the door.

Jim handed her the flowers, and said, "For the Spanish lady who's living here. Just take them up to her; there's a message, too."

She opened her mouth to say something, changed her mind, shrugged.

"We'll wait," said Jim.

She nodded, and shut the door. Ten minutes went by, during

which time Jim flicked pebbles into the fountain, fished them out again, made a little pyramid of them on the edge, and practiced golf strokes with his stick over the cobbles.

Finally the door opened again. The maid said, "Please come in. Fräulein Gonzalez will see you now."

"Gonzalez, now," muttered Jim to Karl, and leaving the other student to keep guard outside, they followed the maidservant up the dark, cabbage-scented staircase to a door on the second-floor landing. Jim had his hand on the pistol in his pocket.

The maid knocked, opened, and said, "Your visitors, Fräulein," before standing aside to let them enter.

Carmen Ruiz was standing beside the only armchair, holding the roses in her arms.

Even if he hadn't known she was an actress, Jim would have suspected it from the way she held herself, from the tilt of her head and the power of her dark expressive eyes. Her black hair was pulled back tightly from her forehead and elaborately arranged behind; her eyes were rimmed with kohl, her lips meticulously rouged. On a stage the effect would have been dramatic, but in this narrow little room in the gray light of late afternoon, with the fireplace empty and one dirty teacup beside a little purse on the table next to the chair, the impression was desolate. She was wearing a frayed and crumpled gown, and her shoes were dusty.

She was shivering. For a moment he thought it was from cold.

"Who are you?" she said in German considerably more approximate than Jim's. "Your name means nothing to me. What do you want?"

"We want to help you get Prince Leopold out of the grotto," said Jim.

A moment's shocked silence; and then she flung the flowers

aside, and sprang at him like a tigress. Her teeth were bared, her nails reaching for his eyes; she was all attack, all hatred, unreflecting and instinctual. If he hadn't moved she would have torn him to pieces and drunk the blood, or so it seemed; but he was an instinctive fighter too, and he sidestepped easily enough, tripping her and sending her crashing to the floor.

She sprang and turned at once, but he was ready: before she could leap again, he had the pistol in his hand. Even her passion didn't stop her registering that. She crouched, blazing-eyed, trembling at a pitch of tension, while Karl watched open-mouthed.

"Sit down," said Jim. "Let's pretend we're civilized. I want to know more about you, Señora Ruiz. Or Menendez. Or Gonzalez. But at the moment I've got all the power, and you've got none. Do as I say and sit down."

"English," she said. "You are English."

"That's right." She still hadn't moved. Jim indicated the chair, and reluctantly, proudly, she got up and walked to it, turning magnificently before sitting down. She was breathing deeply, her bosom heaving under the red silk dress, her mouth pursed in scarlet scorn.

"*She* is English," she went on, her voice filled with poison. "That little nobody, that bit of London scum, that pretty nothing. That should be *me* in her place! A child! A little kitten with its eyes still blind and its face dabbled with milk! What does she know? And her husband the clown! The eternal baby who never grew up! You look at her and you look at me, and where is the comparison? She is a penny candle beside me! Shabby, common, vulgar, coarse, ignorant, stupid—stupid, stupid, vacant!"

"When did you find out that your husband was alive?" Jim said.

She blinked and seemed to make an effort to bring her mind round to it. "A year ago. His old nurse wrote to me. She thought she was dying, and felt guilty. She had kept cuttings! From every performance I had done, all over Europe! Imagine! She looked after him in the asylum, and kept them for him. But then she felt guilty, she wanted to make her peace. So she wrote to me. I was astounded...But I *knew.* I had always known he was not dead. My heart was in prison, but not in a grave. I could feel. And I knew he was alive."

She dashed angry tears from her eyes. Her emotions might have been theatrical, but they were potent.

"The cruelty!" she cried. "To keep him locked away for so long, so secret! Better to have killed him at once! Kinder to cut his throat and let him bleed to death! The villains! The—"

She had been reaching down the side of the chair. Karl saw what Jim couldn't, the glint of a steel blade, and this time it was he who sprang and grappled with her when she leapt up. Snarling, she fell and twisted lithely, and Karl rolled over and kicked the little table down between them, shattering the teacup. Jim stepped down hard on her wrist and bent to pull the knife out of her hand.

"Stop this," he said. "Karl, pour the lady a glass of brandy—I think there's some on the sideboard. Now listen," he went on, bending down to seize her hair roughly and twisting her face up to look at his. "I'm no gentleman. I don't mind in the very least hitting you. As far as I can see you're nothing more than a common murderer, and if I killed you now the world would be a better place. But there's that poor devil locked up in the dark, and I owe him a duty now I've seen him, so you're going to help, you understand?"

He shook her hard. She spat at him. He shook her harder. She twisted and tried to bite him, and he slapped her so violently she could hardly breathe for shock. She looked at him with bewildered eyes. Carefully he let go of her hair and helped her up into the armchair.

Karl brought her the wine, and she held it with both hands, trembling.

"Drink," said Jim.

She sipped. He bent to pick up the purse, which had fallen into the fireplace, and found it light and empty.

She wiped her face with the flat of her hand: no dainty dabbing with a handkerchief but an honest animal physicality. The mark of his hand on her cheek flared red, and with her hair disordered and her eyes smudged with tears she looked suddenly older, but more real, more approachable.

He sat down. He was close enough to smell the scent she was wearing—something heavy and rich, like sandalwood, he thought; and beneath it the smell of her body, for she wasn't over-clean. But it moved him: she was a human being like himself.

"You have to tell me everything," he said gently. "Begin with Prince Leopold."

She drew breath in a shuddering sigh. "He fell in love with me in Paris. We married almost at once. Why should I not marry a prince? I was worthy of being a queen. But they would not allow it. They tried to annul the marriage, they tried to bribe me to give him grounds for divorce, they tried blackmail, they tried threats. No good. So they kidnapped me and had me taken to Mexico, to a dirty little town on the Pacific coast a thousand miles from anywhere. They had the power to do that! And the next I heard, my husband was dead. But I *knew* all the time he was not dead. I knew they would do anything; they have no scruples, no conscience. None of them! They were all behind it, the whole corrupt mess of stinking inbred fear and decay and rotten putrid *disease* of the court, every one of them..."

"Count Thalgau as well?"

"That name I don't know. Who is he? He is not important."

"Otto von Schwartzberg?"

"A cousin. He means nothing. They despised him as a wild man, uncultivated. I mean the corruption at the heart of it all, the court itself. The old king, he knew what they'd done with Leopold. He didn't have to say anything to Gödel or anyone else; just a nod, a flutter of the fingers—" she acted it— "and they understood, and it was done. Lock him up, pretend he's dead. Anything *I* have done—" she pressed her hand to her heart and sat up straight, flashing proud defiance from her eyes—"was *clean.* Dynamite and bullets are *clean,* not that sort of filthy cowardice of imprisoning a man until he goes mad. I killed them! Yes! And I would go on until they are all dead and all in hell!"

"You didn't do it on your own. You had accomplices."

"I didn't have accomplices. I had money. You can pay men to do anything."

"But you've got none left..." He held out the empty purse.

"I have enough to pay the landlady."

"And what then?"

She looked at him directly, and it was a real, confused, unhappy human soul that looked out of her eyes, and not a confected blaze of passion to strike across the footlights and dazzle the pit.

"I don't know," she said. "I want to help him. The nurse, Frau Busch, she can't get him out; she bribed the guard to leave us alone for five minutes, but she's afraid of Gödel. I'm not, but I have no power on my own."

Not much, Jim thought. He looked at Karl, and back at her.

"All right," he said, "now listen to me. He must come out of that damned hole in the rock—and we'll get him out, tonight. But if you think that gang of parasites around Gödel are ever going to let you near the throne, you're crazy. As soon as he's on his feet again, they'll kill you like a rat. No, don't interrupt. Leopold will never be king, but he's got a chance of living a fairly decent life if you help him. And that means helping *us.* You've really got no choice. That's the only path that's open to you."

She blinked. There was a flutter of not-wanting-to-understand in her eyes like a broken bird trying to escape a cat; but it couldn't reach the air; it could only flap in ragged circles on the lawn. And Jim the cat had never felt more cruel.

She bowed her head.

"What must I do?" she said.

Jim began to tell her. The flutter in her eyes calmed as if an invisible presence had fallen silent, and withdrawn to some deep chamber far inside, and for a while, Carmen Ruiz was contrite and eager to please; so eager and so warm that Jim had to remind himself forcibly of who she was and what she'd done, and found it almost impossible to believe.

In the Council Chamber, the second day of the talks was drawing to a close, and the outline of a treaty was in place. It was an astonishing achievement. Adelaide had persuaded the two powers to guarantee, jointly, the continued independence of Razkavia; to come to her aid if she were threatened; to respect her borders; to extradite offenders against the criminal laws; to enter into a customs union that permitted the free flow of goods and trade; in short, to give up forever any claims either of them might have had on the little kingdom that lay between them.

The clerks and secretaries of all three teams went away to draw up the treaty in its finally agreed form, for a signing ceremony on the following morning. The queen and the delegates, together with representatives of the other major powers, went to a gala performance at the opera. Becky, worn out and nearly voiceless, asked to be excused and went to bed.

At eight o'clock, our acquaintance Herr Bangemann (of the five daughters lined up in order of size) blotted the last page he had been writing, handed it to the chief secretary, and put on his hat and coat ready to leave.

The chief secretary checked the work. It was impeccable; every word, every comma was in place, in the finest copperplate on the smoothest vellum. He put it together with the other two completed copies in the safe, locked it carefully, and hastened to change for the opera.

Herr Bangemann, meanwhile, was in a cab on his way to a large house not far from the casino, on the wooded hills at the western edge of the city. His plump wife was waiting placidly in their apartment; there was venison soup and dumplings on the stove; the five daughters were lined up ready to tell him of their day's work at school.

But Herr Bangemann's clerkly salary would not have paid for Gretl's piano lessons, for Inge's new calico dress, for Bertha's winter hat, for Anna's satin slippers, for Marlene's dancing class, never mind the chocolates Frau Bangemann enjoyed. They thought their man had an important post, to work so late and to buy them the little luxuries they liked. And in a way they were right.

Herr Bangemann paid off the cab, rang the doorbell, gave his hat and coat to the servant, and was shown into a study where a warm fire was burning. Two men were sitting there: one in an armchair, the other at a table where a curious selection of apparatus was laid out: mahogany boxes with brass terminals, copper-bound induction coils, and an instrument like a piano keyboard, the keys each marked with a letter of the alphabet. From the terminals, wires bound in gutta-percha trailed up to a corner of the ceiling, and then through a dark hole. An efficient electrical hum came from it all.

Herr Bangemann glanced at the apparatus with polite curiosity before bidding good evening to the man in the armchair.

"Good evening to you, Herr Bangemann," said the host. "Please be seated at the other table, and begin when you like."

There was a smaller table, with a carafe of water and a glass thoughtfully provided. The keyboard operator was flexing his fingers. Herr Bangemann sat down, cleared his throat, closed his eyes, and summoned up on the screen of his photographic memory the entire text of the Tripartite Treaty.

"Whereas," he began...

A wintry landscape: in the background, a castle on a pine-covered mountain; in the foreground, a row of ancient houses, with snow swirling out of a low sky to settle tentatively on the cobbles and rush up and around and down again.

It might be Razkavia. In fact, it's only three inches across, and it's contained in one of those glass toys filled with liquid, which you shake to make a snowstorm. At present, it's in the hand of another acquaintance of ours: the banker from Berlin, Herr Gerson von Bleichröder.

He holds it up to his eyes, peering closely in, and then puts it gently back on the desk. It's the only snow that's falling in Berlin just now; the weather is cold, but the streets are dry. Bleichröder crosses to the window, looks down toward the well-lit Behrenstrasse below, taps a hand into the palm of the other behind his back, waiting.

He's waiting for the energetic clatter of the tape machine in the corner of the office to come to an end, and presently it does. Julius the secretary, who has been patiently gathering the yards of paper tape into a wicker container, snaps off the end and says:

"Ready, sir. It's all here."

"Good. Read it to me, Julius."

Julius raises his eyebrows, but sits obediently and rustles through the tape to find the start. As he reads, the banker comes back to his chair and sits in his usual posture, leaning back, hands behind his head. His prominent nose and chin are immobile, but his fine hooded eyes dart this way and that, as if trying to see every implication of every clause that Julius reads out.

Finally Julius reaches the end, and drops the tape into the basket.

"That's it, sir," he says.

"Well, well. Is the messenger waiting?"

"Yes, sir."

"Good. Send it off to the chief, then."

Julius rings a bell, and instructs a clerk to roll up the tape neatly, put it in an envelope, and give it to the messenger waiting in the lobby. Bleichröder sits up, rubbing his hands.

"Now, take a letter, Julius. Can you see all right? Would you like some more light?"

"I can see perfectly well, thank you, sir."

"To His Excellency Count Emil von Thalgau...Special messenger, Julius. Address it to the palace in Eschtenburg."

Julius, at his smaller desk, inscribes his neat shorthand on a piece of heavy paper.

"My dear Count Thalgau," begins the banker, "it is with great pleasure that I learn of the imminent accession to the throne of His Royal Highness the Crown Prince Leopold. I trust that his health has benefited from the devoted medical attention that he has no doubt been receiving.

"The various constitutional...give me a synonym for obstacles, Julius."

"Impediments, sir?"

"That will do. The various constitutional impediments that might prevent his immediate resumption of the throne are not, of course, of the slightest concern to the House of Bleichröder, nor, more importantly, to Prince von Bismarck."

He breaks off, and strokes the little glass toy for a moment. The secretary waits, pencil poised.

Bleichröder goes on: "Here's a little test for you, Julius. I've learned from the British Ambassador that London wouldn't give tuppence to preserve this little English girl who finds herself queen; that she's a profound embarrassment; in short, that if she meets with a fatal accident, the British lion won't even twitch its imperial tail. Now, Julius, say that diplomatically."

The secretary frowns faintly, composes his thoughts, and says, continuing the letter: "Nor, for that matter, to the British government. Private sources at the highest level have disclosed a decided preference on the part of London for a resumption of the normal dynastic arrangements."

"Excellent, my boy! Write it like that."

The secretary's pencil moves, and Bleichröder continues:

"As to the matter of the Tripartite Treaty, no doubt His Excellency the Chancellor Prince von Bismarck will make his dispositions known in the near future. In accordance with our agreement, I can confirm transmission of the first half of the agreed sum, namely eighty thousand marks, in a draft on the House of Rothschild. The remainder will be paid in full on the day following the coronation of Crown Prince Leopold.

"With my cordial regards, Gerson von Bleichröder, and so

on. There you are, Julius. Special messenger. It will be in Eschtenburg by the morning."

"Very good, sir."

Bleichröder leans back again, hands behind his head. Julius waits deferentially.

"Now, Julius, tell me what you read into this correspondence."

"Firstly, that Count Thalgau has been in financial trouble, from which he expects to be rescued by the House of Bleichröder."

"Correct. A mortgage on his entire property; he could not meet it; he would have been ruined. He is a patriot, none more so, but his estate, his castle will now be his whatever happens to Razkavia. So far correct, but easy, dear boy; you have seen the file. Carry on."

"There is a plot to remove the English girl and substitute Prince Leopold...Is he a genuine prince, sir? I thought he was dead. And surely the English girl's claim is good?"

"Yes, he's perfectly genuine, though probably insane by now. And her claim is as good as it could possibly be. You know about their picturesque ritual, with the flag and so on? Charming; I wish I could see it...But why must she go? Come on, Julius, the hidden motive. Look *beneath.*"

"The treaty..."

"Yes. What will the chief think of the treaty?"

Julius tries to think: the treaty looks good for all parties—therefore something must be wrong with it; official German policy is to negotiate and settle—therefore Bismarck's private policy must be to disrupt and subvert. Unless of course he's really doing what he pretends to be doing, in which case...

"The chief wants to prevent the treaty in order to...get a better deal?"

"Not quite, Julius. This is the true plan: the chief wants to restrict the power of the German parliament. The Reichstag is getting too dominant, and the treaty is a Reichstag affair, not a Chancellery one. If it collapses, the chief's judgment will be vindicated. And the incidental outcome will be favorable too: the chief wants all the nickel they produce in that funny little country. Krupps needs it. Therefore they must have it. The treaty would prevent that; therefore the treaty must not be signed. You understand so far?"

"Indeed, sir."

"Furthermore, there will be a disturbance tomorrow in the Razkavian capital. As a friendly gesture, the chief will dispatch a regiment of Grenadiers to help restore order. The soldiers are currently boarding the trains."

Julius marvels. To sit in this quiet office, at the heart of Europe, and learn of these complex, hidden maneuvers of state! It is a rare and mighty privilege.

"I see, sir. But...Count Thalgau and the mysterious Prince Leopold. How are they connected?"

Bleichröder laughs. It's a merry laugh, like that of a fond grandfather at a Christmas party.

"They're not connected at all, Julius! When poor Thalgau reads the first paragraph of that letter, he will be thunderstruck. And when he reads the last sentence—thunderstruck again! No, I happen to know that the conservative elements have had Prince Leopold up their sleeves for a long time, as a desperate card to play. They had him ready on the day the English girl was crowned, but she was too strong for them."

Julius is amazed. "Do you mean that...the assassination..."

"Was planned, yes. You remember the Spanish actress I told you about? She was married to Prince Leopold, you know; passionate, hot-blooded. And clever, too—not an intellectual cleverness, but cunning beyond anything you could imagine.

Women, Julius! But *suggestible.* Even a little unbalanced. A word in her ear—a friendly murmur of encouragement—a pretend fact or two to fuel her passion for vengeance, and the thing was done. She has no scruples, any more than a torpedo has when it's fired. Yes, she was responsible for the death of Prince Wilhelm and his wife; it was all planned. The only thing we didn't anticipate was the English girl. She was too strong, and she's been too popular with the common people. Well, it'll all fall apart very soon. And poor Count Thalgau, who imagines that all that will happen is a six-month delay in the treaty..."

"That's what he's been told?"

"Oh, yes. He wouldn't want to harm his little English queen. We told him we only wanted a slight delay, that everything would be safe after that. And now to find the ground falling away beneath his feet...Oh, dear, dear. And to find us seeming to assume that *he knows about it and is part of the conspiracy...*"

Julius is silent. Bleichröder, smiling to himself, is gazing upward, but he presently coughs and sits up.

"Come, come, my boy, this kind of thing happens all the time. In a year or two I'll have a word with the chief on his behalf. We'll create some kind of position for Count Thalgau—provincial governor, something of that sort. I believe in making friends, Julius, not enemies. Banking thrives on peace, you know. That's a very important lesson to learn. Now read me back the letter."

The secretary does so. Bleichröder leans back, listening, suggests a minor change or two, and sends the young man away to have the letter transcribed and dispatched to the house in the woods near the casino.

Then he picks up the little glass toy and shakes it once more. Holding it up an inch or two away from his right eye, he tries to make out the swirling white flakes, but it is no good: only the vaguest blur is visible. He lost the sight of his left eye some time ago, and now the right one can only just distinguish dark from light. The snow in the little glass globe swirls and dances and settles on the pretty landscape, so like that of Razkavia, and he sees nothing of it.

14
Betrayal

Becky, deep in sleep, heard a knocking, and muttered, "Go way. *Hau ab! Leine ziehe!*"

But whoever they were, they didn't. They knocked again and her door opened a little way.

"It's me," said Jim's voice quietly. "I need to talk to you. Asleep? Tough luck. I'll stir the fire up and pour you a glass of something."

She growled. He closed the door and, still nine-tenths submerged, she felt for her dressing gown. When after a minute she dragged herself through into the little sitting room, tousle-haired, sleepy-eyed, barefoot, she found him standing by the rekindled fire, holding a bottle of wine and two glasses. He looked like a sailor: he was wearing rough trousers, rubber-soled shoes, and the navy-blue jersey Mrs. Goldberg had knitted for him. A heavy pea jacket lay over a chair.

"What do you think you look like?" she said crossly. "'Once aboard the lugger and the girl is mine,' I suppose. I don't want wine. I want cocoa. *Schokolade.* Do you *realize* how tired I am? What's the use of wine to me? And you don't need it, you're full of beer, I can smell it, *ach*, disgusting. If you were a gentleman you'd never dream of bursting into someone's room without *Schokolade*. Go and get some at once. Oh, all right, don't. The servants are asleep and you'd set fire to the kitchen. What do you want?"

"I could make a cup of tea," he said helpfully. "I've got all the doings..."

"Tea—pah. English swill. What do you want?"

"I want you to listen. Sit down and put the poker in the fire."

"Oh—*mulled* wine. That's different..."

He took a twist of paper from his pocket, shook some sugar and a pinch of spice into each glass, and topped it up with red wine. When the poker was hot, he dipped it into the wine, careful not to touch the glass, and the liquid hissed and bubbled angrily.

"Bit sooty, but it'll do," he said, and handed her a glass. She sat close to the fire, her bare feet on the fender, and hugged her knees, sipping the steaming wine as he spoke.

He told her everything that had happened since the moment on the terrace two nights before. She listened, appalled. After the work of the last two days, she thought she knew about politics; that it was complex but open, achieved by painstaking negotiation and compromise. How wrong she was! Because all the time, underneath, a different politics was taking place. And *that* politics was simple but secret, achieved by cruelty and violence.

"I'm...I'm breathless," she said. "Baron Gödel hid that poor man in an asylum all this time? I can't take it in...And what about the woman? You say she's the one who killed King Rudolf? Where is she now?"

"She's with Karl and the others—under guard. We need her to help get Leopold out. They're on their way here now. Once we've got him out, we can arrest Gödel and have done with it. Clear the whole thing up."

"What's going to happen to her?"

"She's a murderer, Becky."

"But what's going to happen to her?"

"We'll hand her over to the police."

"What'll happen to her then?"

"She'll be tried. The penalty is hanging. In fact, I'll make sure she'll plead insanity; then she'd be locked in an asylum instead of him. That'd be ironic, wouldn't it."

"It's hardly fair. She did it because she loved her husband, and now you're tricking her into helping you, and you're going to betray her."

He ran his hands through his hair and stared at the floor, elbows on knees, shoulders tense.

"That's about the size of it," he said. "But loving your husband isn't a good enough reason to shoot someone else. She's not fully there, Becky. If you saw her, you'd soon see how odd she was. Little things that don't fit; her hair, for instance. She must spend hours on it, pulling it back so fiercely from her face that the skin of her forehead's drawn back as well, and it's so tightly rolled at the nape of her neck that it feels like wood—I noticed when we fought. But with all the attention she pays her hair, she neglects her shoes altogether—they're scuffed, muddy, the soles are loose. A dozen little things like that; she's coming adrift. And it's not just that—it's something in her eyes, in the intensity of them.

"But whether she's mad or not, she's just too dangerous to leave at large. And think: If she got what she wanted, would it make her happy? Could she put her husband on the throne, and reign beside him? He's *destroyed,* poor devil. He wouldn't even be able to lift the flag, much less know where to carry it, ten thousand times less deal with these diplomats like Adelaide's doing. If Carmen Ruiz is in her right mind, *that* life wouldn't make her happy; and if she isn't, she'd never know anyway. This is tragic, I dare say—for her, for him, for them both. And we're instruments in the tragedy. But we have to do it. We can't sacrifice everything Adelaide's done, everything you've done, the whole future of the country for the sake of a moment's happiness for her—which would be illusion anyway. So, yes, we've used him as bait to catch her, and we're going to use her as the bait to get Gödel, and then we're going to betray her; but I'll go in any witness box in the world and swear blind she's insane. They won't hang her if I've got anything to do with it."

Becky felt a lump in her throat.

"And the count?" she said. "Does he know?"

Jim shook his head.

"He was looking very pale today," Becky went on. "Quite ill, in fact. Even Adelaide noticed. I'm sure he feels guilty about whatever it is."

Jim gnawed his lip. "The old fool. I thought we could trust *him*, at least. Listen, Becky, I'm...That morning back in St. John's Wood, when the bomb went off...I'm damn glad it was you. You've done a cracking job. But I wish you were a thousand miles away."

"Why?"

"Because things are getting dangerous. I'm thinking of your mother, I suppose. If anything happens to you, I won't forgive myself. How is she? Does she write to you?"

"Of course she writes. And I write to her, twice a week, great long letters. Wouldn't you?"

"My old Ma wouldn't have been able to read anyway," he said. "She died when I was ten. Consumption. She was a washerwoman, up in Clerkenwell. It was my Pa who taught me to read...Dickens, mainly. He used to love *All the Year Round;* took it every week. I remember him taking me to one of Dickens's readings once, the great Inimitable himself giving out with Sikes murdering Nancy, sending shivers down our spines...What am I talking about this for? Your mother. That's right. So that's why I wish you were a thousand miles away. Listen, Becky, will you sleep in Adelaide's room tonight?"

"Well...all right."

"Just in case."

He got up, wandered to the window, and lifted the edge of the curtain aside to look out.

"Becky, how's this going to end?" he said with his back to her. "What are you going to do when the treaty business is signed and sealed?"

"Me? I want...I want to go to university and study languages properly. But for the moment I just want to see that treaty signed tomorrow morning. It's been the most exciting thing in my life, Jim, you can't imagine what this *means.* My own country, and I'm at the very center of things, of great important discussions—there's nothing that could ever be better than that!"

He shook his head. He was still looking out the window.

"And what about you?" she said. "What do *you* want to do?"

"I want to fight, Becky. Can you understand that? I want struggle, I want danger. You know, Sally said something to me once: we were talking about happiness and what that might mean. She said she didn't want to be *happy,* that was a weak, passive sort of thing; she wanted to be alive and active. She wanted *work.* That's the spirit I like. That's what I want; and my work is a rough dirty dangerous kind of work. Oh, I want other things too. I want to write a play and see Henry Irving perform in it. I want to swank about town smoking Havanas and have supper with pretty girls in the Café Royal. I want to play poker on a Mississippi riverboat. I want to see Dan Goldberg get into Parliament. I want to see you go to university and get a first-class degree. Sally...Sally can do anything she wants, by me. There's a whole world I want, Becky."

"You haven't mentioned Adelaide."

"No."

He looked in from the window. His green-blazing eyes and tousled straw-colored hair gave him the look of some electrical spirit, charged with urgent forces. Then she realized that his attention was focused on something outside the room, and as she listened she heard it too: the sound of hurrying footsteps in the corridor, followed by a swift tap at the door.

"Come in," she said, sitting up.

A maidservant, looking anxious, opened the door.

"I'm sorry, Fräulein," she said. "A message for..."

She looked at Jim, embarrassed at Becky's state of undress, and handed him a note.

"Thanks," he said, and she bobbed and went out.

He unfolded the note, read it swiftly, tossed it into the fire, and stood up.

"Time to go," he said.

"What are you going to do?"

"Fight, of course!"

And he bent to kiss her swiftly on the cheek. She felt a flash of some complicated mixture of emotions: *How dare he?* was part of it, and so was envy of the clarity of his task, the beautiful instinctive energy with which he leapt to it; and so was a shiver of fear. All her daydreams of piracy and brigandage suddenly seemed childish and tawdry. Jim was real.

He was pressing something into her hand. It was a pistol.

"Go and sleep in her room," he said. "And keep this hidden.

If you have to use it, hold it in both hands and be prepared for the kick. I'll see you later."

And he was gone, running lightly down the corridor. The maid was still in sight. Becky concealed the pistol under her dressing gown and summoned her.

"Is Her Majesty back from the opera?"

"Yes, Fräulein. They are all back except Count Thalgau."

"Except...But why? Where is the count?"

"I couldn't say, Fräulein. He didn't come back with the rest of the party. That's all I know. Will that be all, Fräulein?"

"Yes, Ilse. Thank you. That's all..."

She watched the maid go, and went back into her own room with a racing heart to gather what she needed for the night.

Karl and a dozen others, together with Carmen Ruiz, were waiting in the ruined chapel above the entrance to the grotto. They were all wearing dark clothes, as he'd asked them to; the heavy sky let no moonlight through, and all he could see was the blur of pale faces in the gloom. Anton had been detailed to keep a special eye on the woman, and Jim saw him now, standing warily a foot or so behind her.

"Good evening, Señora," he said softly, and she inclined her head. "All quiet?" he whispered to Karl.

"Not a sound. No—that's not quite true—you can hear him crying out from the top of the shaft. Like a troll or something under the earth. Hansi's guarding the trapdoor with his group."

Jim had found the top of the steps, concealed among bushes in the little copse where he'd first heard the scream.

"All set, then?"

"All set. We'll leave Jan in the mouth of the grotto with three others to guard our backs."

Jim nodded. "Good. There's a boat hidden in the rushes down there—we'll take that and bring him out in it. He's too weak to walk far. And then to the forest, and away."

He shook hands all round, they wished each other luck, and the dozen shadowy figures set off with him down the slope toward the grotto. The air was still tonight, there was no lashing wind among the trees, and as they reached the foot of the slope Jim could hear the ripples of the river. A bird called far off in the forest, a high distant scream, and a small animal splashed softly as it entered the water.

They stopped to let Jan and his three move on ahead into the mouth of the grotto, and Jim felt among the rushes for the rope anchoring the boat.

Karl, Anton, and the woman got in, and Jim led the rest along the path and into the profound darkness of the grotto itself. He had drilled everyone to keep close to the right-hand wall; they had lanterns, but they were for using on the way out.

"Good luck, my boy," Jim whispered into the darkness once they were inside the mouth. "If you need to, yell at the top of your voice."

"With pleasure," came back Jan's whisper. "Good luck."

The long, cold, silent walk through the enfolding darkness was no less unpleasant now that Jim had companions and a known goal. The constant drip of water, the clammy air, the slime on the rock under his hand, the continual apprehension about projecting rocks at head-height were just as oppressive as before. Occasionally a soft knock or bump from the water to his left told him that Karl hadn't succeeded in keeping the boat clear of the wall, but the sound wasn't loud enough to carry, and it was reassuring to know how close he was.

Finally Jim stopped. There was the faintest of gleams on the wet rock ahead. He put out a hand and stopped the man behind him.

"Careful now," he whispered. "Nearly there."

Since they didn't know how the dungeon was guarded, they were going to have to improvise when they got there; the second essential thing was to give Jim enough time and room to work at the padlock. The first essential thing, of course, was surprise.

Jim took out his pistol. Eyes fixed on the gleam on the rock, he moved ahead more slowly, beckoning the others on behind.

Coming out of the dark, they had the advantage that the scene around the corner seemed well lit. Jim, reaching it first, took in at a glance the flickering lantern on a hook, the little table, the pair of soldiers, the greasy cards, the huddled figure behind the bars.

He walked up quietly and said, "Sit quite still and put your hands on the table."

The soldiers both jumped in shock, and exclaimed so loudly that they woke the man in the dungeon, who sat up at once and cried in fear. The other students were hurrying up; Karl was helping Carmen Ruiz out of the boat while Anton held it steady, and then she flung herself at the bars, calling the prince's name passionately. He cowered away.

"Don't move," said Jim to the soldiers. "Don't make a noise. Don't do anything. Karl, take my pistol and keep them covered."

Another student moved the rifles out of reach of the two soldiers, who sat white-faced and openmouthed, one twisting to stare over his shoulder at Jim, who was already busy at work on the lock.

"Please, Señora," said Anton, "move aside a little, let him work..."

"What have you done to him?" she cried suddenly, and turned like a tigress to the soldiers, who flinched. The students could see that the prince's face was bruised and swollen. "Who has hurt him? Who dared do that?"

"Señora!" Anton said sharply. "We'll get him out in a minute. They'll be punished, don't worry about that."

"Nearly there," muttered Jim, twisting, prodding, bending his wire and prodding again. "Nice new lock. Oily. Just as I like—"

And then there was the sound of a shot from behind them.

It was muffled and magnified by the echoing tunnel, but it was unmistakable; and then there was another, and Jan's voice, shouting. Heads snapped round, eyes widened. The woman fell still.

Into the shocked moment Karl said, "Heini, take three men and run back to help Jan. Peter, take a light and run along the other way till you find the steps. Wait for us there."

Jim didn't look up once. While the others did as they were ordered, he calmly withdrew the wire from the lock, looked at it carefully, bent it a little more, and slid it back in. More shots came from behind. Prince Leopold was cowering in the corner, clutching a blanket and whimpering like a beaten dog.

Jim murmured quietly, "Take it easy, mate. Another little tweak and we'll have you out. Go and climb the stairs, eh?"

He coaxed and spoke softly, and little by little the man shuffled forward. More gunshots thundered, and more closely. Shouts echoed down the tunnel.

The padlock sprang open. Jim said, "Prince, you're going to have to come. It's your duty. Come on now."

Beside him, Carmen Ruiz was quivering.

"Come, Leo!" she murmured. "Come on, my prince!"

He came to the door and glanced fearfully down the tunnel, where someone was shouting orders, and where the pounding of feet echoed louder and louder.

Jim seized the prince and pulled him out; no time for delicacy now. Dragging the man between him and Carmen, he shoved past the two terrified soldiers and on to where Karl was beckoning urgently at the foot of the steps. Another student, holding a lantern, stood beside him peering anxiously up.

"They're nearly here—" someone said from behind, but then there came the explosion of a shot from above, immensely loud, and a cry; and the tumbling sound of a body falling.

"Watch out!" said Karl, and Hans fell out of the darkness to the foot of the steps, dead.

"Run!" came a despairing cry from above. "Run! They've trapped us—"

The boat, unnoticed, was drifting past. Out of the corner of his eye Jim saw the woman seize the rope and pull it to the bank, and leap in, dragging the prince with her by his shirt. Leopold fell with a cry to the edge of the bank, and then the frail cotton tore, leaving him sprawling and scrabbling for a hold on the slippery rock. Anton bent down and heaved him back, and the last they saw of the woman was her white face, mouth open in a silent scream of loss, and her pale hands reaching back; and then the current, much faster here, swept her away into the darkness.

Jim cursed.

"Bring the prince!" he shouted, and sprang for the steps. If he could fight his way through, the others might be able to get Leopold away. Pistol held high, he leapt up the narrow steps three at a time, and butted his head into the midriff of the first man he saw.

The soldier fell with a heavy grunt. Jim leapt over him and grabbed for the side of the trapdoor, which showed as a dark edge against the scarcely lighter sky. A body lay across the gap; he heaved it aside, and then something struck him hard on the head.

Dazed, he fell and rolled aside into the cold wet grass. Shouts, the glow of lanterns, running feet; and then he was up, crouching, firing at the blaze and bang of gunshots around him in the dark, diving aside and rolling over to come up a few yards away and fire again; and at the edge of his sight, he was aware of the pale figure of the prince in his torn white shirt being dragged out of the trapdoor by two figures, who might have been Anton and Karl.

"Run!" he shouted. "Run!"

But there were more shouts, heavy figures crashing into him, bearing him to the ground, and another sickening blow to the head; and the last thing he thought was, *Who betrayed us? Count, if it was you...*

15 Saucepan

Becky woke up, stiff and cold, on the little sofa at the foot of Adelaide's bed. Her Majesty was still asleep. As Becky stretched and yawned she dislodged the pistol under the cushion at her head, so that it fell to the floor with a thud, and Adelaide opened her eyes at once.

"Who's that?"

"It's me," said Becky, retrieving the pistol and hiding it again.

"Why? What are you doing here?"

"I—Jim told me to come up and guard you in case—oh, I don't know. Did you know you snore, Your Majesty?"

Adelaide, sleepy-eyed among deep pillows, cast her a look of contempt and closed her eyes again.

"Where's me soldiers?" she muttered. "Why aren't they guarding me? What's the use of you doing it?"

Becky was about to reply when there came a knock at the door, and Adelaide's maid came in and curtsied, blinking with surprise as she saw Becky. She was carrying a breakfast tray.

"Good morning, Your Majesty," the girl said. "Good morning, Fräulein..."

Adelaide grunted as the maid threw open the shutters and

crouched to stir the fire. Within a minute she had it burning up brightly. Adelaide's black kitten woke among the folds of the eiderdown, and showed his pink needle-filled mouth in a wide yawn.

"Come here, Saucepan," said Adelaide, and lifted the soft little thing up to her face to kiss while the maid arranged the pillows more comfortably.

"It's a cloudy day, Your Majesty," said the maid. "I think it's going to snow. Was there anything else?"

"No. What's the time? Never mind. Fräulein Winter will tell me. You can run the bath, that's what you can do. Got to look posh today," she said to Becky. "And you have to, as well. Sleeping on sofas—you'll get a stiff neck. You'll be standing there behind me looking like an umbrella. What's Jim on about?"

From behind the closed bathroom door came the sound of water splashing into the tub. Becky lifted the breakfast tray onto Adelaide's lap and sat on the bed to be able to talk quietly.

"I haven't been able to tell you before. I didn't want to distract you. But the night before the talks began, I was out on the terrace with Jim, and we saw a woman talking to one of the servants..."

Adelaide had put the kitten down on the tray, and was lifting the lid of the butter dish for it.

"I'm listening," she said. "You saw a woman with one of the servants. Who was that, then?"

"A woman who turned out to be the wife of Prince Rudolf's eldest brother Leopold."

"*King* Rudolf. He was king." Adelaide, a stickler now for precedence and etiquette, except where Saucepan was concerned, was buttering a roll, in between little kitten-paw dabs. "And you said wife. You mean widow."

"No. Wife. Because Jim's discovered that Leopold is still alive."

Adelaide, suddenly pale, dipped a silver spoon into the apricot jam. Saucepan was lapping at the cream. Adelaide's hand moved more and more slowly as Becky told her what Jim had found out.

"And where's Jim now?" she said when Becky had finished.

"They were going to rescue him from the grotto. He and the students—"

They both stopped, Becky in mid-sentence, Adelaide with the roll halfway to her mouth. The kitten had given a little cough, then a racked, choking cry, and stumbled clumsily onto its nose. Unable to move, they watched it gasp and kick at itself in a spasm of pain, and then, with a little soft meow, thrash over onto its back, curling, twitching, and die.

Beyond the door, the splashing water stopped. The handle turned; the maid came in, bobbed, and said; "The bath is ready, Your Majesty. Shall I lay out the silk, or..."

But before she could finish, the door burst open, and there stood Countess Thalgau. The maid's head turned in astonishment. The countess, wide-eyed and pale, saw her and, distracted, waved her out. The maid bobbed swiftly to Adelaide and fled, and the next moment the countess was at the bedside.

Neither Becky nor Adelaide had moved a muscle. The countess was breathing heavily; she was still in her dressing gown and her gray hair was disordered.

"Oh—thank God—" she said, and took the roll from Adelaide's fingers.

Then she saw the kitten. Her eyes lost focus and she swayed. Becky leapt up and helped her to a chair.

"What—is—going—on?" said Adelaide in a dangerous voice.

Becky had never seen the countess like this. Her normal glare of icy disapproval was melted; she was weeping openly now, and she couldn't sit still. She pushed up from the chair and lifted the breakfast tray off Adelaide's lap and carried it to the far end of the room, putting it down in the furthest corner from the bed as if its very presence were toxic.

And all the time she sobbed and gasped, brokenly: "A plot—I learned of it only now—my husband—I cannot bear the shame—Your Majesty is safe? You haven't tasted anything? God be praised—oh, this is too much to bear—"

Becky hurried to the door and turned the key. Then she helped the countess, now crying freely, to the sofa.

"My husband—I didn't realize—he was doing something wrong—but not this! He did not do this! It was Gödel—they never meant you to succeed—they thought you'd crumble, you'd break and fail—but you didn't do what they expected, you *succeeded*—and now the talks, the treaty—they're never going to let you sign it!"

"But the count?" said Becky. "He's not behind this poison business?"

"He confessed to me this morning that he had arranged for the treaty to be postponed for six months—but never this! He discovered that Gödel was up to something much worse—but he, I, we didn't learn of it till just now, I swear it—"

Adelaide's hand was automatically stroking the dead kitten. As Becky translated the countess's broken words, her expression gradually darkened until she was finally looking thunderous. Then she lifted the little creature and laid its body on the bedside table before swinging her legs down and standing barefoot on the floor. Her dark eyes blazed out of her flushed face as she confronted the countess.

"They were going to poison me? The queen? So that's what the Leopold plot was all about?"

"Leopold?" The countess was bewildered; it was plain she hadn't heard all of it.

Becky explained quickly. The countess put her head in her hands.

"Where is the count now?" said Adelaide.

"He is ill. He was explaining to me, and his heart—I don't know—he collapsed. I came straight here..."

"And you. You're on my side?"

"Ja! Ja, natürlich! Auf alle Zeiten!"

And she curtsied clumsily, that big, cold-mannered, warm-hearted woman, before hastily draping Adelaide's dressing gown around her.

"I'll get dressed at once," Adelaide said. "Never mind a bath, I'm clean enough. Becky! Put out the white silk. I'm not in mourning today, I'm in a temper, that's what I am. And a hurry. Where the bloody hell's Jim? Why isn't he back yet?"

Since Becky couldn't answer that, she didn't, and in any case Adelaide was already in the bathroom brushing her teeth. Becky found the white silk dress—ordered before Rudolf's death, but never worn—and laid it on the bed, together with clean stockings and underclothing.

Ten minutes later, Adelaide was dressed, and the countess was trying to arrange her hair. Becky was running from dressing table to armoire, bringing now the jewel case, now the atomizer of scent, now the rouge, and then Adelaide started as if she'd remembered something, and said:

"Becky—listen—in the bottom drawer of the bureau—there's a velvet purse there. Fetch it out, there's a pal."

Becky found it: a heavy velvet bag no bigger than her palm, embroidered in gold thread, with a gold clasp and lock. She gave it to Adelaide, who tucked it away in her bosom just as a knock sounded loudly at the door.

The three of them looked at one another. Adelaide stood up. "How's me hair?"

"Tidyish. Shall I open the door?"

"Yeah, go on. Stand here, countess. Guard of honor, that's the style."

Becky unlocked the door and stood back.

The Baron von Gödel stood there, with a captain and a squad of soldiers. The Chamberlain was breathing fast; a pulse in his neck was beating like a little fist against the high starched white collar. His eyes flicked around the room, looking for something, and Becky realized it was the breakfast tray. Perhaps they should have hidden it as evidence; but it was too late now.

Before anyone could speak, the countess stepped forward angrily.

"Baron von Gödel! What is your explanation for this—this despicable act of treason and attempted murder?"

Without looking at her, the baron turned and spoke to the captain.

"Take the countess to her husband," he said. "He is ill. She is not needed here."

The countess drew herself up and said with powerful clarity, "I am staying by the side of the queen. That is my duty, that is my choice. I shall not move."

The baron, still avoiding her eyes, gestured to the young captain, who said unhappily, "I have power to compel you, Your Grace."

"And no doubt you would. Well, you will have to do so, young man. I'm not going to make it easy for you."

She lifted her chin and glared. Adelaide, following their words, clapped her hands, and both the captain and the baron started guiltily.

"You had better not lay hands on anyone," she said, eyeing them with cold anger. "Countess, I don't wish to see you hurt. I am very grateful to you. Your loyalty is very precious. But please go with the captain without arguing. Go and look after your husband, who needs you. No doubt we'll see each other soon when this nonsense is over. In the meantime, you can tell anyone who cares to listen that I am queen and I will never surrender."

She spoke in careful, clear German, and although the countess looked like rebelling, she curtsied low. On an impulse, Adelaide leaned forward and kissed her. Tears came to the woman's eyes, and her hands reached forward involuntarily to clasp and squeeze Adelaide's; and Becky marveled at the change, from that marmoreal monster of disdain who'd first taken Princess Adelaide's training in hand.

The captain clicked his heels as the countess came out of the room, and detailed two soldiers to escort her away. Gödel turned back, and at that moment Becky saw something that nearly made her heart stop: it was the pistol Jim had given her, in plain view on the blue silk sofa. She stepped across as if to stand beside Adelaide, but in fact to hide it from view. Perhaps she could pick it up unseen...

Gödel said to the captain, "Place them under close guard. Both of them. Take them to the castle."

Adelaide saw what Becky was intending, and spoke to distract him.

"Perhaps you're surprised to see me up and about, Baron, after the poisoned breakfast you sent in. It was you, wasn't it?"

Becky, pretending to fold Adelaide's nightdress, picked up the pistol and hid it inside her dressing gown, turning around in time to see Gödel's haggard expression as he tried to find a reply.

Finally he snapped, "Hurry up, Captain!"

The young officer saluted and stepped forward.

"I must ask you to accompany me to the carriage downstairs.

If you resist, I shall be obliged to order my men to take you by force."

His voice shook: Adelaide was still the queen to him. In other circumstances, she'd have given him one of her looks and he'd have been her slave for life, but some shame was preventing him from looking at her. Instead, his eyes fixed on the middle distance, he stood with drawn pistol, waiting unhappily.

"I am not stupid, Captain, and I hope you're not discourteous," she said. "You must give Fräulein Winter time to get dressed before we leave; you're surely not going to take her across the city in her dressing gown."

The captain actually blushed.

Gödel said impatiently, "Escort her to her bedroom and wait outside while she dresses. Then bring her to the carriage. You have five minutes, Fräulein."

Becky left, clutching the dressing gown tightly around her. She didn't look at the soldier beside her, and she slammed the door loudly once she was in the room.

She washed her face and brushed her teeth quickly, and flung on some comfortable clothes: no need to look smart if she was going to prison, but plenty of need to keep warm, she guessed. She hastily threw some spare things into Mama's old carpetbag, and tucked the pistol into her waist.

In a very short time she opened the door and went out, cloaked and bonneted. The soldier gestured for her to follow, and together they marched stiffly through the strangely deserted corridors toward the East Door, a side entrance hidden behind the Orangery, where a closed carriage was waiting with a mounted escort.

Gödel stood beside it. "Give me that," he said, and took the carpetbag from her. She watched indignantly as he fumbled through the stockings, the underwear, the nightgown she'd thrown into it, and then he gave it back. She snatched it from his hands, and glared contemptuously.

A soldier opened the door. She climbed in, and the carriage began to move away at once, so that she swayed and fell onto the seat. The only light in the interior came around the edges of the blinds, and she said, "Who's in here? I can't see—"

"Just me," said Adelaide. "Stop bouncing around. You're making me feel ill."

Becky stood up carefully and felt inside the waist of her skirt. She drew out the revolver with a sigh of relief.

"At least it won't perforate me if it goes off," she said, putting it in the carpetbag. "There's only six bullets in it. We'll have to make them all count."

She sat down beside Adelaide, who—she saw dimly—was looking murderous. The carriage swayed as they went through the gate of the palace grounds, and then gathered speed as they swung away toward the castle.

Shortly after that, messengers arrived at the German and the Austro-Hungarian embassies. Profound regrets—Her Majesty taken suddenly ill—unable to perform signing ceremony as planned—have to postpone it for three days at least, on doctor's orders—final session of talks to be held in abeyance until her recovery, which of course was most earnestly wished for, etc., etc.

A similar message, more tersely worded, was handed to the representatives of the press in the offices that had been placed at their disposal. Twenty or so correspondents were gathered there, two-thirds of them from abroad, including a gentleman from *The Times* and three reporters from the popular press of London, eager for news of the Cockney Queen, as they called her.

The correspondent of the *Wiener Beobachter* read aloud the message the official had handed him. At once his colleagues began to question the official, who had to hold up his hands and say helplessly, "Forgive me, gentlemen, but I can tell you no more than I know, which is that Her Majesty was taken ill in the early hours of the morning—that her doctor was summoned at once—that a full bulletin will be issued at midday—that in the meantime, the talks are suspended—more news at midday—midday, gentlemen. Excuse me. Midday!"

He left, and the reporters and foreign correspondents began to scribble at once. Some of the quicker-witted, who could do two things at the same time, gathered their hats and coats and ran to be sure of a cab, composing the first sentences in their heads.

The clerks and scriveners, including our acquaintance Herr Bangemann, received the news with loyal concern, and in the absence of any work to do, occupied themselves with speculation, or cards, or the composition of light verse. One of Herr Bangemann's colleagues showed him how to fold a Chinese mandarin out of a square of paper, and Herr Bangemann at once set about making five of the little fellows, in decreasing order of size.

Jim had had no idea, not the faintest far-off dawning of a glimmer of suspicion, of how much he would loathe being a prisoner. It was entirely and profoundly hateful. You were as helpless as a baby, as much in the dark as poor Leopold had been. Jim felt his eyes fill with hot tears when he thought back to the scene by the trapdoor in the copse; he'd seen the prince cling desperately to Anton, sobbing like a little child as the soldiers tore him loose. Or had he imagined it after his second bang on the head?

Nor could he clear from his mind the picture of Carmen Ruiz reaching back helplessly from the boat as it floated more and more swiftly away and into the dark. He had no idea whether it flowed on to join the river or indeed whether it ever reached daylight again, and that was hateful to think about.

Jim brushed his face angrily and tried to turn his mind to Adelaide instead, but that made him nearly roar with frustration. It was no good; he got up off the plank bed, tore it from the rusty brackets holding it to the wall, and belabored the door with a chunk of wood till a voice shouted:

"Stop that row! Any more of it and we'll come in and beat you senseless!"

Jim replied with an even louder volley of blows, and a paragraph or so of Billingsgate invective, which made the voice change its mind about coming in and go and ask for orders.

Tiring of the exercise, Jim clambered over the ruins of the bed and tried to jump up high enough to reach the bars of the little window above his head. He could touch the stone windowsill, but it sloped so much that he couldn't get a grip. He spent ten minutes constructing a step with the bits of broken bed, but as soon as he put his weight on it, it collapsed. He yelled with fury and kicked it across the cell.

The light coming in was gray and dismal, and from the amount of time he thought had passed, he guessed it was about ten o'clock in the morning. As for where he was—it might be the castle, but that idea was only suggested by the stone walls; and any prison might have had those.

After another hefty kick at the door, he cleared a space and sat down.

"Work it out," he said aloud. "Use your head."

If he couldn't reach the window or the ceiling, and he couldn't scrape a hole in the walls, and if the floor was made of stone, it only left the door. They'd opened it once, after all, to put him in, and they'd have to open it again sometime.

He got up to examine it more closely. It was made of ancient, heavy oak, and there was neither keyhole nor handle on the inside. At eye level there was a rectangular peephole or Judas window about as broad as Jim's hand, with stout wire mesh over the inside and a sliding wooden cover over the outside—which was about three inches away; and that was a lot of oak, Jim thought.

The cover was closed. He couldn't reach it with a finger, but a few minutes' twisting and snapping produced a long splinter from the broken plank.

Poking it through the mesh, Jim managed to move the cover sideways a fraction by stroking the splinter along its surface. Once there was a gap, he slid the end into it and levered carefully.

After five minutes, he had the cover open. The view was hardly spectacular: a dismal corridor of stone, lit by the gray light coming through a high barred window at the far end. It was empty of furniture, empty of guards, but there were other doors into other cells, and they were open.

He was the only prisoner, then. Perhaps that was worth knowing. He looked hard at the locks on the other doors: hefty black iron things, secured to the outside of the doors by staples. Medieval rubbish, he thought scornfully; if his lock was like those, he'd have it open in seconds with a bit of wire, if only he could reach it. And if he had a bit of wire. He slid the cover back across the Judas window, so as not to reveal that he could undo it: the least advantage was worth holding on to; and then he tapped his teeth with the splinter of wood and looked around the cell: was there anything he'd overlooked?

Well, his pockets, to start with. Empty, but for a handkerchief; they'd pinched his clasp knife and the skeleton keys, naturally. No help from there, then. What was he wearing? Shoes, trousers, belt, shirt, jacket, jersey...

Sally's knitting! And there was an idea. He couldn't help grinning; the work she'd put into it...

Whistling softly between his teeth, he took off the heavy dark blue jersey and sat down to unpick it.

The door of the governor's chambers closed behind Becky and Adelaide, and a key turned in the lock.

"Well," said Becky. "Prisoners. And it's cold in here. *Vexing*, I call it. D'you know, my father was a prisoner here—I've just remembered. He died—"

Suddenly and without any warning she found herself sobbing: not for herself, but for that father she'd hardly known, dying of typhus in this very building. She would have been able to take up the cause of democracy and carry on his work, but now everything was coming apart, and it was unjust, it was cruel...

Adelaide, scowling, paced up and down the threadbare rug in front of the cold and dirty fireplace. The castle had had no governor for a hundred years, ever since the palace was built, and this room had probably been empty all that time. Adelaide took no notice whatever of Becky's tears, and after a minute or so Becky calmed down and mopped her eyes, and sniffed hard.

"All right," she said. "Tears over. I won't do it again. I wonder if they'd bring us some breakfast? Shall I ring the bell?"

For there was a bellpull by the mantelpiece, a shabby old rope of faded velvet. Adelaide seized it herself and jerked it savagely, and the whole thing came down in a shower of plaster and dust; but a satisfactory jangling resounded in the corridor.

"Useful," said Adelaide, looking at the rope. "We can take

turns to hang ourselves. Me first. You'd break it."

The door opened, and there was the captain.

"Captain, are you aware that someone tried to poison us this morning?"

The man blinked and gulped, and shook his head, and shrugged.

"And that we have had nothing to eat or drink as a result?"

"I—I shall arrange for something to be sent up."

"Do so at once."

He began to bow, caught himself, changed it to a polite nod, clicked his heels anyway, and left. The key turned again.

"Huh," said Adelaide, and sat down on the edge of a moldering armchair, having whisked away the dust. "I suppose, if they've gone as far as arresting us, Jim's plan can't've worked. I hope he's all right."

Becky felt a cold bolt of fear in the pit of her stomach. She hadn't realized how much of her own confidence depended on knowing that Jim was free.

"Course he's all right," she said shakily.

"And poor little Saucepan...I wonder what it'll be next? Something quick, I hope. I wouldn't mind a bullet. I don't fancy having me head cut off..."

"Stop it," said Becky, trying to rally herself as well as Adelaide. "Stop being silly. Wouldn't mind a bullet—you bloody well *should* mind a bullet. Don't you *dare* get resigned. They've got no right to do this. What we have to do is work out what they're doing, and how to stop it."

Adelaide's eyes flashed dangerously. She'd been queen just long enough to have forgotten what it was like to be spoken to like that; but she nodded.

"All right. Well, they can't do anything without some kind of ruler. They got to have someone to sign papers and ratify laws and...to carry the flag. To be the *Adlerträger.* That's where the authority comes from, innit?"

Becky, watching her, nodded. "So you think they'll take it down and get Leopold to carry it to the Rock—if they've got him?"

"Yeah. They were really hoping I'd guzzle that breakfast and turn me toes up, like Saucepan. Then they could have said, Oh, what a pity, look, the queen's kicked the bucket, and given me a posh funeral and everyone would've cried their eyes out. Then they'd look good, see, they'd look innocent, they could join in the mourning with everyone else. And then bring on this Leopold geezer and make him do what they wanted..."

"But we don't know that they've got him. If Jim's rescue plan worked—"

The key turned again, and one soldier held the door open for another to bring in a tray containing a jug of coffee, two cups, and a plate of rolls. He set them down on the table, saluted, and was about to turn and go when Adelaide got up and said, "Wait."

She picked up a roll and held it out to him. His puzzled eyes flicked to the sergeant in the doorway.

"Eat this," said Adelaide. *"Essen Sie."*

The sergeant nodded, and the soldier took a small bite, chewing it politely and swallowing hard before smiling uncertainly. Adelaide was pouring some coffee.

"Now drink," she said.

It was hot, and he had to blow on it. He sipped once, and twice, and smacked his lips.

Adelaide looked at Becky. "How long should we give him? Saucepan keeled over at once."

"He was only little. I should think it would take longer on a person."

"Especially a great hulk like this one. More!" she said to him. *"Trinken Sie mehr!"*

Trying not to look surprised, the soldier drank it down, with Adelaide watching every movement through narrowed eyes. When he'd finished it, she took the cup, still watching him, and finally nodded.

"All right, send him away," she said to Becky.

The man clicked his heels and saluted, still puzzled, before leaving. Adelaide fell on the rolls at once, and Becky poured out the rest of the coffee.

"We'll have to share the cup," she said.

Adelaide nodded, her mouth full. But her eyes were gleaming; she had an idea. Becky ate a roll—they were dry and stale—as patiently as she could, and waited for her turn at the coffee before saying, "Well?"

"I was just thinking. What I said before they came in—about the flag."

"All the authority comes from the flag. Yes, and all they've got to do is collar it and give it to Leopold to carry, and the whole game's over."

"Only if it's there to take," said Adelaide.

"What?"

"Suppose they woke up tomorrow morning and found it gone?"

Becky stared at her, but she was quite serious.

"You're suggesting what, exactly? That we get out of here without being seen and steal the flag from under the noses of the guards—and then what?"

"Dunno," said Adelaide. "I've only got that far. It's a good start, though, innit?"

She calmly took the last roll. Becky crossed to the window, which overlooked a narrow courtyard in which a single sentry was patrolling. On the other side of it, the building rose high against the gray sky. All the windows were barred. Apart from the sentry, nothing moved; there was no life to be seen. Becky felt desolate. As she was about to turn back, her eyes caught a movement in the air, and then another and another, and the first fat flakes of snow began to fall.

16 Wool

Nine of the students, including Karl, Anton, and Gustav, had survived the fight at the grotto, although Karl and Gustav had been slightly wounded. It had been hand-to-hand fighting; the soldiers, unwilling to shoot at them in case they shot the prince, had had to rely on fists and swords, where the students were on more equal terms. However, the fight didn't last long, for the soldiers were only interested in capturing the prince. As soon as they had torn him away from Anton, they hustled him away toward the palace, beating off the students who gave chase.

And then the main party of soldiers emerged from the tunnel, and the students, outnumbered and with no firearms, had to flee. It was then they discovered that Jim had been captured, as well, and a heavy sense of guilt and failure descended over the ragged, aching band who stumbled back to the alleys and courts of the university quarter.

They woke next morning to find the city seething with rumor and counter-rumor. Knots of people stood at every street corner discussing the situation, scanning the few newspapers, and being dispersed by police. The queen was taken ill, they heard; a closed carriage had been seen turning into the castle; troops had been moved in from the garrison at Neustadt; a demonstration by Glatz and his friends had begun noisily and been broken up almost at once; the Stock Exchange was closed; a bulletin was expected hourly from the palace on the state of the queen's health.

Karl and the others, who knew far more than most, felt electric with anxiety about what they didn't know. The one thing they could do was inquire among the watermen for any knowledge of a tributary stream joining the river, for each of them who'd been in the tunnel was haunted by the picture of Carmen Ruiz drifting away helplessly in the boat: assassin she might have been, but no one deserved to die like a rat in the dark, as they were all convinced she would. But even those inquiries came to nothing, and, miserably, the students of the Richterbund drifted back to the Café Florestan, as the city fragmented with fear and speculation around them.

By the time the afternoon light began to fade, Jim's preparations were complete. A guard had looked in twice during the day, once to bring in a tray of food and once to take it away again, and each time he had found Jim apparently slumped in apathy on the mattress. He'd eaten the half-cold, greasy goulash and dumplings to keep his strength up, and had given the impression of lethargy and hopelessness, and that was useful; and he'd watched the routine the guard went through, which was even more useful. And all the time he'd been patiently undoing the wool of his jersey.

It was strong stuff: thin and oiled and tightly knitted, and hard to see in the dismal light. When he'd finished, Jim found himself shivering for lack of its warmth, but in possession of eight balls of tough yarn. Now, how could he use them?

Whistling softly, he picked out one of the longest and toughest splinters of wood from the broken bed. It came to a sharp point, and he sat down to wind enough wool round the other end to give it a comfortable grip; and there was a dagger.

Next, he turned to the cell wall, where he had noticed one or two loose stones. Using another length of wood, he prized out a stone about the size of his head, and reached behind it to find what he was really looking for: smaller, loose rubble. He pulled out a few handfuls until he found a stone the size of a goose's egg, and roundish, and then kicked the rest of the rubble under the mattress and replaced the large stone he'd taken out first.

Next, by knotting and reknotting the damnably twisty wool he made a little net into which the stone fitted, and tied it firmly to a handle he'd made by plaiting together three strands of wool, and plaiting that length with two others: a nine-stranded cord, with a loop for his wrist, from which hung a weight heavy enough to stun a horse, if he swung it accurately. He tried it time and time again on the mattress until his muscles were familiar with the weight and the movement.

So now he had two weapons. By the time he'd finished, it was dark, and he was cold and thirsty. Presumably they didn't intend to starve him, or they wouldn't have brought him the earlier meal; so presumably they'd be in again at some stage. He considered banging the door and shouting for attention, but decided that that was more likely to bring them alert and curious, and he wanted them relaxed, expecting the apathy they'd seen before. Better wait, he thought; and, giving the mattress a shake to dislodge the insects, he tucked the dagger in his sock, lay down, curled up, and, like a cat, was peacefully asleep in a moment.

• • •

Adelaide, chewing a thumbnail, turned away from adjusting the little lamp they'd been given, and scowled.

"You made them chessmen yet?"

"Nearly."

"Well, hurry up."

Lacking anything else with which to keep Her Majesty from fretting herself into an apoplexy, Becky had suggested a game of chess. They had marked out a board in the dust on the floor, and Becky had begun to fashion some pieces from scraps of paper and twists of frail cotton from the edge of the curtains. It wasn't easy, and she'd broken a fingernail rubbing half the pawns in the fireplace soot to blacken them.

"I've run out of tassels," she said. "We need four for the kings and queens. I've only got two. Look, can't we just shoot the guard and run for it?"

"If there's any shooting, I'll do it. But not guards. He's just doing what he's told. Mind you, he's not doing what I tell him. Perhaps I *will* shoot him. Where's the bishops?"

"Bishops?"

"You ain't done any bishops. Get out the way, let me have a go."

Tucking her hair back behind her ears, Adelaide knelt in the dust and began twisting and folding. Becky wandered to the window. It was nearly dark, but down in the courtyard below a party of soldiers was coming out of a door with a lantern. She watched idly as they cleared a patch of snow by the far wall. Two of them began to dig a small square hole, and then four others brought a stout, heavy post and leaned it against the wall. Becky, with a sudden sickening knowledge, realized what she was seeing and turned away busily to distract Adelaide.

"How are you getting on?"

"I've done the bishops," said Adelaide, looking up. "You can tell who they are cause they've got little thingies on their heads. Where's that gun?" She got up and took it from Becky's carpetbag. "By God, it's heavy, innit? How many bullets in it? Six. I wish Miss Lockhart was here. She'd know what to do."

"I'm sure she would." Becky swallowed hard; she was thinking of her mother, and a picture came to mind: the shabby sitting room at home, warm and familiar, with Mama's colors laid out on the table in the lamplight and a muffin on the toasting-fork, with granny nodding in her chair, and Tom-Tom purring on the hearth...It was so vivid that she sniffed and then had to swallow hard.

"No good weeping, Becky," said Adelaide, returning the pistol to the carpetbag. "Pull yerself together. I ain't cried since...I dunno when. Oh, yes, I do. The last time I cried was in Mrs. Catlett's, in Shepherd Market."

"Was that..." Becky didn't know how to put it.

"She found me in the street, starving. She took me in and fed me and cleaned me up...I couldn't understand why, at first. I soon found out. That's when I cried, when I realized how low I'd fallen, though it was silk sheets I was lying in. There was a lot further I *could* have fallen. I was lucky it was old Bessie Catlett and not anyone else. She'd been in service, she knew all the dukes and earls and such like, she knew how to flirt, how to please...She taught us. Drilled us. And kept us clean. She had a doctor in once a month to look us over. But one girl, she was my friend, she got infected. She was out that day. Bessie Catlett never spent any money on medicine; she never wanted a girl sitting around when there was dozens, hundreds more out there in the streets. So poor Ethel was slung out. I've often wondered what happened to her. I hope she got better and found a decent bloke, but Gawd, there's bloody few of them..."

"And that was where you met Prince Rudolf?"

"Yeah. Some toff brought a party in, and Rudi didn't want to, you know, join in. So him and me sat talking. He was so nice...Well, you know the rest."

"How long were you there?"

"Two years, almost."

"And what were you doing before that?"

"I forget." She looked down abruptly. "We going to play chess, then?"

Becky knelt to face her across the board. It was only dimly visible, so she brought the little lamp down beside it on the floor.

"I'll give you a rook odds," said Adelaide. "Go on, you're white, you start."

Becky could hear a faint, regular hammering from the courtyard. Chattering inanely to cover the sound, she moved her king's pawn out two squares. Adelaide tucked her hair back and began to concentrate with a little sigh of satisfaction.

Jim awoke. There was a rattle of keys outside the door, and a dim gleam showed where the Judas window had been opened. He was awake in a moment, his right hand feeling for the stone on its thong. The door creaked open. Through narrowed eyes Jim watched the guard let the keys fall to the chain at his waist and pick up the tray of food, leaving the lantern on the floor outside.

Even better: there was only one man. There'd been two of them before. A bit of luck, at last...

Eyeing Jim warily, the guard came in and stooped to put the tray on the floor. He was too canny to turn his back, but he was too old to move fast, and when Jim suddenly rolled off the mattress and sprang up, swinging the stone, he couldn't dodge it in time.

Jim had had to steel himself to do it: he didn't like hitting people on the head. But the thought of Adelaide lent him ruthlessness, and the stone cracked into the side of the man's skull and sent him sprawling.

With a powerful tug Jim ripped the bunch of keys from the man's belt. Taking a slice of bread from the tray, he stuffed it into his pocket for later and slipped out.

The key of the cell door was easy to pick out: it was the biggest and oldest. Jim locked the man in for good measure, and then picked up the lantern and set off down the corridor, silent on his rubber-soled shoes, stone in hand.

He paused at the corner, listened, looked around. Light shone through an open doorway at the top of a flight of steps, and he tiptoed up and stopped to listen outside it.

There was nothing to hear except the occasional rustle of paper. Looking through the crack, he saw part of a man's back as he sat bent over a table, and then he moved, and Jim saw that he was turning over the page of a newspaper.

Silently he put the lantern down, put the stone in his pocket with the loop outside, and took the dagger from his sock.

Then, moving with no more sound than a ghost, he stepped through the doorway and into the little guardroom, where a stove glowed and a pot of coffee simmered. Before the man heard a thing, Jim's hand was clamped over his mouth and the sharp wooden point of the dagger was jammed hard against his throat.

"Make a noise or move a muscle and this knife'll cut you wide open," Jim whispered.

The man stiffened. He was a stout, slow-looking fellow, and the number of cigars he'd smoked would have done nothing for his wind.

"Now bend down and take off your boots. Move slowly. My dagger's going to stay at your throat, so don't you so much as twitch."

The man did as he was told.

"Now your socks," Jim said, and prodded harder to encourage him.

Off came the socks, to the guard's embarrassment; he hadn't washed his feet for some time. Jim had no time to feel sorry for him on that account, though.

And then he saw a prize: a revolver, in a holster, hung on a nail behind the door.

"Put the sock in your mouth. Yes, in your mouth, all of it. Quickly."

Reluctantly the man did so. Jim leapt for the gun and had it out before the guard could react. It was loaded, too.

"Right," he said. "Take that sock out so you can speak, and if you even take enough breath to shout there'll be a bullet in your heart before the first word comes out. Now tell me: what is this place?"

"The castle," said the man in a shaky voice.

"Where is the queen?"

The guard opened his mouth and shut it again, but he'd glanced involuntarily upward.

"Upstairs," said Jim. "I see. Where?"

The guard clamped his mouth shut.

"Put the sock in," said Jim.

His ferocity must have scorched, because the guard did it at once. Then Jim kicked him on the shin as hard as he could, and a sudden muffled grunt broke from the man's throat.

"That hurt? Well, next time I'll break one of your fingers, and that *will* hurt. Take the sock out again and tell me where she is."

His eyes watering, the guard dragged the sopping lump of wool out of his mouth and mumbled, "There's a staircase just along the corridor. It's up on the fourth floor. The old governor's apartments. Big double door."

"And what's the quickest way out?"

"Other end of that same landing—door to the servants' staircase. Out through the kitchens. Please—"

"Put it back. Hurry up or I'll make you swallow it."

With his fat face wreathed in misery, the guard shoved the sock back. It bulged over his lips disgustingly.

"Now stand up and turn around."

Moving as slowly as he dared, the man did so, and Jim rapidly wound some wool from one of the balls in his pocket around the man's head, holding the gag in place.

"Put your hands behind you."

He bound the man's thumbs together before lashing them as securely as he could to a stout iron pipe set in the wall. The wool was as strong as whipcord; he wouldn't break loose.

With a quick glance around to see that there was nothing for the guard to kick over and make a noise with, Jim blew him a kiss, took the lantern and the pistol, and left.

"Check," said Adelaide. "You ain't paying attention."

"I can hardly see. What's that? A bishop? That was a pawn a minute ago! And one of mine, at that!"

"Suit yourself," said Adelaide, putting it back and moving another piece instead. "Checkmate. I was just spinning it out. D'you want another game?"

Becky got up, stretched, yawned, shivered. She had no idea what the time was; she was cold, hungry, tired, and frightened, and, she thought, Adelaide was much more use to her than she was to Adelaide. It was time to earn her salary, if only she had the remotest idea how.

She looked at the lamp, to see if the wick needed turning up; it was beginning to flicker. Perhaps the oil was running low.

She had just bent to look, and Adelaide had begun to gather

up the scraps of paper and cotton they'd been playing with, when both of them heard the same sound: a scratching, scraping, clicking noise from the door. Adelaide stood up, smoothing her skirt.

Then the lock opened as if with a key, and the handle turned.

"Jim!" cried Becky, and at once he raised his finger to his lips.

He was unshaven, filthy, and bruised; there was a cut on his forehead; his hair was tangled. He carried a pistol in one hand and a lantern in the other, and there was a hardness, a grim determination of purpose about him that she'd never seen so clearly in anyone. It made him formidable.

And Becky was conscious of something else, and turned quickly to Adelaide to verify it. A charge of some kind, like an electric spark, seemed to pass between Adelaide and Jim. It was physical, like an animal smell; the two of them were looking at each other with such intensity that Becky felt they'd forgotten her and the castle altogether. But then Jim blinked, and, to her surprise, bowed.

"Your Majesty," he said quietly. "Put your cloaks on, if you've got 'em. Then follow me, and don't make a sound. Becky—you got that pistol? Good. Don't fire it unless I tell you. The main thing is quiet—we'll talk later."

They threw their cloaks around them in a moment. Becky took the carpetbag and they followed Jim on tiptoe out of the room that had been their prison into the wider castle that still was.

About two minutes later, the captain sent a man down to the guardroom to order them to bring Jim out. When the messenger saw the stout soldier barefoot, struggling at the wall and apparently in the act of eating a sock, he laughed; but the grunting, snorting noises, the anguished heaving of the pinioned arms, and the rolling eyes soon stopped the laughter.

"Where's he gone?" was the first question.

"Upstairs—to her room—the queen—and then out through the kitchens—wait! What's he done to Trautmann? He never come back from taking his food—"

"*You* go and see! Damn fine guard you are—I don't fancy being in your shoes when the captain finds out—" The newcomer stumbled over some empty boots on his way out, and flung them at the guard with a curse. "So you better put 'em on yourself."

And he ran off to raise the alarm.

Endless corridors, endless staircases; archways, vaults, blind doorways, windows barred with iron; and at one point a hall whose dusty wooden floor was big enough, Jim thought, to play a decent game of cricket on. Vast columns of stone rose to the distant ceiling, carved like entwining plant stems. Immense windows thick with grime—some of their panes broken many years before—overlooked the snowbound city, and all three of them stopped to gasp at the icy beauty, and then caught their breath again as they saw a line of silent watchers along the opposite wall behind them.

Jim's finger tightened on the trigger—and then he caught the dull gleam of armor.

But which was the way out?

He'd lost them in this abominable maze.

"Hey, Jim?" whispered Adelaide.

"What?"

"Remember the Animal Charcoal Works? When we were running away from Mrs. Holland?"

"I'll never forget it."

"Nor will I. I was just thinking—at least this is clean."

"Same result if they catch us. Let's try that door over there..."

A high archway led to a wide, shallow, stone-flagged staircase leading down. They moved along it silently, three ghosts, only the faint glimmer of the lantern—which Jim kept masked as much as possible—to give them away.

"Here—what's this?" he said, stopped by a window.

It overlooked a garden, or the ruins of one; bare trees and shrubs held up their arms of snow, and a leaden statue or two, a silent fountain-basin sheathed in ice, and a broken pergola gave off an air of deserted melancholy.

But more to the point, the window was only ten feet or so above the ground, and beyond the garden wall was the open street, where dim lights glowed behind the shutters of the old houses.

"Hold the gun," he said to Adelaide, and took the wooden dagger out of his sock.

It took no more than a few seconds and a creak of rust to prize open the catch. The air they breathed in was fresh and welcome.

"What are we going to do? Not *jump?*" said Becky.

"It's only ten feet, and snow to land on. You first, then the queen, and I'll come last. When you land, keep your knees bent and roll over. Then you won't twist an ankle. When you've got up I'll drop the bag to you. Go on, don't think about it, jump."

Encumbered by her thick skirt and cloak, Becky struggled to get through, and fell more suddenly than she expected to. She hit the ground with a thump that shook a loud gasp out of her, and fell on her face in the snow, but got up unhurt as soon as she'd recovered her breath.

Jim dropped the bag to her, and then helped Adelaide out—far more considerately than he'd done with her, she thought.

Adelaide fell lightly, almost like a bird landing, and rolled over as Jim had told her, to get up in a moment. Jim was fiddling with the handle of the window; Becky couldn't see what he was doing, but when he'd jumped, he looked around in the snow and picked up a ball of dark wool that was attached to something above. Rolling it up, he tugged carefully, and the window seemed to pull itself shut. He snapped the wool and put the ball in his pocket.

"We can't hide our prints in the snow," he said, "but there's no need to draw attention to them with an open window. Come round to that door—and keep in the shadow of the wall—that's it."

Retrieving the lantern, he led the way along the edge of the garden.

"Stay behind this bush. Don't come out till I've got the door open."

When he looked at the padlock, he saw at once that there was nothing to be done with it; the thing was fused into a mass of rust. He took the dagger, inserted it through the staple, and twisted hard. Sure enough, the flimsy hoop snapped at once, and there was the door, open, with the street beyond it.

Adelaide and Becky waded through the powdery snow and joined him, and then they were through the door and hurrying away down the narrow street.

"Any idea where we are?" said Jim.

"I think if we follow this down we'll get to the river..." said Becky doubtfully.

"There's the Rock!" said Adelaide.

They stopped to look. Between the tall buildings, and some way off, the white-crowned Rock gleamed under the black sky.

"Right, we'll navigate by that," said Jim. "We'll make for the Café Florestan. Come on, step out lively, and keep your hoods up."

• • •

Fifteen minutes later, Becky and Adelaide stood in the shadow of a doorway. Jim bent and took a handful of snow to clean his face with, and when he was reasonably free of dust, he pushed open the door of the Café Florestan and entered the steamy, beer-flavored warmth.

The place was full, and there was an air of tension about the customers; a lot of talk but no laughter; frowns and drawn faces. One or two looked up curiously as Jim threaded his way through the tables and toward the corner where the students sat, and put his hand on Karl's shoulder.

Karl leapt.

"Jim! Thank God! Come and sit—"

"Not yet. Hello, gentlemen. Karl, come outside a minute."

Karl followed him out at once.

"What happened?" he said urgently, in an undertone. "You know the queen's missing? There are all kinds of rumors. They say Gödel's going to have her shot...Who's this?"

Adelaide pushed back her hood and moved forward six inches so that the light from the gas lamp over the café door fell on her face.

Karl gasped and bowed his head, but Jim caught his arm and said, "Not here. Listen, we need to go indoors. Is the back room safe? We've just escaped from the castle. We need food, drink, warmth, in that order, but we can't just go in and sit down."

Karl nodded. "Give me a minute. I'll get Matyas to open the back door—it's that one down the alley there."

He went back inside; and two minutes later, the door in the alley opened, and a minute after that, Karl showed the three of them into a small room where a porcelain stove glowed with heat, a lamp on the table shone warmly over the clean checked tablecloth, and a tabby cat purred on a rocking chair.

Karl pushed the cat off, and Adelaide sat down gratefully.

"I've told Matyas, the landlord. He'll keep quiet. He's bringing some soup and a bottle of wine. May I take your cloak, Your Majesty?"

There was a soft knock. Karl opened the door, and in came the landlord with an immense tray, which he put down before bowing to Adelaide. He was a stout, blue-eyed man of fifty or so, and as wonderstruck as a child at Christmas to see the queen in his own parlor.

"Ma'am—Your Majesty—I hope you'll forgive these rough arrangements—if there's anything else you'd like, just let me know and you'll have it at once. You're safe here, Your Majesty, as safe as in your own palace."

"I hope I shall be safer than that," said Adelaide in her best German. "But I am sure I have never felt more welcome. Thank you."

The landlord bowed again and left. He'd brought soup and bread and wine, and as the three of them ate, Karl found some glasses and opened the bottle.

"By God," said Jim, "that was the best soup I've ever had. I could eat a gallon. When did you two last eat?"

"This morning," said Becky. "Jim, they tried to poison her! The *queen!*"

She told them everything, and Jim exchanged grim glances with Karl. Karl told them of the fight at the grotto, and of the students who died. Jim looked murderous.

"There's the woman too," he said. "We shouldn't have let her drift off into the dark like that."

"No one could have stopped her," Karl said. "We've been over and over it. We've asked the watermen to watch out for her in case the stream reaches the river, but—"

Karl broke off, because there was a knock at the door. He got to his feet, and so did Jim, who raised the pistol. Karl opened the door, and a student came in, breathless, and bowed hastily when he saw Adelaide.

"I beg your pardon," he said, his voice shaking. "I've just come from the Tristan-Brücke Station. They're blocking it off—no one's allowed in—and a number of trains are coming in from the north. I managed to hide and see what was happening—German troops are getting off, hundreds of them, with guns. As soon as I could I got out and ran here—but Your Majesty—what's happening?"

"Thanks, Andreas," said Karl. "Well done." But he looked bemused, as if it were too much to take in. He turned to Jim and said, "Well, what do we do *now?*"

"Listen," said Adelaide. "How many of your friends are there in the café now?"

"About a dozen."

"Are they armed?"

"Most of them, yes. They'll fight whether they're armed or not."

"I'm sure of that, Herr von Gaisberg," she said. "But I'll need their help, because I've got a plan. I thought of it in the castle, to stop Baron Gödel, but it's even more important now. I mean the flag, of course."

Jim looked at her with sudden understanding. She saw his grin, and went on:

"While the eagle's in my hands, Razkavia's free. I want to do what Walter von Eschten did back in 1253. We can't defend the Rock like Walter did, not against howitzers and Gatling guns. But we can take the flag to Wendelstein, and rally the people there. So that's what I want to do. Will you help?"

Karl stood, on fire with excitement, and nodded vigorously. "I'll go and get the others!" he said, and left.

Jim was looking at Adelaide with true admiration. Dirty and untidy as she was, she looked more beautiful than any girl he'd ever known, and yet still the same frail little ghost of a thing he'd first seen all those years before when she'd slipped into the offices of Jim's employers looking for Sally. The determination that had taken her there, when she was so nervous she could hardly raise her voice above a whisper, was sustaining her now; but now she was the embodiment of a nation, proud and angry and beautiful. She smiled at him, and he knew the smile meant *I trust you, Jim. We can do it.* He smiled back.

Then one by one they came into the crowded little back parlor of the Café Florestan, the students of the Richterbund, and knelt to Adelaide their queen and kissed her hand as a commission. They stood around the table and peered over each other's shoulders and tried not to dislodge the ornaments from the sideboard with clumsy elbows as they all listened to her.

She spoke swiftly through Becky, telling them that they were going to rescue their country's flag, the most sacred emblem of the nation, from falling into enemy hands. Any one of them who did not want to take part could stand down now and leave with his honor unstained; those who stayed might well not live to see the next day dawning. Not one of them moved, and when she saw it she had to blink rapidly and turn away. Then she said in German, "Thank you, gentlemen. I expected courage, but you have given me hope as well. Please sit down while we discuss the best way of carrying out the plan."

She sat herself, and awkwardly they perched on the arms of chairs or sat cross-legged on the floor.

"We must work out what to do in detail," she said. "So if anyone knows anything about the Rock or the funicular railway or anything that might help, speak up, for God's sake. Oh, and if anything happens to me...if anything happens to me, the flag is to go to Herr von Gaisberg. He's the *Adlerträger* next."

There was a tremor of understanding and approval. Karl looked as if he were about to say something, but held his tongue. His cheeks were blazing.

Jim said, "Right, gentlemen. Speak up. The more we get right now, the less there'll be to go wrong later. Who's first?"

17
The Funicular Railway

All through the city, rumor was spreading like fire along a thousand fuses. In café, *Bierkeller, Weinstube,* in private parlor and kitchen, in hotel lobby and opera house foyer, on street corners and squares, voices spoke and ears listened:

"Ten thousand German troops—"

"Guns on railway carriages!"

"The queen's run away with a lover—"

"Count Thalgau's dead! He's shot himself!"

"No he hasn't—he's under arrest!"

"Have you heard about the treaty? It was going to give our sovereignty away! No wonder they didn't want it made public!"

"They shouldn't have shot her like that—"

"*Shot* her? The queen's been shot?"

"In the castle. I saw the squad going in. They had to draw lots, and even so half the men refused to obey orders!"

"You'll never believe this—Prince Leopold's alive! My cousin, he's a footman in the palace, and he says Leopold had a terrible disfiguring disease, but he's come out of hiding to save his country at the last hour!"

"Have you heard—"

And so on.

The streets were busy, but patchily: some places deserted, others thronged. A big crowd was collecting outside the station, for example, from which the German troops had not yet emerged, though sounds of heavy equipment being moved came from inside. Another crowd, less concentrated but angrier, was beginning to move toward the palace, and (in the way of crowds) tilting in mood from one passion to another as the cry "We want the queen! We want the queen!" was taken up. Individuals who'd had no idea what they wanted ten minutes before were now infused with the desire to see Adelaide and defend her against—well, against what no one knew; but they were passionate to defend her against something.

In the palace, Baron Gödel was trying to retain command of the situation, without knowing from minute to minute what the situation was. The German invasion had taken him horribly by surprise: he wasn't expecting them to march in, but to support him from a distance when he restored Leopold to the throne. This wasn't the plan at all. Seeking someone to blame, he had burst into the private apartments of Count and Countess Thalgau. The countess tried to hold him back, but he forced his way into the count's bedroom, to find the old man lying down, his face drawn in pain, his eyes shadowed, the fierce mustache like wisps of straw. Even Gödel was taken aback by the change in the old warrior.

"What was your agreement with Berlin?" he demanded. "I insist that you tell me at once."

The count looked at him briefly and then closed his eyes.

"Where is the queen?" he said hoarsely.

"Damn you, Thalgau! Answer my question! What did you agree with Bismarck?"

The count sighed. It was a deep, groaning sigh that seemed to rake out his entire soul.

"I had no agreement with Bismarck. My agreement was with his banker. I was to let him know the substance of the treaty twenty-four hours in advance, that was all. In return...sum of money. I regret it bitterly. I didn't know...ought to shoot myself...But what you've done, Gödel...Prince Leopold...thousand times worse...*Where is the queen? What have you done with her?*"

As he said that, he raised himself up by sheer willpower and confronted Gödel like a specter, blanched with the pallor of the grave. Gödel took a step backward.

But before he could reply, an aide ran in, saluted clumsily, and thrust a piece of paper at the Chamberlain, who took it with trembling fingers.

"General von Hochberg to Baron von Gödel..." he read. "Who is this General von Hochberg?"

"The officer commanding the German forces," the aide stammered. "This message came by hand from the Tristan-Brücke Station a minute ago."

The Chamberlain read:

"I understand that the instrument by which legal authority is transferred is the flag that flies on the Rock. Please arrange to have it conveyed to my carriage at Tristan-Brücke Station within the hour. Failing that, my troops will remove it by force."

Gödel tottered. The paper fell from his hand, and he clutched the arm of the young aide.

Then he pulled himself upright again. Ignoring the count and countess, he ran for the door, the aide following after.

Halfway down the corridor, the Chamberlain stopped suddenly. He was a subtle, cautious, fearful man, not used to act-ing on impulse, and when he had to, he felt unsure of his ground. He beckoned the young man.

"They want the flag," he said. "They want me to give them the flag. But if I have it—if it's in my hands..."

His eyes prompted a response from the aide.

"You needn't give it to them at all?" he said.

"Quite. Now, listen carefully. I want a carriage at the West Door at once to take me to the Rock. Then tell the nurse to wake Prince Leopold and have him dressed. The moment he's ready, have him taken in a closed carriage to the Botanical Gardens Station. Got that?"

The aide repeated it. Gödel continued:

"Finally, go to Tristan-Brücke Station and arrange for a locomotive to be attached to the royal train so as to take it to the Botanical Gardens, and then on to Prague. And for God's sake don't let the Germans see what you're up to."

"Locomotive—royal train—Botanical Gardens—Prague," said the aide dutifully, and hurried away.

Baron Gödel mopped his brow, and hastened to his own apartments to pack a bag.

Behind him, the countess picked up the paper he'd dropped and read it aloud to her husband.

He listened somberly, and then said, "Minna, has that soldier gone from our door? Are we still under arrest?"

She looked. "No one there," she said.

"Where are my field glasses?"

Perhaps it was all too much for him, she thought. She had prudently removed the bullets from his revolver earlier in the day, when his despair and self-loathing had been at their peak, but he couldn't harm himself with field glasses. She brought him the leather case and sat down wearily.

• • •

Through the dark streets, Adelaide and the little band of students moved toward the Rock. Most of the disturbance was elsewhere: distant shouts, the breaking of windows, the occasional crack that might have been a gunshot. The party kept to the shadows, slipping through the snow-filled lanes and alleys in silence.

When they reached the foot of the Rock, each person went to a different spot. One student went off to the Tristan-Brücke Station, to report on what was happening there; another went to find a carriage and horses. Karl, with four others, set off around the riverside to climb the path up which Adelaide had carried the flag on the day of the coronation. The risk here was that they would be clearly visible, because the whole of that side of the Rock was open to the river and to the bridge. The rest of them, with Jim, Becky, and Adelaide, made for the funicular station.

They weren't going to use the train: that would be even more conspicuous than walking up the path. Besides, it would mean involving the stationmaster, and they didn't want to risk it. However, the train ran on rails laid on horizontal ties of wood that ran up the side of the Rock like a staircase, and against the dark track the climbers would be less conspicuous.

When they reached the little station they found the stationmaster's house, which doubled as a ticket office and waiting room, dark and quiet. One of the carriages rested at the platform, at the end of the long cable that joined it to the other carriage waiting at the summit.

Becky was to remain at the bottom, hiding among the bushes next to the track. "Here," Jim said, and handed her a ball of wool.

"What's it for?"

"Signaling. You hold on to the end and jerk hard if there's

any danger. Fritz here is going to unwind it as we go up."

She tied the end of the tight dark wool around her forefinger to make sure she didn't drop it. Then Adelaide, tucking up her cloak, climbed over the wooden fence and onto the steeply sloping track above the carriage. There was only one carriage-way, shared by both the ascending and descending carriages. Where they met halfway up, the track split into two, the carriages each swerving neatly out of the way of the other.

"Good luck!" Becky said softly. *"Viel Glück!"*

She settled down on a discarded beam of wood in the shadow of the bushes. Level with her eyes were the wheels of the carriage, seeming to lean upward on its angled track, and across the buffers the station lay silent, with its shutters closed and the snowy roof gleaming faintly under the dark sky. A little stream ran past her feet, and she dipped her hand into it and brought up the icy water to her lips, thinking, *Walter von Eschten drank from this spring when he was fighting here...*

The end of wool in her hand twitched and tugged gently as the others climbed.

Halfway up the track, the ball of wool ran out. Fritz called softly, and Jim handed him another. Fritz tied the ends together.

Snow lay thickly on the wooden ties they were treading on. They were high above the nearby roofs, and Jim was anxious in case they could be seen. From this side of the Rock the main streets and squares, the cathedral and the bridge and the palace were out of sight, but the iron-and-glass roof of the Tristan-Brücke Station was glowing dimly a little way off, and Jim thought he could see a bustle of movement in front of it. Under the darkness of the bushes behind them he could hear the running of a stream, and realized it came from the spring that fed the tank of the carriage at the top.

"How does the railway work?" he said quietly to the student beside him as they climbed on.

"The tank in the carriage at the top fills up with water, and then it's heavier than the one at the bottom, so it goes down and pulls the other one up. The driver controls the speed with a brake. While the passengers are getting in and out they fill the tank at the top, and empty the one at the bottom. Simple."

"And do they keep the one at the top filled and ready to go?"

"That I don't know. You're not thinking of coming down in it?"

"Just curious."

They said nothing more till they were nearly at the little station on the top of the Rock. The carriage above them looked as if it would hurtle downward at any moment and crush them, and Jim was glad to step off the track and climb up onto the station platform. Like the carriage, this was built in two sections at different levels. Fritz crouched at the lower end, wool in hand, while Jim and Adelaide and the others crept up the steps toward the upper platform.

This was on the same level as the summit of the Rock itself, the little flat space where Adelaide had been crowned. At the center of it stood the flagpole, with the flag hanging stiff and still. The only other structure on the summit was a sentry box.

The flag guard consisted of two soldiers, who kept guard in watches of four hours, night and day. For much of the time their job was to stand at attention and look ceremonial, but when it was cold the guardsmen would march briskly to and fro to keep warm.

A little wicket gate separated the station platform from the summit. Keeping under the shadow of the platform roof, Jim crept along until he was nearly at the gate. The sentries had trodden a path into the snow in a square around the flagpole; he could hear the regular stamp of their boots, but for the moment they were out of sight, hidden by the wall of the station building.

Behind Jim came Adelaide and the others. Each of the students held a pistol.

Suddenly there came a harsh command, very loud in the still air:

"Halt! Who goes there?"

They still weren't visible, so the sentry must have been challenging the party from the other side. Before Jim could react, Adelaide stepped quickly to the gate and said clearly, *"Die Königin,"* the queen.

Jim was at her side in a moment. The sentries had swung round in confusion, and their rifles pointed now at Karl, coming onto the summit, and now at Adelaide, who was opening the gate.

"Put that rifle down!" Karl said. "Can't you see who this is?"

Both men now gazed openmouthed as Adelaide lowered the hood of her cloak and stepped forward. A student held up a lantern so that the soldiers could see her face. One looked at the other, doubtfully, but his companion was already presenting arms, tense with astonishment. Finally the first man gathered his wits and did the same.

"I wish Becky was here," Adelaide muttered. "Jim, tell 'em it's my command to take the flag down. Because the country's being invaded, and—and we're going to take it to Wendelstein, and if they want to save the country they can come and join us."

Jim translated, with Karl's help. The two sentries looked at each other, doubt clear on their faces.

"But, Your Majesty—the *Adlerfahne* is here throughout the life of the monarch! We're here to keep it flying, not to take it down!"

Adelaide nodded briskly and said, "I know. And you're good guards, the pair of you. But that's why I've come here, see. I'm going to carry the flag myself. If we don't take it away—"

She broke off, because from the direction of the railway station there came a volley of shots and then the deeper boom of an artillery piece. Everyone's head turned at once. Jim quickly translated her words, and added:

"That's the Germans you can hear. A traitor in the palace tried to put the queen under arrest and invited them to invade the country. They were going to shoot Her Majesty, but we escaped in time. Now will you do as she commands and take the flag down?"

One of the men looked up at the flag almost in anguish.

"We're here to guard the flag!" he said. "It's more important than any king or queen! It's been here for five hundred years, and all that time...All that time there's been men like me guarding it, and...I *can't*, Your Majesty! Even if that is the Germans down there, we've got to keep the flag flying on the Rock!"

Adelaide understood enough of that to know what she must say in reply.

"You're right," she said. "And if Walter von Eschten was alive he'd be proud of you as I am. But he never had to face guns like those down there—"

For another gun had boomed. They could hear shouts as well now, and smoke was rising near the station.

"If the flag stays here," Adelaide went on in an urgent mixture of German and English, "the country will last about an hour. If they come up here now, I'll stand side by side with you and fight to keep it flying. But if we take it away they'll never be able to say they've conquered, because they won't have the flag! And think—think what Walter von Eschten did all those years ago. *He* took the flag down. He took it to Wendelstein, remember? To the castle there. And he fought the Bohemians and beat them. So that's what *we'll* do. We'll take the flag to Wendelstein. Everyone in the whole country will know what that means, and they'll come and join us and beat the Germans. See? Join us! Come with me to Wendelstein and save the flag!"

There was a pause of several seconds. No one moved; the doubtful soldier was enduring a wrestling match between his discipline and his imagination, and finally, after nearly half a minute, his imagination won.

He slammed the butt of his rifle down beside him and saluted.

"Private Schweigner," he said. "At your command, ma'am."

"Corporal Kogler," said the other. "We're with you, Your Majesty."

She couldn't restrain a little clap of delight.

"Bully for you!" she said. "Take the flag down quick, then..."

They turned swiftly to the flagpole. As they did, Jim heard a soft whistle from the platform behind, and ran to the gate.

"She's tugging the wool!" Fritz called up in a clear whisper. "Something's happening below!"

Jim leapt down to the next level, at the edge of which Fritz was crouching, and the two of them peered down the slope. The dark track, shadowed by bushes, led down as straight as an arrow to the station at the foot, with the passing loop the only deviation.

"There's someone on the platform," whispered Fritz. "Two of them—more—they're getting in the carriage! They're going to come up!"

From under the carriage beside them, Jim and Fritz heard a

clanking sound, and the carriage jolted very slightly against the brakes clamped to the rails. Then came the sound of water gushing into a tank.

"Open the carriage doors," said Jim, "and quick."

He ran to the steps, scrambled up to the higher platform, and found Karl and two others already opening the wicket gate, having heard the sound of the filling water tank.

"Quick!" said Jim. "We'll ride down in this as they ride up—it's controlled from below—"

Behind Karl, the two soldiers were reverently unfastening the flag from the halyard. Adelaide was helping them, folding it like a sheet fresh from the laundry, and finding it hard to do; the cloth was stiffly brocaded with frost.

"Hurry up!" Jim called softly. "There's danger! Move! Bring it onto the platform!"

Adelaide was just folding the last corner over to make a tidy bundle. No one wanted to move until she did; the soldiers had picked up their rifles again, the students were standing aside to make room...

Another loud clank sounded from the carriage as the increasing weight settled it further down against the brakes.

Adelaide set off. Jim, impatient, put his arm around her and almost lifted her through the gate. Karl held it open, and when she was through, the rest followed, some leaping over the fence. All four carriage doors were wide open, and they scrambled inside just as the carriage jerked forward.

"Shut the doors quietly and keep down!" Karl said. "Lie on the floor and keep out of sight!"

Becky, shivering with anxiety, crouched under a snow-laden bush and watched as the men—three of them, the Baron von

Gödel, a young aide in a top hat, and an officer with a sword and plumed helmet—got into the carriage followed by the grumbling stationmaster, hastily buttoning his tunic.

She pulled the wool off her finger distractedly; it had served its purpose. She knew Fritz had felt her tug because he'd responded, but she could see nothing of what was happening at the summit.

The stationmaster, having checked the tension on the cable, swung the brake lever forward, and the carriage moved upward with a jerk. It moved more smoothly during the day, when he was fully awake, when frost hadn't bound the wheels. Still, it was moving upward, and Becky came out of the bushes, brushed herself down, and scrambled across the track to climb up on the platform and get a better view.

She was in time to see the graceful way the lower carriage swung to the left, making room for the descending one to pass it on the right and then swing back onto the main track. Thinking that the carriage coming down would be empty, she didn't pay it any attention; all her anxiety was focused on the summit. So when the carriage bumped to a halt in a squeal of brakes, she was still gazing upward, and she nearly fell over with shock when all four doors opened and a dozen dark figures got out beside her.

"What—oh my God! Jim, is that you?"

"Yeah. And we've got to get away *quick.* They'll be staring at the flagpole right now, and—"

"The beam!"

"What beam?"

"Lay it across the track and—"

She leapt down and scrambled across to the bushes. Karl and another student followed, saw what she was doing, and bent to help. As they did, they heard water cascade out of the carriage tank and into a culvert somewhere below the track. They tugged and hauled at the beam Becky had sat on, and heaved it out from the bushes and onto the rails.

"Jam it under the wheels—" Becky said, desperate, ignoring the scratches and grazes she was collecting.

Two more students joined them, and the log fell awkwardly in front of the wheels just as the cable snapped tight and the carriage jolted forward.

"Watch out!" cried Karl, and pulled Becky out of the way just in time. The carriage was lurching upward, dragging the log with it.

The other two tipped up the beam with a last effort, and it fell between the ties and jammed tight. The carriage stopped with a jerk that made the cable twang like a harp string.

"Back here, quick," Jim called softly, and they scrambled back across the rails to be helped up to the platform by several hands.

"Listen," Jim went on, "Willi and Michael are back. There's no carriage or horses anywhere, but in one of the sidings they've been making the royal train ready. I reckon someone's going to do a bunk, but if we get there quick enough, we can commandeer it. We'll split up now and go in separate parties: me and Private Schweigner with Becky and the queen; Corporal Kogler with Karl and his group; the rest on your own. Make for the station. Meet under the statue of whoever it is—those naked women—you know the one. It'll be crowded—we'll have to pretend we don't know each other and talk in whispers. But I've got a plan. Now split up and go! Run!"

The others scattered. Jim helped Adelaide down the slippery steps to the street, and then, holding the heavy bundle in her arms as if it were a child, she set off quietly with the others to walk to the station. Jim was scribbling something in his notebook as he walked.

From the windows of Count and Countess Thalgau's private apartments, it was possible to see across the roofs of the city to the summit of the Rock. The old man put down his field glasses and straightened up.

"Minna!" he called. "My uniform. Set it out, please, my dear."

The countess sat up. She had been dozing fearfully on the sofa.

"But what are you going to do?"

"I'm going to wash and shave and get dressed. Then I'm going to the stables to find a horse."

"You're not well!"

"I'm better than I've ever felt in my life," he said.

His color was dark, his eyes bloodshot; a tremor shook his left hand, and his foot dragged a little on the carpet. But as he stood in front of her, his chin high, his shoulders thrown back, she knew what he was going to do, and knew it was the right thing, after all. Her eyes seemed to be failing; she couldn't see him clearly; she couldn't see the traitor. All she saw was the proud young soldier she had loved for forty years, still there inside him.

She hastened to find his best uniform, the tight dark green trousers with the glossy stripe, the jacket with its gold buttons and braid, the black shako with the red plume. Then his riding boots and cloak; and then the sword-belt, with the long curved cavalry saber. She helped him dress. That left hand was bad; he couldn't manage the buttons, but in order to prevent his embarrassment, she did them for him and didn't speak about it.

"My little girl," he said gruffly, and touched her cheek.

He took out the leather holster containing his revolver, and she clipped it to his belt, reloaded; and finally he swung the dark cloak around him, and flung it over his left shoulder.

He faced her. It wasn't easy for either of them to speak. However, the simple intimacies of dressing, buttoning, brushing, the simple openness of standing up straight with one's chin high, the simple tenderness of a familiar hand on one's cheek—these things go deeper than shame.

He kissed her gray head and marched out.

The German general had given Gödel an hour to bring him the flag, and he was a man of his word. When after sixty minutes were up no one had come back with it, he called for his horse.

Leaving the crowded, jostling, shouting confusion of the station to the capable hands of his second in command, the general and his aide-de-camp left by a side exit. The young officer consulted a plan of the city, and pointed, and the general turned his horse's head toward the Rock.

"D'you know, Neumann," he said, as they made their way through the excited streets, "I think there's something else going on. I shouldn't be surprised if that man Gödel had planned a little coup of his own. All the better."

"Why, sir?"

"Politics, dear boy. If there really is something to rescue them from, and we do it, we smell of roses. Is that the Rock? Railway carriage at the top? Men waving lights?"

They peered up through a gap in the houses. The general courteously made his horse step back out of the way of a young couple: a slender girl in cloak and hood with, it appeared, a child in her arms, and a young man in a pea jacket who put a protective arm around her as they hurried past.

"Something seems to be wrong," said the young officer. "On the summit. Look, I think the railway's broken down or something."

The general had seen it too. He shook the reins, and the horse's hooves clattered loudly as they cantered toward the funicular railway station.

It was at about that time that an elderly pair of brothers from Marienbad, river thieves who specialized in breaking into waterfront buildings and carrying the stolen goods away in a skiff, found their oars snagged by a corpse.

There was money in corpses, if they got them to the School of Anatomy before they fell apart, so it was worth abandoning the promising-looking tobacco warehouse and hauling this one over the stern.

She was a fine-looking corpse, too: dark hair, red lips, full figure. It was natural to be disappointed when she began to revive and cough up water, and they were tempted to knock her on the head and make a proper corpse of her, but they were a sentimental pair, these Bohemians. While Miroslav rowed them back to the crumbling ruin they inhabited in the Old Town, Josef patiently rubbed her hands, helped her sit up, held a flask of plum brandy to her lips. Presently she was breathing properly, and then her eyelids fluttered open.

"I think she's going to be all right, Slava!" said Josef. "Yes, my dear, save your breath, we'll have you dry and snug in a few minutes. Aren't you lucky we were just going for a little boat ride, eh? Nearly home. You'll be all right now..."

The statue Jim had referred to was an allegorical figure of Peace, receiving tributes from Commerce and Art, cast in bronze and set on a marble plinth. It had no obvious connection with the railway company, but the three stout and cheerful nudes were a favorite meeting place, and now, with the crowd beginning to taunt the German troops who were drawn up outside the station entrance, Peace, Commerce, and Art were more popular than ever. Several youths had climbed up the monument, and one sat astride the comfortable shoulders of Peace, shaking his fists and yelling obscenities at the invaders.

So it wasn't hard for Jim and the others to confer unobserved among the jostle. He spoke to Anton first.

"Anton, you stay in the city. Take these notes—very rough—use them as the basis of a leaflet. Set it up in type and print as many as you've got paper for, and stick them up, shove them through doorways, get them all over the city. The essential thing is that people know what's happened: the queen was arrested on Gödel's orders, and was about to be executed, but she escaped; she's got the flag safe; like Walter von Eschten, she's taking it to Wendelstein. The flag is free—that's the message. Let no one think she gave in or betrayed the country herself. Do that straightaway."

Anton nodded, bowed swiftly and inconspicuously to Adelaide, and vanished. Jim nodded to Karl, who said:

"Now we must get to the sidings on the right of the station, beyond the hotel over there. Make for the signal box. Michael says the royal train's drawn up in front of it, with steam up in the locomotive. Obviously Gödel was going to run, but we'll beat him, as long as we get there quickly. Willi's uncle is an engine driver; Willi knows how to work it, and Private Schweigner does too—they'll go to the locomotive and take it over. The main thing is to get the queen aboard. As soon as she's on, we'll leave, never mind who else hasn't made it. So split up now, find your own way in, and the best of luck."

It took five minutes to force their way through the crowds around the hotel and slip down the side street beyond, twenty seconds to break into the empty baggage hall, and thirty to break out the other side into the station. Then they found themselves on a dirty little platform under a great water tower, and no more than a hundred yards away, in front of the dark signal box, there were the two maroon carriages of the royal train. Steam drifted from the stack of the little tank-locomotive, and as they watched, the shadowy figures of Willi and Private Schweigner, swathed in his overcoat, leapt up inside the cab.

"Right, move," said Jim, and they darted down the slope at the end of the platform and across the rough ground toward the train.

The student Michael was waiting beside the open carriage door. He said quietly, "We'll stay here and block the other trains as long as we can. The switches are set to put you on the Andersbad line, and you'll be clear as far as that. Good luck!"

Hands reached down to pull them aboard, and Michael waved to the engine. A hand waved back, and with a jolt, the train began to move. They'd got away.

18 Wolf-light

Shouts from behind, the crack of rifles—but the train was gathering speed, and then they passed out of the siding and onto the main line. Two figures, dark against the snow, waved briefly and then hastened to throw the switch behind them. Jim relaxed and looked around.

They were in the rear of the two carriages. He couldn't see much of it, though, because the only light came from outside until Karl struck a match and turned up the gas in one of the lamps. As the burner took the flame and flared and settled, the interior came softly into view: an open, comfortable sitting room or saloon, with plush seats, a carpeted floor, and mahogany paneling.

Adelaide was laying the flag carefully on one of the tables. When it was neatly folded, she looked up.

"Herr von Gaisberg," she said, "would you ask everyone to come and see me in here, please?"

Then she saw Becky, white-faced with exhaustion, holding on to the back of a seat.

"Sit down," she said, sitting herself. "You can have a snooze in a minute, but I want to talk to everyone first."

Karl came back, bringing with him five other students and Corporal Kogler. She asked them all to sit down, and they did, the corporal most uncomfortably, holding his rifle upright by his side.

With Becky translating, Adelaide spoke to them.

"Well done, all of you. You can see how close we came to losing the flag; it's obvious what Baron Gödel was going up the Rock for. But we've still got it, and Razkavia is still free, and I'm still queen. What we're going to do is this. We're going to take this train into Andersbad and go straight to the garrison. I'll speak to the troops there, and I'll call on all the loyal people of the town to support me. Then we'll march up to the old castle at Wendelstein. The whole country'll know what that means."

Karl coughed. "Wendelstein is only a few miles from Schwartzberg, Your Majesty. Count Otto..."

He hesitated. Adelaide said, "Go on."

"Well, are you sure of his attitude to you? We all know he expected to succeed. Has he been involved in these plots?"

Adelaide's face set firm and her eyes blazed darkly. Jim and Becky recognized that expression.

"I don't know what Count Otto will do. I have been queen long enough to know the importance of the flag, and what Walter von Eschten did at Wendelstein. So does Count Otto. The part he chooses to play is a matter for him. Has anyone else got any questions?"

She looked around the little carriage. The faces that looked back were somber. No one spoke.

"Very well. Now we all need some rest. I suggest we try to sleep between here and Andersbad. Make yourselves comfortable wherever you can. And I'm proud of you all..."

Becky had reached that stage of tiredness when you begin to

imagine things, or perhaps to see things normally invisible. She seemed to be seeing a kind of look on Adelaide's face when she looked at Jim, and on Jim's when he looked at her, that was fierce and tender and greedy and shy and somehow *animal,* all at once. They couldn't keep their eyes off each other. When she and Becky had gone through to the front carriage, and Becky had lit the lamp in the main sleeping compartment, she turned to see Adelaide chewing a fingernail, her cheeks flushed, breathing deeply.

"Go and fetch Jim," was all she said.

Becky did so, and when they came back Adelaide was opening the little velvet bag she'd asked Becky to fetch from the bureau that morning, so long ago, when they'd awoken in her suite in the palace. Jim was trembling, his green eyes red-rimmed but blazing with the same emotion as hers. *Really,* Becky thought, *it's positively indecorous; if they touch each other, they'll explode...*

Then Adelaide surprised them both.

"I was going to do this on me birthday, but I'm not sure when that is, and none of us might live that long anyway. And if you feel like refusing or anything I'll scratch your bloody eyes out, because I'm the queen and I can do what I like. Now, Jim, you're supposed to kneel, go on. Kneel!"

He did, slowly, and she took out a gold star-shaped decoration on a dark green silk ribbon.

"This is the Order of St. Stephen. It's an order of nobility. It means you're a nobleman, a baron or summing, I can't remember. Because of everything you done, right from the beginning, for King Rudolf and for the country, not for me."

For once in his life, Jim was utterly without the power of speech. His eyes flashed with what Becky thought was anger, but then he took the hand Adelaide held out and kissed it.

She put the ribbon around his neck and turned to Becky.

"And you," she said. "I got one for you and all." She fumbled in the bag and brought out a gold medal on a crimson ribbon. "Come here," she said.

Becky came, and Adelaide pinned it on her breast.

"It's the Most Noble Order of the Red Eagle," she said. "Second Class. That's for civilians. 'Cause you been a good interpreter. Now you go out and sleep in the other compartment, Becky, cause I want to—I want to talk to—"

Becky left, and as she shut the door she heard a soft half-choking sigh, or gasp, or both. She felt shut out, to be sure, but not by being made to sleep next door; it was that the other two so urgently wanted to…to what? She knew, but she blushed to think of it. They wanted it with an intensity that she could only marvel at. Perhaps she wasn't old enough; perhaps passion came with another couple of years' life; or perhaps there was one particular person whom she hadn't yet met, and with whom…

With a blush on her cheeks and the Most Noble Order of the Red Eagle (Second Class) on her breast, Becky fell asleep. The train chugged on through the snowy silence of the night.

In the cab, Willi the student checked the controls. The pressure gauge was hovering around the hundred and twenty pounds per square inch level, which was a little low, but on the other hand the water level was low too. They hadn't had time to fill the tank properly. Could they afford to stoke the furnace and raise the pressure? It might mean having to stop and take on water; but where could they do that? However, if they kept the speed down, they might be caught…It was a puzzle.

It wasn't the only puzzle, either. Was the line clear? There were no trains scheduled, but a special could come along at any time; and would all the switches be set in their favor?

And then there was the soldier, Private Schweigner. Willi found it hard to make him out. He'd been stoking like a Trojan, but he'd said little, answering in monosyllables when Willi spoke to him. And now he was leaning out of the cab on the left, shading his eyes against the smoke and the snow, which had begun to fall thickly again.

The heavy flakes swirled into the cab, and Willi was glad of the roaring furnace in front of him. Curious to see where they were, he leaned out on the right as Schweigner was doing on the left, hand sheltering his eyes. A roaring speckled darkness was all he saw. And a second later, a blow from the shovel struck him so brutally on the head that he heard it ring, or was it his imagination? He seemed to be kneeling suddenly. His hand reached for the rail, everything happening with extraordinary soothing slowness, and then came another blow that brought with it all the pain the first one had just begun to remind him of.

"The queen—" he started to say, but got no further, because he was on his face and then he was sliding and then the wind tore him out of the locomotive and into the thundering darkness, where there were gravel, and tree roots, and ice, and under the ice, deep still water.

Private Schweigner stood up, shaking. He could barely hold the shovel. But he'd done his duty, or the first part of it; the rest wouldn't take long.

He gripped the handle firmly, threw several more shovelfuls of coal into the furnace, and swung the door shut. He checked the speed: twenty-five miles per hour, but they were going up a steepish gradient here. The pressure was rising. He traced the steam line to the safety valve and beat it flat with the shovel. Then, as the locomotive slowed to just over twenty miles an hour at the top of the gradient, Private Schweigner jumped from the cab and rolled down the snow-covered bank, coming to rest with a thump that knocked the wind out of him.

He struggled up, holding on to the tree he'd bumped into, and wiped the snow from his eyes as he watched the train roll past above him and gather speed over the crest of the hill. There was a long run downward now; Schweigner knew the line well. He couldn't predict when the boiler would explode, though; that was a matter for God.

Wincing, he clambered back up the slope and began to trudge the half-mile back to the little town of St. Wolfgang, where he knew there was a telegraph office.

From the basement of a jobbing printer's in the university district, figures carrying bundles of leaflets with the printer's ink still wet on them slipped through the streets, thrusting rough paper into hands, through letter boxes, into pockets, pasting them up on walls, lampposts, doors. Here and there people stood reading them, or tugged at a neighbor's sleeve and pointed them out:

"The queen's taken the flag! She's gone to Wendelstein like Walter von Eschten!"

"What a coup! It's as good as the Middle Ages!"

"That'll fox 'em..."

The streets were in confusion; there was open fighting in a number of places. The commander of the German force, General von Hochberg, was keeping the larger part of his troops in reserve, because he thought that at some point the Razkavian army might gather its wits and come out to support the ragged little groups of civilians with their hunting rifles and cobblestones.

As soon as he'd learned what had happened on the summit of the Rock, he put Baron Gödel under arrest. The Chamberlain, astonished and bitter, could hardly bring himself to resist.

Immediately afterward General von Hochberg, seeing a large fire burning in the banking quarter, sent in a company of grenadiers with orders to put out the blaze and protect the civilians, and he was about to deal with the barricades around the university when an excited major galloped up accompanying a closed carriage.

"General! Look who's in here! We found him by the Botanical Gardens Station..."

The general looked in at the figures of Prince Leopold and the nurse.

"Who's this?"

"Prince Leopold," said the nurse, anxious to protect the prince, and anxious too in case she was doing something wrong.

"Ah! Now I see." Here was the rest of Baron von Gödel's plan. The general cast a glance at the pitiful figure of Prince Leopold, and turned back to the major. "Take this poor man back to the palace, give him a great deal of brandy, and let nature take its course. Neumann, where are you? Let's deal with those barricades..."

And the students with the leaflets moved on, into the Old Town, through the alleys and warrens and hidden little courtyards with their message of escape and hope. Miroslav Kovaly, one of the elderly river thieves from Marienbad, was out scavenging for some scraps of food for their guest from the water when a young figure thrust a leaflet into his hand.

"Here you are, Grandpa! Read this! Take it home and show the family!"

"I will, I will. Thank you..."

The swaying of the train shook Jim into wakefulness. His arm was under Adelaide's head, still asleep, and when he tried to withdraw it she stirred and murmured, "Don't go..." But he kissed her and sat upright, shrugging his shoulder to restore the circulation.

There was no doubt about it: the train was rocking from side to side like a boat on a stormy sea, and jolting so hard that Adelaide's velvet bag and his own jacket had shaken off the pegs they'd hung on.

"Wake up!" he said, and shook her silken shoulder. "Come on, love—for God's sake—"

"What is it?" She sat up drowsily, felt the motion of the train, and threw an arm around his neck for support. "Jim—what's happening?"

"I think the train's out of control. I'm going to go forward and see. Get your clothes on and mind the flag. Stay near the bed in case we crash—it'll be soft, at least."

He dragged his jacket on, laced his shoes with quick rough movements, and then caught her up in his arms.

"I love you," he said. "You understand? More than anything. Life, death, Razkavia, England, they're nothing beside this. I didn't tell you just now, but I've got to say it at least once."

Her face was buried in his neck. Blindly he stroked her rich dark scented hair, and heard her say, "Jim, of all the men I've ever known, I only loved you, and I loved you from the first day I saw you in Lockhart and Selby's...I never stopped. I love you, Jim—"

Then there came an explosion that took them back several months to a sunny morning in St. John's Wood, for it sounded as if a bomb had gone off. An instant later came a jolt bigger than any yet, and then the whole carriage swayed and toppled, with a splintering crash that hurled the pair of them against the wall; but which was wall, or floor, or ceiling, neither could have said. A breathless struggle against enveloping bedclothes—and then the smell and hiss of escaping gas, and the blaze of spilled coals, the heat of red-hot iron—

Jim gathered himself in an effort of painful wrestling. His leg was trapped. Tugging it free from something, he fell backward and shattered a pane of glass. He tore himself up again, found Adelaide all but unconscious, cut over the eye, and roughly hauled her free.

She was in her chemise. In the tangle of bedding Jim caught sight of her dark cloak and pulled that out as well, and then, standing, banged his head and cursed before knocking out the glass of the window above him.

"Come here," he said, and lifted her up. She was as light as a child. He pushed her through the gap, and then lifted her feet so that she could scramble free.

"Move! Get away from the engine, and I'll look for Becky!" he shouted, and then he saw one of her boots. She was barefoot in the snow, so down he went, the jumbled sideways carriage lit now with flickering red, the hiss of gas louder every moment. A few seconds' scrabbling and he found the other boot, and then leapt out with them.

"Get back! Go and fetch the flag, but *move!*"

She nodded, looked up at him with those black beloved eyes, and slipped her boots on before clambering back to where the second coach lay, even further over. Other voices came back to Jim, and there were arms and heads and bodies emerging from the shattered coach, but he turned back, scrambling along the upturned side of the carriage toward the next door.

He found it, wrenched at the handle, flung it open, and called, "Becky! Becky! Where are you?"

She said quite calmly from the darkness, "Don't shout. I think I've broken my arm or ribs or something. Collarbone. I don't know. I can't move."

He let himself down into the darkness, and felt down the length of her free arm down her side to her hips. She was trapped under the upper bunk, which had broken from its retaining straps. He heaved it clear and said, "Can you move now?"

She tried, and cried out, and tried again while he strained to hold the bunk clear of her. When she was out, he let it fall again.

"Got your boots on?"

"No..."

"You'll need 'em."

He felt around till he found them, threw them out through the open door above, and then put his hands on her waist ready to lift her out. She fainted. It made her easier to lift, and he felt the grating of her broken ribs as he did so, but shoved mercilessly until most of her body was out; then he clambered up over her and hauled her free.

By that time most of the students had got out of the second carriage, and Corporal Kogler was anxiously handing Adelaide the flag, one of its edges torn and trailing a length of crimson silk.

"Is everyone safe?" she said.

"Michael is dead," said Gustav shakily. "His neck's broken. He's dead..."

Behind him, two others were carefully lifting out the body. They laid Michael under the trees and covered him with a blanket. Jim put his hands on Gustav's shoulder and shook it gently.

Karl said, "Where's Willi? Is he still in the cab?"

They looked along the twisted track. The glow of the spilled fire was lurid, the dark tree trunks looming like the wings of a stage set. Jim, at the edge of exhaustion, anger, passion, wouldn't have been in the least surprised to see Henry Irving suddenly appear in his sleigh from *The Bells,* or the trees draw apart like painted scenery to reveal Louis dei Franchi wounded after his fatal duel in *The Corsican Brothers.*

"Pull yourself together," he muttered, and shook his head. "Willi's nowhere to be seen," he said in German. "Nor's that soldier, what's his name...?"

"Schweigner!" said the corporal. "He wasn't convinced from the start! Damn it, I should have gone in the cab with him..."

"We didn't have time to get everything right," said Jim. "Get everything you need out of the train, and quickly."

As if to underline what he said, there was a sudden *whoomp* of flame behind them: the gas leaking from the tank had caught, and the force of the combustion pushed them off balance for a second.

While two of the others climbed back inside to retrieve their weapons, Jim said to the corporal, "Do you know where we are?"

"Not more than a couple of miles from Andersbad. Look, there's the distance post."

Nailed to a tree trunk was a rectangular tin plate in the faded colors of the Razkavia Railway Company. Jim looked past the blazing engine, shading his eyes against the heat, and saw only rank upon rank of dark pines in a gloomy recession toward utter darkness.

"We can't be far from the castle, then," he said to no one in particular.

"It's on top of the hill," said a strained voice below him, and he looked down to see Becky sitting on a tree stump and holding her side.

"If it's that close, we'll go there straightaway," said Adelaide. "We got to get the flag up—"

She stopped, hearing the same sound they all did: the distant beat of a steam locomotive from the direction of the capital. The night was still, and it was some way off yet, but it was unmistakable.

"That decides it," said Jim. "We'll go up there now."

Karl said, "What about Fräulein Winter?"

Becky sat still. Jim could see the tears glinting on her cheek.

"Can't move?" he said softly.

She shook her head. "Leave me here. I'll hide or something."

"Don't be stupid!" Adelaide stormed. "You don't think I'd let anyone leave you behind? Don't even waste time thinking it. Get some blankets out the carriage, go on, someone. Make a stretcher!"

Karl and two others leapt inside while Jim and Corporal Kogler pulled over a couple of saplings and tore the twigs off them.

A minute or two later, Becky was lying in a blanket suspended by its four corners between the two poles. It was excruciatingly painful, and when her four bearers began to stumble up the rough slope it was all she could do not to cry out loud.

But they were moving, the ragged band, and before long they were some distance over the railway line among thick trees. Jim looked back; he could see the glow of the burning engine, and strained to listen for the other train. He heard it more distinctly now. It seemed to be slowing down, which meant either that they had seen the crashed train or that they were expecting to; which meant that someone must have warned them. Schweigner...He shrugged.

"How far up is this castle?" he said to Karl.

"At the top of the slope. We're on the right path."

"I wish we *were* on a path. This is bloody murderous stuff to walk on. Here! You want to change over, you fellers?"

The four stretcher bearers gladly gave up their poles to Jim, Karl, Gustav, and the corporal. Becky was still, though Jim could hear a barely audible moan that seemed to be tearing her heart out.

"Not long now, gal," he said, knowing it was a lie.

Over rocks and tree stumps, slipping on icy moss, floundering through gaps where the snow concealed the footing, they stumbled ever upward, each focused on the ground in front of him. Vague blurs of gray and black were all they could see. Soon the knee Jim had injured years before was hammering with pain, but he kept moving, shoes full of snow, face scratched by brambles, holding his pole as still as he could. Adelaide, just ahead and clutching the flag to her breast, was muttering a string of quiet, concentrated curses, talking to herself.

Then, from a long way below, there came a change in the sound of the approaching train. There was a faint squealing of brakes, a long hiss of steam, though both were so muffled by the trees that the listeners might have imagined them.

"They've reached it," said Karl.

"Keep going, then," said Jim, and they stumbled on.

Poor Becky seemed to have fainted again, because there was nothing but silence from the heavy blanket. Jim noted it grimly. No doubt it was dangerous to carry her like that; no doubt she ran the risk of having a lung punctured by a broken rib. It was a little picture of the whole muddle. He was practically certain that they were going to die, here in this forgotten little corner of Europe, for a struggle that was pointless anyway. Dan Goldberg was right: Germany would inevitably crush Razkavia, or Austria would.

And if you could trace cause and effect accurately enough, he thought, you might be able to follow the thread of it all back to the starting point, and it might be a thousand miles away and many years ago, in the bankbooks of a financier or the childhood of a frustrated princeling; but more probably there were a million such threads, and if any one of them had snapped or twisted differently, the outcome would have been utterly different, too. There was no pattern in things, Jim saw, no sense; everything was random and chaotic.

Which left a ragged band of wounded people struggling to plant a rectangle of silk in a heap of ruins, and die defending it. Since nothing made sense, that made as much sense as anything else.

The climbing was a little easier now. The trees were thinning ahead; the sky had not lightened, but something in the air spoke of the approach of dawn: a freshness, a stir in the breeze. It was bitterly cold. Jim felt the sweat chilly on his face.

"Change over," said someone, and the four bearers gave up their poles to the ones who'd had a rest. Jim looked at Adelaide, whose head was down, whose cloak trailed bedraggled, whose white chemise was torn and muddy at its lacy edge, but who was clutching the flag to her breast with firm arms.

"All right, gal?" he said.

She pulled her head up and lifted her chin. In the wolf-light, the ghostly pre-dawn hour when the world turns gray, her great eyes glowed black, and brimmed with feeling.

"Yeah," she muttered. "How much farther?"

"Dunno. Must be close, though."

He took her hand and helped her up the last tumbled slope of snow-covered rock.

Suddenly they were out of the trees.

They stood at the edge of the forest, facing a wild prospect of jagged mountains. The sky that hung over them was heavy with snow, a dark metallic bruise-gray. Directly in front, across a gentle slope of untrodden snow, lay the ruins of Schloss Wendelstein, which Adelaide had last seen under the warm sun of an autumn afternoon. The place looked more desolate now; the tower thrust up at the sky like a single broken tooth, the lines of tumbled walls confused under the white.

To the left, a path sloped down from the castle and into the forest toward the town. Darkness was clustered thickly under the branches; the world was wrapped in silence.

And silently, having taken stock, the little band set off across the snow. The going was easier here—easy but cold, and terribly slow, for the snow was knee-deep. Becky had woken and asked to be set down, and Karl supported her as she walked. They took nearly ten minutes to cross the four hundred yards or so to the first tumbled wall of the castle.

It was no good taking refuge in the tower, for it was only a hollow shell. The roof had fallen in, and the ground floor was filled with a heap of rubble laced through with bramble stems.

Adelaide looked around, and it was clear that she had never ceased to be the queen; she was the queen now, deciding things.

"Take one of them sticks you was carrying Becky with. Fix the flag to it, that's the first thing, and set it up among the stones over there. I'll feel happier once it's flying again."

There was nothing to tie it with until Jim remembered his last ball of wool. The corporal's eyebrows rose at this unsoldierly substance, but it worked well enough. However, the flag hardly flew; it hung limply in the still air, its lower edge trailing on the snow. Jim and Gustav lashed that pole to the other with lengths torn from the blanket, and that raised it off the ground, at least.

It was important to keep warm. Jim was shivering hard, having been without his jersey since leaving the dungeon, and Adelaide, even with her thick cloak wrapped around her shoulders, was shaking. Jim made her sit next to Becky, so they could share each other's warmth.

Then Corporal Kogler saluted and shyly said, "I beg your pardon, Your Majesty. I didn't think I ought to tell you, but I did something wrong. See, it's so cold, up there on the Rock, that sometimes on sentry duty we take a little nip of something. Normally you should have me court-martialed, I reckon. But I haven't touched it yet, and if it'll help keep the cold off you or the young lady, you're welcome to it..."

He brought out a battered gunmetal flask and unscrewed the top.

"Plum brandy," he said. "My granny makes it up in Erolstein. You won't taste anything better than that."

Adelaide looked stern. The light was gathering now, and they could see her almost clearly.

"You're a bad man," she said. "Give it to me. I can't have my soldiers boozing on sentry-go. I'm shocked." She sipped it, blinked, took a deep breath, and swallowed several times. "But I forgive you. You can tell your granny that I'll give her a royal warrant. Becky, have a sip, go on."

She held the flask to Becky's lips, with the same result. As Becky moved she cried out softly, and Adelaide said, "D'you want to lie down, dear? I'll clear a space. You can have all the rest of the blanket, I'm nice and warm..."

But Becky shook her head. Adelaide nestled closer.

"You haven't got a length of sausage in that pocket, have you?" said Gustav to the corporal. "Imagine, that, eh! A piece of hard sausage, with lumps of fat like pearls, and well-peppered on the outside..."

"Not for me," said Karl. "Give me a pastry. Apple strudel. With a dusting of cinnamon and icing-sugar, and whipped cream oozing over the top."

"Too sickly," said one of the others. "Meat for me. A plate of venison in a goulash sauce—big lumps of it—hung for a fortnight first—with onions and garlic and paprika, like they do at the Florestan, with sour cream over it—and dumplings..."

"No, you're all wrong," said someone else. "The best thing of all is bread. Warm bread fresh from the oven. You break the crust and it steams a little and you lift it to your mouth and—"

"That's enough of that," said Adelaide. "We can't eat words, and you're making us hungrier. How far's the town? It's only a mile or so, isn't it? We'll send someone down to buy some bread and suchlike as soon as the bakers open. And meanwhile—"

But there was going to be no meanwhile. Adelaide had seen a movement under the edge of the trees where they'd emerged from the climb, and then another, and the students and Jim and the corporal saw her expression and turned to look. Then they straightened and stood closer together, and Adelaide stood up too and put her hand on the flagpole. Becky, huddled under the blanket, wished with all her heart that she could stand with them—she tried, but she couldn't—as they prepared to defend the flag against the gray-clad German troops, one after another, who came out of the trees, rifles held across their chests, and began to advance steadily over the snow.

19 Ghosts

The first flake of snow settled on Becky's eyelashes. She blinked it away, but almost at once there were others. The sky was light enough now to show the heavy flakes dark against it when she looked up, and the army from the trees—a hundred or more, it looked like—was suddenly rendered ghostlike by the veils of swirling featheriness, as if someone had burst a million pillows.

Becky felt as if she were seeing visions, having dreams. This white world—white and gray—shifted and drifted, and figures from other worlds walked through it, became visible, faded again. This was the spot where Walter von Eschten had fought, and there he was, a gigantic figure with his plumed knights around him, still here after all this time. Becky was proud beyond measure that they'd come back to help. For there were other figures striding among the tumbled walls and emerging from the white confusion of the air, and Jim and the others had noticed too, and looked around in bafflement.

Becky watched, her heart knocking against her painful ribs like a smith's hammer, as the leading ghost approached Adelaide and stopped as Jim leapt in front to defend her, pistol in hand.

"The Englishman!" came a deep growling voice, a voice with laughter in it, the voice of no ghost there could ever be: the voice of Otto von Schwartzberg.

Becky brushed the snow away from her eyes, straining to see and hear, and thought she saw Adelaide extend a hand and the giant bend low to kiss it.

"Cousin," said Adelaide. "Nice of you to drop in. I thought you'd gone to Africa to shoot lions."

"Oh, there's better sport here! I heard about your trick with the flag—nice joke, to steal it from under their prying noses! And where would you come but Wendelstein?"

"How did you hear of it?"

"A good servant of yours told me," said Otto, and stood aside.

Behind him was the figure, gray with pain and fatigue but still upright and soldierly, of Count Thalgau.

As Adelaide looked steadily at him, his eyes dropped, and then the old warrior knelt down and took off the black shako so that the snow fell thickly on his iron-gray hair.

"Your Majesty," he said roughly. "I've done wrong. I betrayed you, and I betrayed the country. I am more ashamed than I can tell you. You...you've got a better heart than I have. You did right instinctively, and I did wrong. But I won't fail you again. Trust me now, Your Majesty, and I'll fight beside you till I fall dead. Every drop of my blood, every remaining minute of my life, is yours, and I beg you to forgive me and let me serve you properly, at last."

His voice shook, and gave out. She reached forward and gave the old man her hand. He kissed it fervently.

"Of course I forgive you. Now get up and do as Mr. Taylor tells you."

"So you're the general?" said Otto genially to Jim, and then, seeing the gold star on the green ribbon, added, "My congratulations, Baron."

"Thank you, Count. Have you come to talk or to fight?" said Jim.

"To fight. We'll talk later, over breakfast. How many are you?"

"Six men. One rifle, six pistols. That's it. When we run out of bullets we'll throw stones."

Otto looked around. Becky, watching from where she sat huddled against a corner of the wall, was still unsure about him: he seemed to be flickering back and forth between the nineteenth century and the thirteenth, Otto and Walter, air and snow.

"So," he said, and turned back. "Well, Baron, since you're in command, I offer you two dozen men all armed with rifles, and myself and my crossbow. How many bullets have you got?"

"Six only."

"Take this then."

Otto slid his sword out of its scabbard and offered the hilt to Jim, who took it and saluted him, holding the hilt to his forehead in the classic style before tucking it through his belt.

"We're all looking forward to that breakfast," he said.

And Becky saw Jim turn into a general. As if he'd been born to it, he disposed the men about the ruin, hiding one here, ordering two to wait in reserve there, concentrating the main force in the center behind the low wall in front of the flag. Otto stood and watched, nodding.

Finally Otto said, "And the queen?"

"I'm staying with the flag," she said.

"Keep your head down, then, cousin. But the little girl must hide in the tower."

Becky was too weak to protest: little girl indeed...But Count

Otto lifted her as if she were a baby, and put her safely behind the pile of rubble inside the door.

"Don't fire till I give the command," said Jim.

It was the last patch of clarity Becky knew. There was a moment of profound silence, in which the snow whirled in a million directions so thickly that there seemed more snow than air, and even the closest figures were ghost-gray.

Then there came a sound like a firecracker exploding in a garden on a winter's evening, heard through a curtained window by a child inside in the warm. The shot was muffled and made kindlier by the uncountable drifting flakes of down. Then another, and another; little explosions—crack, silence, crack—sounding harmless, as if all they engendered was a spray of pretty sparks.

But each little crack launched a bullet, and each bullet sped ahead of the sound like a hawk released from the hunter's hand. They cut straight through the air and through the tattered flakes, leaving invisible eddies of heat behind them, which dissipated into randomness, tossing the snow this way and that long after the bullets had flattened themselves on stone or plunged into the cold soil far beyond.

Becky, her chest on fire and her mind frozen, was aware of a swirl of details, like a mosaic broken apart. There had been a picture once and there would be a picture again, but there was not a whole picture now.

She saw the scuffling lope of a rifleman clad like a hunter all in green, as he dropped on his knees behind a low wall and lifted his rifle to aim through the world of swirling white.

She heard the crying whine of a bullet as it spun off a rock.

She saw two figures lumber through the encumbering knee-deep snow, long overcoats hampering their legs, using rifles as sticks or crutches.

She saw the ancient flag lift slightly as a breeze from the upper airs caught its stiff folds, and she saw Adelaide look up at it like a child proud of a parent.

She heard a ringing clash, steel on steel, again, a gasp of effort, clash, half-grunt-half-cry, another clash, ring, gasp.

She saw plumes—a man with an iron face—a rearing horse, hooves stamping at the air.

She saw a hand that twitched, palm uppermost, saw the fingers clench and then relax profoundly, and saw the open palm fill up in under a minute with snow flakes, like coins thrown to a beggar. They melted at first, but then as more and more fell into it, they stayed, covering the palm entirely until there were just the fingers, then the fingertips, then four shadows, then nothing.

She saw Otto von Schwartzberg stooping over a wounded man, a giant with a child, a huge hand soothing, an arm scooping him to shelter.

She saw him bend, haul back the heroic string of his bow, raise it, shoot; heard the whizz of the bolt, heard a peal of mighty laughter as it struck.

She saw a soldier, broad red face, pale eyes, bloated with astonishment as a sword point slid through felt, serge, linen, skin, and into the grate of his ribs to put out the fire of his heart.

She saw Jim, bloodied, leap down from the rocks around the flag, aim his pistol, fire, fire again, pull the trigger a third time, and then hurl the empty weapon in the faces coming at him through the snow—saw one go down—saw Jim switch the sword to his right hand, sweep it to left and right to feel the balance, then leap again to slash, thrust, parry, a gray ghost fighting shadows.

She saw blood; she saw a mound of snow turn red from

within; she saw drops fall heavily and plunge their red heat deep into the soft white, leaving dark holes like wounds themselves.

She saw Count Thalgau, his stout old man's courage stalwart against the enemy, steadfast even as his strength failed, look up at Adelaide and sense her thanks, and fight on dauntlessly, into the gathering dark of his own death.

She remembered the pistol in her bag, and, moaning, hauled it out, and holding it with two hands, fired, and felt a fierce joy as a man fell.

She saw Adelaide struck; she thought she saw the very bullet, a little black thing the size of a bee, spinning its way through the yielding air to its home in her breast. She saw the bright blood gush, she saw a pale hand fling out to grasp the flag, she saw Jim catch her, the flag dip and topple, wavering, dropping; she saw Otto spring to catch it and wave it mightily above his head in one hand, clearing the air for the pistol in his other hand to blaze in.

She saw Jim above Adelaide's body, sword point whirling, eyes not human any more but cat-like, demon-like, afire with emerald rage. He seemed to be fighting the air itself, hacking, slicing, cutting, thrusting; and the sky, the enveloping flake-thick air, seemed to swirl more closely around him, peopled by grappling shadows that clung and hung and tugged, dragging him down, struggling, fighting, down.

Then there were acres of silence.

The flakes sifted endlessly soft from above, filling the crevices in the walls, settling on eyes and teeth, covering upturned faces with a filmy veil that became a white Pierrot-mask that became a nothing, a smooth blank space. The blood that had blossomed in the snow, in the old fairy-tale way, soon faded to pink and surrendered to white, and vanished. Soldiers and students, bodies and stones, huntsmen and horses, were little more than hillocks in the snow.

But voices came.

At first she thought they were snatches of dream, or fragments of conversation from another world, the next world:

"...gone..."

"...heard them shooting from the farm..."

"...Count Otto von Schwartzberg..."

"...dead! So many..."

"...a German uniform..."

"...off the train down there..."

"...the queen? Surely not..."

"...a nobleman—look—the ribbon and the star..."

"...breathing?..."

"...can't be alive..."

"...the brandy! Fetch it, quick!"

"...can't loosen his hand..."

"...grip like a baboon—all right, we're friends—take a sip..."

"...Count Otto—he's got the flag..."

"...sent a man down for help..."

"...what was that? Did you hear a voice?"

"...in the tower—quick..."

"...alive!"

For Becky had wanted to speak, even if she was speaking to phantoms.

A man appeared in the ancient doorway, elderly, whiskered, anxious. He saw her, turned to call for help, began to clamber clumsily up, holding out his old shaking fingers that beckoned as a grandfather might gently urge a little child to move forward so that he could pick her up.

Then she realized that, truly, it was all over.

20
The Swiss Clinic

The people from the town of Andersbad carried down those who were still living and those who were dead, both German and Razkavian. It was a cold, uncomfortable, melancholy journey, and the Medical Institute of the little spa became more and more crowded, with wounded men sitting slumped in the corridors or lying unconscious in the wards, the hydrotherapy clinic, the steam room.

The doctors worked hard, but they were more at home with archducal gout and baronial indigestion than sword cuts and bullet wounds. The medicinal waters were good, but not miraculous, except in the brochure. The director ordered his staff to divide the patients into those who could wait, those who would die anyway, and those whom surgery could help if it came at once, and concentrate on the third; and at half-past three in the afternoon, they got round to Jim.

"How are they ever going to kill this fellow?" said the surgeon. "Two bullets—"

"Three," said his assistant, dropping something into a china bowl with a loud clink.

"Three bullet holes, four wounds—sword cuts? Looks like it—requiring stitches, multiple abrasions, exposure... Who is he?"

"No name. He's got the Order of Something-or-other around his neck; a nobleman of some kind."

"Ours or theirs?"

"Oh, ours. Theirs are clean and tidy."

"Keep him tucked away then. Found any more punctures?"

A stocky young man with a sword cut over his eye and a broken collarbone forced his way through the crowd of people in the lobby to where Becky was lying, dizzy with pain, on a sofa in a draft.

"Fräulein Winter..."

"Karl! Is that you? Thank God! Are you..."

"They're going to set the broken bone in a little while. Otherwise I'm well. How is—"

"Have you heard whether—"

"The queen? I don't know. I saw her fall; I think they put her in the steam room. That's where they're keeping the..."

She knew what he meant: those who were dead. "Oh, don't... But what are you going to do?"

"I'm going to join Count Otto. He told me to come and get patched up and then join him in the hills outside Neustadt, but I think they're going to take too long to get round to the ones like me who can still walk. I want to leave now."

"Take care! Do take care!"

Karl had been crouching to talk quietly. Now he took her hand and kissed it formally.

"Good-bye, Fräulein Winter."

"Oh, please call me Becky! If you're going to leave..."

"I hope so much I see you again, Becky. When all this is..."

They were awkward, shy. Then she caught a glimpse of uniforms through the crowd by the door: clean uniforms, not wet dirty ones, and unfamiliar: German?

"Be careful," she whispered. "Go. Count Otto will be a good leader. Please stay alive..."

He kissed her hand again, and vanished.

It was hours later, and the doctor wouldn't listen.

"Rest," he said. "Keep still and quiet. There's nothing better for broken ribs. They will heal again, but if you agitate yourself—"

"Can't you see that you're making me more agitated?" Becky cried. "I want to know where she is! Is she dead or alive? Can't you even tell me that?"

"She? Who's this she? I think, Fräulein, I had better prescribe a sleeping draft. Too much anxiety at the moment can—"

"The queen! Queen Adelaide! Dead or alive? You *must* tell me! I'm her secretary, her companion, her friend—this is too cruel! You *must* tell me!"

The doctor turned to the nurse. "Nurse, please go and bring me some tincture of valerian from the pharmacy. And some papaverine syrup."

As soon as the nurse had left, the doctor laid his medicinal hand on Becky's forehead and said softly, "Alive, and out of the way to be safe. She was very badly hurt: the bullet passed within an inch of her heart. We're not sure yet how well she'll recover; we're sending her on somewhere else. If we keep her here she'll be arrested again for sure. As it is we've had policemen from Germany looking all over the hospital, and there's been some crazy woman...Fräulein?"

Becky didn't need the tincture of valerian; at the word *safe* such a flood of relief passed through her that her system couldn't absorb it. She was fast asleep.

• • •

The doctors making the first crude separation of patients into those who would live and those who would die had put Adelaide unhesitatingly in the latter class—if indeed she wasn't dead already. They laid her frail, chilly body in the steam room, and it wasn't until late in the afternoon that anyone suspected she might recover. An attendant laying out one poor man who certainly wouldn't heard a slight intake of breath, and turned to see her eyelids fluttering, her lips parting, her fingers moving faintly.

Ninety seconds later, a doctor was feeling her pulse, and two minutes after that, he was joined by two of his senior colleagues.

"Should we operate?"

"Yes. At once."

"And what then?"

"You mean—politically?"

"I heard they tried to execute her yesterday. She got away with the flag. Passed it on to Schwartzberg. If they find out—"

"The city's in chaos. There's no one to give orders but the German general. That's what I've heard."

"If they know she's alive—"

"They'll want her back. She's a symbol of the freedom of the country—even more than the flag, I'd say."

"They'd force her to submit."

"She never would!"

"Then they'd imprison her and let her die of starvation. They can't let her survive."

"Well, we can't let her die."

"Agreed...What *do* we do?"

"Operate. Then send her secretly into Austria. Schwann-hofer's clinic in Vienna."

"Switzerland would be better. The Austrians..."

"Might use her as a bargaining counter? Yes, good point. I know a man in Kreuzlingen; the St. Johann..."

"Excellent place. Come on, let's get her in the operating room."

And four days later, Jim Taylor was sitting in an invalid chair, glaring balefully at the skaters on the ice outside the great windows of the colonnade leading to the Trinkhalle in the Swiss lakeside town of Kreuzlingen. The atmosphere inside was heavy and clinical, a combination of hush, steam pipes, and carbolic soap. Ferns grew prosperously in glass containers beside the wicker tables; an elderly gentleman took nearly five minutes to turn the page of his newspaper, with much fussy rustling. Jim scowled at him.

The string trio playing selections from Strauss and Suppé in the Trinkhalle through the open door, and the scatter of polite applause, covered the sound of approaching footsteps. The blond young woman in the fox-fur coat sat down on the iron bench a yard or two from Jim, and waited for him to turn and see her.

He looked pale and battered. There was a rug over his knees. But his straw-colored hair was neatly plastered down, his high "masher" collar was immaculate, and his three-buttoned jacket in dark lovat was the very glass of fashion.

Then he turned and recognized his oldest friend, and a little cry broke from him, and he reached with both hands. She took them, and leaned across to kiss him.

"Sally!"

"What's been *happening*?" said Sally Goldberg. "Is Adelaide—"

"She's in bed. Not allowed to move. I tell you—"

He stopped, aware of the waiter standing attentively by with a tray of glasses and a jug of the sulfurous water from the spring.

"You're too healthy for that muck," said Jim to Sally, "and I'm too ill. We'll have some beef tea. *Fleischbrühe, bitte,*" he said to the waiter, who murmured respectfully and hurried away.

"*What* did he call you?" said Sally.

"Baron. It's genuine. It was almost the last thing she did before the fight. It wasn't...I didn't...It wouldn't have been right to refuse. And she had the perfect right to confer it, being queen and all. When they patched me up in Andersbad and sent me on here, all they had to label me by was the ribbon round my neck, because I was unconscious. It makes the waiters hop, I'll say that for it, but it's back to Jim when we get home. But what brought you here? I thought you were still in America?"

"We came back earlier than we'd planned. And the first thing I saw was this." She took out a folded newspaper cutting from her bag. "I wired the Medical Institute at Andersbad and they told me where they'd sent you. And here I am."

He took the cutting and read:

Fall of an Ancient Kingdom.

The Cockney Queen Is Missing.

Flight of the Red Eagle.

News has been received of the annexation of the Kingdom of Razkavia by the German Empire. This little country, scarcely bigger than Buckinghamshire, has been independent since 1314, but civil disturbances in recent days, coupled with an appeal for help from the Chancellor, the Baron von Grödl, have resulted in a response from the German authorities. A regiment of Pomeranian grenadiers is now quartered in the capital city, Estenburg, and discussions are under way with a view to the country's entering the German Customs Union and ultimately its administration from Berlin.

Razkavia became the object of widespread interest six months ago, at the coronation of the last King, Rudolf II. Readers may recall that he was assassinated at the ceremony and that his place was taken by his Queen, an Englishwoman. Queen Adelaide reigned in her own right for six months, but she has not been seen in the capital for some days.

Also missing are several valuable items from the Treasury of Razkavia, including the ancient banner—

Jim angrily crumpled the paper and threw it down.

"They're all saying that! Implying she did a bunk and scarpered with a lot of loot! Bloody liars..."

"That's what I thought. I brought Frau Winter with me, by the way; she's with Becky now. You'd better tell me all about it."

"Mama, you are not to believe what it says in the papers. Believe *me*, your daughter. I was *there*. Oh, it was so *close*, Mama! One more day and there would have been a treaty to keep us safe and independent forever! And they loved her, the people, and you should have seen how we fought—at the end..."

Frau Winter's hands released her daughter's, and smoothed down the rug Becky had rumpled in her agitation.

"I shall never forgive her for leading you into danger. If I had thought—"

"Mama, you will *have* to forgive her if you want to speak to me again. She could only lead if people were willing to follow. And she didn't cause the danger, she was betrayed. Have you *seen* the papers? I never believed they could write things like that. I thought it wasn't allowed, I thought they had to print the truth. It's too cruel, Mama, after what she's done. But Count Otto knows. And the men who fought—they know. Oh, Mama, when will people listen?"

Frau Winter didn't know.

That afternoon, Sally Goldberg went to the British Consul. He was a plump man with snippy manners, mildly irritated to be called away from his study, where he was happily cataloging the dried results of his summer's collecting among the Alpine flora.

"Yes? How can I help you, madam?"

"I wonder if you could tell me about the British government's attitude to the invasion of Razkavia. Are we making any representations to Berlin? What about the safety of British residents? And what of the attempts on the life of the queen, who is of British birth?"

"May I ask what your interest is?"

"I am a concerned British subject."

"I see. Well, Razkavia is not a matter of great or immediate concern to Her Majesty's Government. As far as I know there are few British residents there, but no doubt their interests are being very effectively looked after by Her Majesty's representative in the capital. What else did you want to know? Something about Berlin?—Oh yes. Well, it has long been the policy of Her Majesty's Government to seek and foster the most cordial relations with the major powers. Germany is a nation of immense importance; it would not be in our interests to interfere in what is essentially, I understand, an internal German question. And finally, what was your other point?—Oh yes—the famous Cockney Queen. Well, you see, this is the sort of thing that happens to old, corrupt, played-out regimes—they fall prey to any adventurous confidence trickster who comes along. I gather she made off with half the treasury, did you see that in the papers? Used to be a music-hall dancer, or worse, I believe. Probably halfway to Brazil by now. Make a jolly yarn. But, good gracious me, Mrs.—ah—Goldberg, it's not the job of the Diplomatic Service to give aid and protection to common criminals, even picturesque ones. No, the work of diplomacy is serious, and, if I may say so, grown-up. We have no interest in the Cockney Queen. Was there anything..."

"I see. Thank you. No, there was nothing else. Good afternoon."

As the daylight faded over the lake, the nurse came to change Adelaide's dressing and to tell her that she was allowed a visitor.

"But only for an hour," she said. "You must not move. You must not become agitated. You must rest."

Adelaide frowned, but they'd been good to her here, and in any case she hadn't the energy to argue. The nurse helped her sit up and arranged the nightgown around her shoulders before leaving quietly.

The bed faced long windows that could open in fine weather onto a balcony overlooking the lake. Adelaide wasn't susceptible to the beauty of scenery, or she hadn't been, but in the three days she'd been lying in front of that view she had come to find the changes in the light and the weather almost as fascinating as diplomacy, and to reflect that there were compensations for stillness. A distant low hoot told her to look leftward, and she saw the lights of the last steamer leaving the pier to ply its course across the darkened water.

"Adelaide?"

It could only be Jim. She felt her heart quickening, and turned her head to see him. His malacca cane, his silk cravat, his tender, green, ironical eyes...

"My word," she said. "Neat, but not gaudy—"

"As the monkey said when he painted his bottom pink—"

"And tied up his tail with pea-green. Oh, Jim, I love you!"

"I'm glad to hear it. I've come for a kiss."

He leant over; she reached up. They were both too sore for the kiss to last long, but there'd be plenty of time for more; and each of them had the same impression, as if they were sharing thoughts for a moment: that a prison wall had melted away to reveal an open landscape, that fetters had fallen from them, that there would be no pursuit. They were free.

"Come and sit beside me," she said.

"I don't think I could swing me legs up. We've got a fair bit of mending to do, both of us."

He pulled a chair to the bedside, with some effort, and sat holding her hand.

"I've got no money, Jim. I can't afford to pay for this. I don't know what's going to happen when—"

"I have. Stop fussing."

"How'd you get it? Are you rich?"

"Gambling, mainly. And a bit of writing, and the detective lark brings in a few quid. You'd be surprised. There's enough to pay for as long as it takes us to get well, anyway. Then I can earn some more. I'll need to if we're going to get married."

"Are we? When did we decide that?"

"In the railway carriage. You're not going to change your mind, it's not allowed."

"All right."

She sat placidly, with happiness pulsing along her veins. The steamer's lights moved slowly away towards Friedrichshafen on the German shore.

"Jim," she said, "I need you to tell me this, now. Tell me honestly. I'd ask Becky as well. And in fact I *will* ask her. I've been a queen, haven't I? It was true?"

"Yes."

"And I did it well?"

"You were the best ruler, king or queen, that they could ever've found. You were magnificent."

"Right. *I* thought I was, but...Now then, d'you think I ought to go back and fight? Or be a queen in exile? Or have I finished now?"

"D'you remember anything about the fight at Wendelstein?"

"I remember the cold. And I had snow in me boots. And fixing the flag up in that pile of stones...And the Corporal's plum brandy, bless him. And the poor old Count...And Otto turning up out of the blizzard. I thought he was a ghost. He called me cousin, didn't he?"

"That's right. D'you remember being shot?"

"No. Just a huge bang, and everything vanished."

"Well, you fell one way, and I caught you, and the flag fell the other way. You were holding it up. When you let go of it, Otto caught it. By God, he's a giant, that man. He was waving it around his head like a handkerchief, the last thing I saw."

"So he's the *Adlerträger!*"

"Looks like it."

"And I'm not anymore...I'm free. I'm free! Oh, thank God for that!"

"Didn't you like being queen, then?"

"I loved being able to make things happen...Getting all those diplomats to agree about the treaty. Oh, I adored that, Jim. It was the best job in the world. But...all that ceremony. Stifling. I don't think I could've stuck that for long." She smiled.

"What's the grin for?"

"When I was a little girl, at Burton Street with Miss Lockhart and you and Mr. Garland, I remember the day Mrs. Holland came and snatched me. I'd been for a walk with old Trembler Molloy and he took me to see Buckingham Palace. He said we was going to call on the queen and have a cup of tea, and I believed him. But when we got there the flag, you know, the Royal Standard, it wasn't flying. He said, Gor blimey, she must be away for the weekend. Just like her. And when I was queen, I thought it'd be a real lark one day to go and call at Buckingham Palace. Only properly this time. Red carpet, guard of honor, the whole boiling. But now I don't suppose I ever will."

"You'd have a miserable time if you did. She's a glum old besom, from what I've heard. I'd sooner have a smoke and a yarn with the Prince of Wales."

"Yeah! He'd like Andersbad, wouldn't he?"

"They'd need to spruce up the casino first."

"All right. We'll do that...No, we won't, will we? It's all over. Jim, I saw the paper today. I made the nurse bring me one, and the crafty scheming minx brought me a German one, only I fooled her. I can read German better'n English. I saw what they're saying about me."

"Yeah, but it's just lies. Everybody knows that."

"Everybody who was *there* knows that. But to all the other people in the world, I'm just the Cockney Queen, a bleeding rorter..."

"Doing the flimflam."

"Working the pigeon-drop, yeah, all those things. Just a cheap con girl. I gotta be careful, Jim, else I'll get angry. I can feel me heart going."

Ignoring his own injuries, Jim sat up on the bed beside her and held her in his left arm, laying his right hand on the fragile breast where that heart was beating. He could feel it, like a bird in a cage.

"That's better," she said.

"I've got a scheme for sorting out the truth of it," he said after a minute.

"What?"

"I'll write a book. Not a shocker nor a blood, a serious, proper, historical, scholarly book about the talks and the treaty. I'll put down everything you can tell me and everything Becky can remember, and I'll go to Vienna and talk to the Austrian side, and I'll put it all down in black and white. Then I'll write how you were betrayed, and exactly what happened to the flag. It'll help Otto, too. It'll back his claim to the throne—show how the succession really did pass to him."

She rested against him silently. Her breathing became slower, more regular, and when he looked down he saw that her eyes were closed. He marveled at the great sweep of the dark lashes, the way they lay like artist's brushes tipped with sable against the silk-pink flush of her cheeks. Her thick fragrant hair moved slightly as he breathed, and for the moment, he thought, that was enough; to sit and hold her like this was quite enough. Presently he fell asleep too.

Downstairs, the physicians were glancing at their notes before the evening round; the cooks were mixing their sauces and rolling out their pastries and chopping their vegetables; the musicians were beginning to arrive for the evening concert in the Trinkhalle; the pool attendants, the steam-bath nurses, the masseurs were helping out the last of their patients for the day.

The electric lights were switched on around the ice rink, and men with brooms were sweeping the ice for the skaters who would arrive later in the evening, gliding rhythmically up and down, leaving their breath in little puffs of steam behind them.

The inspector of water quality had just completed his routine analysis, and was closing the laboratory for the night. Below ground, in the pump room, the engineers were turning the wheels that led the continuous flow of the water from the spring into the hygienic tanks of the bottling plant, which would fill overnight ready for the morning shift.

In the ticket office of the steamer company, they were about to lock up for the night, and the ticket collector, who'd been dealing with a problem, was glad to hand it over to the chief clerk.

"She came across from Friedrichshafen and says she lost her ticket. Well, *I* can't take responsibility for her. I says she's got to pay, that's the regulations, but she says she's already paid over the other side. So I says—"

"All right, all right. Where is she?"

The ticket collector nodded toward the waiting room, where the problem was sitting: an intense, shabbily-dressed woman in early middle age, dark-eyed, dark-complexioned, holding a basket on her lap. She might have been Italian or Spanish, perhaps.

"See, the thing is," went on the ticket collector confidentially, "I don't think she's got any money. I think she's trying it on. If you ask me—"

"I don't want to ask you," said the chief clerk, and opened the door of the waiting room. "Madam, we're about to close for the night. I understand you've lost your ticket."

The woman seemed to make an effort to bring her attention away from something more interesting elsewhere. A strange expression she had, too; distracted; torn between this world and another.

"Yes?"

She stood up and waited for the chief clerk to say something else.

"Yes, well, there's a form you could fill in..." He hesitated.

The more he looked at her, the odder she seemed: almost certainly mad, now he had a close look. And time was pressing, and he was due to play the trombone that evening with the Kreuzlingen Silver Band, and..."Oh, never mind," he said. "I'm sure it won't matter. Come on, I'll see you out."

As he held the door for her he noticed that she hadn't washed for some time, and that she was carrying on a silent, and animated, conversation with herself. There was nothing in her basket but a pair of long, sharp scissors.

"Mad," he said to the ticket collector as they watched her cross the road, check a signpost, and climb the hill towards the Clinic. "No point in wasting time arguing with a crack-brain. Come on, let's lock up."

Becky was taking a turn up and down the colonnade with Mrs. Goldberg, watching the men sweep the ice.

"How are you mending?" Sally asked.

"It's still painful. Apparently there's nothing they can do for broken ribs except let them mend on their own. But at least I haven't got pneumonia, which sometimes happens. I must be as strong as a horse. I just feel so...baffled...frustrated..."

"I can imagine."

"You know, before all this began I used to read the penny dreadfuls Mama illustrated, and pretend to be Deadwood Dick or Jack Harkaway, fighting robbers and capturing pirates. I wanted so much to do active things, daring things. And I have, now. I've taken part in important diplomatic negotiations and escaped from a castle and fought a battle...I've fired a pistol and I think I've even killed someone, and I...I don't think anyone could have a more exciting six months than I've just had. And do you know what I feel?"

"Hollow."

"Exactly! Empty, drained, exhausted. It's all been for nothing. The *betrayal*...Adelaide worked so hard for so long, and she was nearly there...And all the time, there was someone working away to undermine it. Just toying with her! Toying with the whole country—even toying with Baron Gödel! And we don't even know who it was."

"It was a man called Bleichröder," Mrs Goldberg said.

Becky stared at her. "Who's he? And how do you know?"

"He's Prince Bismarck's banker. Dan, my husband, has been compiling a dossier for a long time now; Bleichröder's a sort of spy, a secret agent, a...What's the Yiddish word? A *macher*. A fixer. Apparently he's a courteous old gentleman, very nearly blind; Jewish, so he's not really accepted by German society, especially the stuffy people around the court; but he's been looking after Bismarck's affairs for years. This is just the sort of enterprise he's good at. As soon as Dan heard about it he guessed it was Bleichröder's doing. It seems that Bismarck's engaged in a struggle with the Reichstag, the German parliament, and overturning the treaty was part of his plan to outflank them. But we saw it too late to warn you, of course. There'd been nothing in the American papers."

Becky dashed an angry tear from her eye. "So everything we went through was part of something else we didn't know about, organized hundreds of miles away...Oh, that's too cruel. The country had no chance!"

"You and Adelaide and Jim gave it the best chance it could have had. You did everything that courage and wit and imagination could, but force wins. Enough force always does."

"Forever? There's no hope for anything except force?"

"Not forever. For a while. Then cracks appear, and the center loses its grip, and people remember what they once were and feel that they want to take charge of their own destiny again.

Life's not static, you see, Becky. Life's dynamic. Everything changes. That's the beauty of it..."

They stopped at the end of the colonnade. The men on the ice gave a final flourish with their brooms and stepped crabwise onto the wooden floor at the side.

"What's Adelaide going to do?" Sally went on. "I met the ex-queen of Sardinia once. She led a horrid life. Dwelling on the past, getting involved in hopeless plots to regain the throne, surrounded by obsessed exiles in shabby clothes, growing older and older and more bitter and never having a real life at all. I hope Adelaide doesn't do that."

"I think I know what she might do," Becky said. "She doesn't know it yet, and I haven't mentioned it to her. But on the first morning of the talks, when she went into the Council Chamber, she looked just like an actress taking the stage. She commanded their attention, and she held them, and she's got such a quick mind...She's a star. I wouldn't be at all surprised if she went into the theater."

"What a good idea! And Jim can write plays for her. And you're going to university. There are so many things to be done, Becky, worthwhile things...Look, they're setting out the chairs for the orchestra. Shall we go and dress for dinner?"

Becky felt invigorated by her talk with Mrs. Goldberg. She was so much the kind of woman Becky wanted to be; she showed it was *possible;* she brought hope with her, and a sense of wide, continuing, bustling life. When she'd heard what Jim had done with the jersey she'd knitted, she laughed with pure happiness, as if there were no final dark, as if the whole universe were a joyful play of light.

Becky left the colonnade and made her way slowly up to her room, where Mama was resting. Soon they'd be sitting around a table in the grillroom, and perhaps Jim would join them. In a day or two Adelaide would be able to get up. She'd be frail for a long time; no skating yet for her, or for Becky, who longed to skim over the ice—longed to try, anyway.

Daydreaming, she turned into the long corridor, so quiet and clinical, at the end of which her room stood, three doors away from Adelaide's. As she passed the door to the service stairs, a nurse came out with an armful of blankets and hurried ahead of her, and perhaps it was because Becky was relaxed and calm, or perhaps it was because Jim's eye for character had brought Carmen Ruiz vividly to life when he'd described her, or perhaps it was simply luck—but some fluke of perception drew Becky's attention to the nurse now several yards in front of her: her *shoes.*

They were worn down and filthy!

And in this temple of hygiene...And surely her cap was askew, as if she'd just...

Becky caught her breath and tried to shout: "Help! *Zu Hilfe!*"

But her painful ribs wouldn't let her, and only a hoarse cry came out. The nurse heard it, turned in a flash, dropped the blankets, and flew at her like an animal. Becky saw scissors—blades held high—saw a round mouth screeching redly, white teeth, and felt for the handle of the nearest door, anywhere, safety, hide—

She fell through into a dark room full of the smell of carbolic acid. Sprawling on the shiny floor, she tried to scramble away from the woman, who, off balance herself at the sudden turn, fell across her legs and immediately brought the scissors up high and stabbed down, down, down. Becky twisted and writhed away, and felt the stabbing points pin her skirt to the floor. She grabbed the woman's hair—matted, greasy; the nurse's cap came off at once—and was flung this way and that, like a rider on a wild horse, but she clung and clung until she felt the scissors come out of the floor, and then she grabbed the edge of the laboratory table above her and pulled herself up to a silent shriek from her damaged ribs...

But the table wasn't bolted to the floor. It tipped, something slid, something spilled and fell and smashed, and then the heavy edge swung down and down in front of her and Becky could see it was going to break her legs, and then Carmen Ruiz lunged forward with those terrible scissors once again—

The edge of the table caught the woman behind the neck like a guillotine. It smashed her down in a moment. The scissors stopped an inch from Becky's throat, and then there was silence, apart from the drip of the spilled liquid.

Becky couldn't move.

Her legs were pinned beneath the inert weight of the woman's body. Carmen's head lay in her lap, at such a clumsy angle that Becky knew she was dead, and across the woman's neck lay the edge of the heavy oak table. Waves of pain began to throb through Becky's chest, more powerful than ever before: she couldn't even find the breath to moan.

Someone would come soon. It was a busy corridor; open doors were untidy; this was Switzerland. Someone would look in, and go tsk-tsk, and help her out.

And she'd survive. She'd survived the Battle of Wendelstein, and you didn't do that if you were less tough than old boots. She'd have to grit her teeth.

Her left hand was pinned behind her, but her right was in her lap next to Carmen's cheek. It was wet; the woman's face was covered with tears. Automatically Becky tried to wipe them away.

And this unreasonable pain...She drifted in and out of consciousness. It felt so like sleep, and she was so tired. Little dreams appeared, like the dissolving views of a magic-lantern show, pictures that brightened and faded and melted into one another...She imagined Carmen Ruiz entering the clinic and searching for the nurses' cloakroom, finding a spare uniform, hastily disguising herself, checking the list of patients to see where to go. She saw Prince Leopold, stumbling through the empty corridors of the palace, calling in one cold room after another for the servants who'd fled, the ghosts of his childhood. She saw the games she'd played with Adelaide, the tin princess, the dice and the counters and the chess pieces abandoned, gathering dust. She saw the shopkeepers of the Old Town sweeping up the broken glass that littered the streets; and Countess Thalgau, dressed in black, her strong broad face lined with sorrow, slowly packing away the count's possessions; and the students of the Richterbund, gathering silently at the Café Florestan to wait for news of Karl and Gustav and the others who'd died. She imagined the German general—a governor now, or provincial administrator, or whatever they'd call him; a shrewd, courteous, pitiless man, or so her dreaming mind pictured him—summoning officials to the palace and apportioning responsibilities, dealing fairly with everyone under the new dispensation. She saw the stationmaster of the funicular railway, supervising a couple of laborers as they manipulated the great beam of wood out from the wheels of the carriage. She saw offices opening, clerks dipping their pens, waiters flicking snowy napkins at imagined crumbs, daughters lined up to kiss a fond father, coffee roasting, bread baking, beer foaming in earthenware mugs. She saw an empty flagpole; she saw no one look up at it; she saw newspapers appearing at the newsstands, eagerly bought, cheerfully read.

She saw a young man on a horse, his arm in a sling, ride up a forest road. She saw a giant with scarred hands and a swarthy mustache pass his field glasses to a comrade and point down through pine trees to a little fort quiet under the snow. She saw a cave in the mountains, a fire blazing, rifles stacked against a rock, an ancient flag catching the gleams of red light.

But they were only dreams. When a passing doctor spotted the open door of the laboratory, he found the strangest sight: a woman dead, with her head in the lap of a girl who was fast asleep.

Philip Pullman is the author of three Victorian mysteries featuring Sally Lockhart: *The Ruby in the Smoke, The Shadow in the North,* and *The Tiger in the Well.* His other books include *The Golden Compass, The Subtle Knife, Count Karlstein, The White Mercedes,* and *The Broken Bridge.*

A graduate of Oxford University with a degree in English, Philip Pullman has written novels, plays, and picture books for readers of all ages. He lives with his family in England.